A CHOSEN NOVEL

BRINK OF DAWN

JEFF ALTABEF & ERYNN ALTABEF

FIRST EDITION SOFTCOVER

ISBN: 162253316X

ISBN-13: 9781622533169

Editor: Whitney Smyth
Senior Editor: Lane Diamond

Interior Layout & Formatting: Mallory Rock

Printed in the U.S.A.

www.EvolvedPub.com
Evolved Publishing LLC
Cartersville, Georgia

OTHER BOOKS BY JEFF ALTABEF

CHOSEN
Book 1: Wind Catcher
Book 2: Brink of Dawn
Book 3: Scorched Souls

SHATTER POINT

www.JeffAltabef.com

What Others Are Saying about Jeff Altabef's books:

WIND CATCHER:

"This is an enjoyable read for all ages that goes by as fast as the authors can unspool it."

— *Kirkus Reviews*

"Many young adult books revolve around young adult decision-making processes, but the joy and excitement fueling *Wind Catcher* is that Juliet's search for truth doesn't end with its emergence, but with the bigger picture of what she'll choose to do with it. That's the heartbeat of a powerful saga that fully immerses readers in all the possible scenarios that can stem from one's choices in life—and the reason why *Wind Catcher* stands out from the crowd."

— *D. Donovan*

"*Wind Catcher* is one of the best thrillers for YA that I have read in some time. ... If I hadn't had to eat and sleep, I would have read it right through without stopping. It is just that good!"

— *S. Price "Suze"*

"What an amazingly unique story!! I can honestly say I have never read anything like it! I loved the strong Native American themes running through it as well as the deep plunge into the rich culture then and now. This story seemed to quench my thirst for knowledge of the more supernatural aspect to the Native American history and storytelling and I loved the creativity of the authors. Even though this is, in essence, a young adult book, I was literally kept at the edge of my seat while reading. The plot has some very intense situations as well as mature threads running throughout the story. I love that our authors see our "young adult" crowd as more than older kids; they see them as very intelligent and can handle the more mature themes including murder and secret societies. And come on, who doesn't love secret societies?"

— *Amy @ Read to My Heart's Content*

SHATTER POINT:

"An original gripping, saga. From genetic manipulation and twists of fate to cold-blooded murder, scenarios change with a snap but succeed in bringing readers along for what evolves into a wild ride of not just murder and mayhem, but social inspection."

- Donovan, eBook Reviewer, Midwest Book Review

"The book combines my favorite aspects of my favorite authors into one. James Patterson – the master of the psycho killer who kidnaps girls, Patricia Cornwell – scientific thriller, and Dean Koontz – really spooky plots."

– Kat Biggie, No Holding Back

"An amazing read.... This is one of those books that no reader will be able to part with until they reach the end, I guarantee it."

- Reynolds, Readers' Favorite

"The plot immediately exploded a cast of intricate characters, an evolving plot that you don't know where it's going to take you from one chapter to the next. Every time a protagonist emerges a stronger character and story is unleashed and the result is an intriguing book that I just loved."

– Escapology Book of the Month for July 2015

For Karen Altabef, who provides us with inspiration on a daily basis, and the Covenant House and all those who help homeless youth.

CHAPTER

"You don't have to do this, Jules." Troy cocks his head to the side a little, the way he does when he's worried about me.

The warm expression in his eyes melts my heart. *What would I do without him?*

He's always looking out for me. I used to get into fights, but even when they were my fault, he'd always stand up for me. Now I need him more then ever. The fate of the world is at stake, and he's still here beside me, standing up for me. He'll die to protect me if he has to, but I don't need him to protect me anymore. I need him close, to wrap his friendship around me like a blanket, to connect, to feel human.

Lately I've had a hard time feeling human without him.

"When was the last time I did something I didn't want?" I smirk, but my words ring hollow, untrue—at least for me. I'm always stuck doing chores for other people, and now there's an entire destiny to fulfill that's been thrust upon me. I'd rather be normal and have nothing to do with this future, but we don't get a chance to pick our destiny. At least I didn't.

"What's your mom going to say when she finds out?"

"Since when are you worried about my mom? You've been getting me in trouble since we were in kindergarten. Your name has been etched at the top of her *Undesirable List* since we were six. I've seen it. She keeps it posted on the refrigerator."

Troy arches his eyebrows. "Hey, your mom loves me! I'm the other child she's never had."

"Are you *serious*?" I shoot him a half smile so he knows I'm joking.

Everybody *loves* Troy. Still, he's not on the college track, and Mom wants me to go to one of the best colleges so I can make tons of money and become a big shot lawyer, like her or some other *Master of the Universe* that has no fun and works way too hard.

"Mom's back home and we're here. She doesn't get a vote."

He frowns. "It's just that... once you do this, you can't undo it. It's forever."

"*Really.* That's the point." I shove him lightly in the chest. I'm old enough to make up my own mind, but he's just trying to protect me, so I can't get too angry with him.

"What are your classmates at that fancy private school going to think when they find out?"

I pause for a second and look at him. I mean, *really* look at him, and peer past the handsome exterior: the almond-colored eyes, the chiseled chin, and the long raven hair that falls past his broad shoulders in a tight braid.

Beyond his confident shell, deep in his soul, he harbors doubts that trouble him—doubts he'll never share with me. He's making believe life will go back to normal once I fulfill this destiny—*if* I fulfill this destiny—but that's not possible. Normal has become a bad joke, but I won't shatter the illusion for him. He needs to sort events into a pattern he understands and imagine a time when life returns to what it was for us. It's how he's coping with the situation.

I need to be strong for him. I can't weaken his defenses, even if fears riddle my mind at every turn.

I straighten my back. "You know I don't care about what they think at Bartens. I *want* to do this. I *need* to do it." The wind kicks up, and the cool night air sweeps against my skin, leaving an army of goose bumps in its wake.

The almost full moon lights the cloudless sky. We inch toward the store and hesitate at the door. A red neon sign reads *Lost Souls Tattoos* in the front window. I take a deep breath and shove the door open, and a bell jingles above us.

No one's in sight. Pictures of various tattoos line the walls of the small rectangular shop. Toward the front left is a glass case with a cash register on top, and farther in the back are a massage table, some bright lights, and a chair with wheels on the legs.

A woman strolls from a back room. She's in her twenties, gaunt with sharp features, smoky gray eyes, short hair, one nose ring, and small hoops that circle the edges of her ears. She holds a half-eaten wrap as she ambles toward us. "What do you guys want?"

She wears a loose gray T-shirt and tight jeans. Brightly colored tats cover her left arm, mostly eagles and hawks, and on the left side of her neck is a teardrop the size of my palm.

"I want a tattoo," I say casually, as if ordering a cheeseburger at McDonalds.

She points to a sign taped on the cash register. "You've got to be eighteen for me to give you a tattoo, and there's no way you're eighteen."

I'm almost sixteen. In the right light I could pass for eighteen, but she probably has a lot of experience with underage teenagers asking for tattoos. Still, I feel a lot older than eighteen and that should count for something.

"No one else is here. It's late and this tattoo is really important to me." My voice whines slightly at the end. I wish it hadn't.

"Why?" She crosses her arms against her chest and arches her eyebrows upward. Two gold rings, one in each eyebrow, bob up and down.

An invisible door creaks open. I'll only get one chance to persuade her to give me the ink.

Her teardrop tattoo stands out and must be important. Grief dulls the sparkle in her eyes and shows in the muscles that tighten her jaw. She'll relate to my story, *if* it's truthful.

"I need to remember someone who died recently. He was really important to me."

"Who?"

"My grandfather. I called him Sicheii, and he raised me like a father. He died to protect me." Tears moisten my eyes. The tears are real, as Sicheii's death is a fresh wound. People tell me the pain will get better with time, but they don't know what they're talking about. They mean well, but this hurt will always be fresh. He'll always be gone, and it's my fault.

The woman's face softens. "Just for the sake of discussion, what're you looking for?"

Troy drops the satchel looped over his shoulder, smiles, lifts his T-shirt, and reveals his well-muscled chest and copper skin. Across his heart is a blue tat of two twisted arrows in a circle. Each arrow features different feathers and arrowheads.

The woman glides toward him and examines the ink on his chest. It's beautiful in its simplicity and symmetry. She clearly admires it and perhaps wouldn't mind trying to copy it.

Her eyes widen as she lingers over the details. "What does it mean?"

I hesitate. What am I going to tell her, the truth? That the symbol represents the ancient Order of the Twisted Arrows? Or that my grandfather unwittingly injected me at birth with alien DNA, which has changed me forever? Or that I'm one of four Chosen thrust into a battle for our world against a powerful enemy called from a different planet?

None of those explanations will get me a tattoo. She'd probably chase us from the store.

I settle for something bland. "It represents an old society he belonged to. It meant everything to him. It was kind of a... club."

At least it's not a lie. She's probably used to people lying to her and would catch a whiff of one right away.

She traces the circle with her finger. "Is it some weird Native American thing?"

"You could say that." Native Americans use tattoos generally to identify with certain tribes or to honor their animal spirit guide. I'm half Native American on my mom's side, and Sichcii was her father. I have long black hair, an oval face, coffee-colored eyes that are round but not quite round enough to be beautiful, and a long, pointy nose I inherited from my Irish father. I look Native American except for the ghastly nose.

The tattoo artist leaves Troy and slides in front of me. She stands close, no more than a foot away, and traces of vegetable wrap linger on her breath. I'm taller than the average person and stand at least three inches higher than she does.

She studies my face for a long moment; perhaps she's trying to see if I'm serious. "What's your name?"

5

"Juliet Wildfire Stone." I never used to tell people my middle name. It embarrassed me. Now I realize it's who I am, part of my identity.

"Wildfire, huh? I can see that. Where do you want the tattoo?"

I roll up the right sleeve of my T-shirt. "My shoulder would be great."

She nods. "It'll cost you two hundred cash, and you can't tell anyone you got it here."

"Done." I hand her four fifty-dollar bills.

She locks the door to the shop, guides me to the table in the back, and places a pillow on one end. "You want it the same color?"

I jump on the table. "Yep."

She gestures for Troy to come close. "Keep your shirt up. I want to get it just right."

Two hours later, she wipes my arm with a towel. "That's so weird."

"What's wrong?" My heart jumps. *Did she just totally mess up my arm and leave me with some ugly circle thing?*

Troy's smiling, so how bad of a job could she have done?

"Usually it takes a couple weeks for the tat to heal. It always bleeds a little or gets puffy, but your arm already looks perfect, as if the ink had been on it forever."

She hands me a mirror, and I smile. My tattoo is exactly the same as Troy's. Exactly the same as Sicheii's had been.

6

I shrug and hop from the table. "I've always been a fast healer."

My DNA's been changed, so my body can regenerate itself almost instantly. I didn't know that before. It's just another one of my *abilities*, as Sicheii would say. I've started to think of them as *aberrations*.

I have five so far: I can hear other people's thoughts and read their emotions; I can possess animals for a short period of time; I have increased strength and speed; can move things with my mind; and heal instantly. There will probably be more, but they scare me. With each new one, I become less human.

"We'd better head out."

I step toward the door, and she grabs my wrist. "Wait. I want to take a picture of the ink for the wall."

"You can't." I yank my arm away from her.

"I won't take your face. Just the ink."

"Tough." She scowls at me, but I ignore her and march outside.

When we leave the store a sharp pain stabs through my head, as though someone has taken an axe to my skull and cleaved it in two. A wild rage burns through me, and all of a sudden I'm inside a villa next to a piano.

Breath catches in my throat, all the strength saps from my body, and I plummet to the ground.

CHAPTER

Troy catches me before I hit the pavement.

Air comes in bursts, and then the pain vanishes. A cold sweat coats my back as I lean against him.

"Are you okay? What was that?" He holds me gently by the shoulders.

I want to shout that I'm not okay, that I'll never be okay again, but he doesn't deserve that. "They've found the Seeker I killed five days ago. They're in the villa. They're coming for us."

His face twists into a question mark, as his eyebrows squish together and his nose crinkles. "How do you know they've found the dark spirit you killed?"

I step back and stand on my own, but he slips his hand on my hip just in case. "One moment we're outside the tattoo parlor and the next I'm in the villa where I killed the Seeker. I felt a connection with one of them. I could see what he saw and sensed his rage. I don't know how else to describe it, but I'm sure they know about me. They'll start to hunt me."

"You saw through the eyes of a dark spirit? That can't be good."

I shrug. "Good or not, it happened. I can't undo it now."

Troy likes to call the Seeker I killed a "dark spirit" because killing dark spirits is a good thing, a noble pursuit, whereas killing an intelligent being, even if it comes from another planet like the Seeker did, is a different situation altogether. It involves a certain moral gray area. Different questions pop to mind: did you have to kill him; was he intelligent; did he have a soul? None of those questions are relevant when talking about *dark spirits*. Kill as many of those as you like—you get a totally free pass, the more the better.

"Do they have a way to track you? Some trail or signal they can follow?" His hand tightens around my waist as if he's trying to chase away the Deltites with his presence.

He wants me to feel safe, and my blood warms with him so close. I'd like to melt into his courage and let him lead me, but that won't work. I'm the Chosen, not him.

I shake myself free from his grasp with a burst of willpower. "I don't think so, but if I can see visions from their minds, they might be able to do the same from mine. Maybe they can use see something that will help them figure out where we are or where we're headed."

He swings his head from side to side and scans the empty street. Since we left Arizona we've been looking for Deltites in the shadows. It's silly, because they can't possibly know where we are, but it's hard not to imagine the worst.

He takes my hand. "We'd better get back to the room."

We march toward the hotel in silence, lost in our thoughts, our steps brisk as if we need to race back to keep ahead of them, which is totally dumb. It's late and we both could use some rest before moving on.

We trudge across an empty street, avoid the puddles that slick the concrete, and turn right into the parking lot for *Roy's Red Roof Inn*. The hotel is a shadowy place with mildewed walls, cracked windows, and showers that never get hot—the type of establishment that exists on the edge of society, where no one worries about two teenagers who stay the night so long as they pay with cash. Thanks to Sicheii, we have plenty of that.

We plod our way up the stairs, which creak from our weight. "Do you think the other *Spirit Walkers* will reach New York before us?"

"Who knows, and why do you keep calling us that?"

"Spirit Walkers can shift between the spirit world and our world. Since the Wind Spirit has blessed you, you have a strong connection to the spirit world. That's why you have these gifts and see these visions. Once you succeed, they'll probably all fade away and your connection to the spirit world will return to normal."

Argh! There's that word again—*normal*.

We move down the hallway and look for room 247. None of the lights are working, so we're left with only the moonlight to illuminate the brass numbers on the doors. Troy bumps into me on purpose and I hip check him back. We both crack smiles and some of the tension evaporates from us.

"I was thinking," he says.

"I hope you didn't hurt yourself."

"*Funny.* Now that you have one tattoo, you should get another one on the other shoulder to match. How about my name in a big heart?"

I punch him on the arm. "Only if you get one that says Juliet in pink."

"No way! Those things hurt. Your grandfather wasn't so deft with the needles."

"You're a big wuss." We pass 245 and stop outside of 247.

"Don't tell anyone. I have a certain image to protect." We both chuckle as he unlocks the door and pushes it open.

We shuffle into the dark room and I freeze, the laughter stuck in my throat as Troy bumps into me.

We're not alone.

A shadow sits on the bed and flips on a light switch. Light floods the room and bounces off his short blond hair, wide shoulders, and arctic blue eyes. He's movie-star-handsome except for a rage that simmers behind his eyes. When the light reflects off them, they almost generate heat.

"Stay cool or I'll shoot." He nudges a gun barrel at Troy and then toward the door. "Be a champ and shut it. We don't want any unexpected visitors. That'll only complicate matters."

Troy swings the door closed with a thud.

The hilt of my crystal sword lies next to the burglar on the bed. It's called the *Seeker Slayer*, the only weapon that can kill our enemy. Anytime I touch it, a weird connection forms and a blade materializes from the hilt. Now I need it back, and feel stupid for leaving it behind in the room, but it drains me when I carry it around, and we were only going to the tattoo shop.

He points the gun barrel at Troy. "Drop that satchel."

Thump.

I lock my eyes on the burglar and push into his mind, as if his skull is a curtain I can part. I start to concentrate on his internal thoughts to get a better sense of what we're up against, but only muddled sounds come through. I try to mold them like clay to focus them into words and images, but they're fuzzy.

"I'm guessing that's the bag with the money. Never let anyone see you grab money from a bag. It makes them curious. They wonder how much you have in there. My cousin called right after you checked in." He shakes his head and clicks his tongue. "But I'm not interested in the money as much as this jeweled thing. What is it?" He glances down at the hilt.

I fidget in place. "It's nothing... just a toy. Something I got at one of those conventions they have for science fiction stuff. You don't want it."

He points the gun at me. "You're a bad liar."

His thoughts coalesce in my mind and images appear—violent images. I've touched a hot stove, wince, and retreat immediately. The thoughts and emotions are so violent and so extreme, my stomach churns and I have to force the bile back down my throat.

Panic creeps into Troy's voice. "What're you going to do now?"

A small drop of sweat trickles down the gunman's cheek.

"You can have the money." Troy kicks the bag toward him. "If you leave, we won't say anything."

The gunman clenches his jaw. "You've both seen my face."

He doesn't have to continue.

The muscles tighten in his hand and he smiles. "I'd say I'm sorry, but I'm not."

I ball my hands up into fists. Power surges through me, and the world slows.

Troy leaps in front of me and trips on the bag on the floor.

The weapon fires.

Troy moans as he crashes to the carpet.

Using telekinesis, I mentally grab a lamp and bash it against the gunman's head. The light bulb shatters. He wobbles and I smash it against his skull a second time.

Crack!

He collapses onto the bed.

I drop to my knees and cup Troy's face in my hands, my chest tight.

He moans, but his eyes open.

I look for blood, expecting to find puddles, but there's none. I check again and run my hands over his shirt just in case. Still nothing. I breathe for the first time. He's safe; I must have created a force field that blocked the bullet. He'd been close enough to fall within my protection. I've never done that before, but then, no one has tried to shoot me either. Sometimes these abilities come to me when I need them.

My aberrant traits tick up to six. This time I'm grateful.

Troy's voice sounds husky. "How bad is it? I see a light."

"Well, don't go toward it," I chide him. "The bullet missed. You'll be fine." I let go of his head and it clunks onto the carpet.

"Oh." He brushes himself off and sits up.

"Stop doing that."

"*What?*"

"Trying to save me all the time. I've changed. I can handle myself." My voice starts out hard, but softens like a pillow at the end.

How can I be angry with him? He just risked his life for me. Again.

"Old habits and all."

He grins, but I barely notice because I'm standing over the prone body of the burglar who's out cold. I grab the hilt of my sword, and a tingling sensation runs up my arm as the crystal blade appears, sharp and real and lethal, as if it had always been there.

"What're you doing?" Troy moves beside me.

I grip the hilt so hard my hand hurts. "I saw into his mind, Troy. He's bad. He likes hurting people. Even children." Tears brim my eyes. "I want to kill him." I point the edge of the blade at his chest. It won't take much, just a short thrust to puncture his heart and he won't be able to hurt anyone again.

"Hold on a moment, Jules." He lifts both of his hands palm out. "Cool down. This is just your temper flaring. Let's give this some thought."

I slide the tip of the blade against his shirt. "If I let him live, he'll hurt more people. *Children*. Those lives will be on my head."

"You can't know that for certain. You can't *see* the future."

"I *know*." The tip of the sword dips lower and cuts through his shirt as if it isn't there. "He's a psychopath. He enjoys hurting others."

Troy's voice drifts soft and gentle as a summer breeze. "This is not what the people do. What would Sicheii do?" By "people" he means American Indians.

"He'd talk to him for days if that's how long it took to make him see the error in his ways. He'd try to change him, so he could fit in with the Tribe."

"Right," says Troy. "He did it with my dad, and my dad stopped beating us."

My hand tightens on the hilt. "We don't have that much time, Troy." I stare at him.

His eyes are wide. He doesn't want me to do something I can't live with, that I can't walk back.

A powerful tug of war erupts and threatens to rip me in two. *Can I live with myself if I kill him? Can I live with myself if I don't?* Both sides pull at my soul. I look for the light, but everything is gray.

"Right, but the people do other things too. They warn the rest of the Tribe about the person's issues, so they can guide him and are wary of him at the same time. If he can't change they would banish him, send him on his way without any weapons to face the unknown."

I know what he's hinting at. "Calling the police won't do any good, Troy. We've got no proof against him, and we don't have the time." Blood seeps from the monster's chest as the tip of the blade punctures his skin. The blood reminds me of my tattoo. "But maybe there's another way to make sure children won't trust him."

I press the edge of the blade to his cheek and, with two quick flips of my wrist, carve an X into it. The blade dips in deep enough that the scar will never fully heal. Small frozen crystals form around the edges of the cut, as if the sword were made of dry ice.

"At least that'll make him seem scary to children. They won't trust him anymore."

Troy grabs my hand and guides the sword to my side. "Sicheii would be happy."

"Are you sure I shouldn't kill him?" I shoot him a lopsided grin.

"You've done enough. We'll call the cops on the way out and find a new place to sleep for the night. With any luck they'll arrest him for the gun and trace it back to other crimes."

"Okay." Still I'm not totally convinced this is best.

He doesn't deserve to live—some people are defective and we'd be better off without them.

But could I really have killed him?

I'll have to murder the Deltite leader. That's the only way to stop them. It won't be a moment of passion or self-defense.

It will be planned out.

It will be murder.

CHAPTER

The train's constant rhythmic chugging does little to calm Akari's frazzled nerves. She looks at the seat next to her, half expecting to see her grandmother, and sighs.

On all four of her previous train trips, her grandmother sat beside her and spun a story to pass the time. Each tale focused on their destination and the wonderful adventures they were sure to have. None of them came true. Their outings could never compete with her grandmother's imagination, but they were fun, unique, and safe.

Now, everything's changed. Akari is alone and her world has become impossibly large and dangerous. She's on the run—*that* she knows. She just doesn't know whether she's running *from* those who wish to destroy her or *toward* an uncertain destiny the Order has chosen for her. Both are rotten choices, but that's all she has.

Usually a strong-minded person, her indecisiveness bothers her like an itch she can't scratch. Just when she thinks she's decided on her path, her thoughts storm in another direction and her answer changes. It's driving her nuts.

To chase away the storm roiling through her mind she precisely folds a corner of paper, completes a perfectly formed horse, and drops it into the small bag at her feet with the rest of her origami zoo.

Before the figure lands in the bag, icicles tickle the back of her neck, so she glances up. A new traveler stands by the doors. He's in his mid to late thirties, wearing an expensive navy suit, white cotton shirt and yellow silk tie.

She immediately dislikes him and turns her head toward the window, hoping he didn't notice her looking at him. The last thing she wants is company, and her gut says this guy is trouble. She sneaks a look a second later as he slithers past numerous empty seats to plop down next to her.

Great.

Once the train lurches forward again, he shoots her a bold look—an arrogant smile, eyebrows raised, mustache curved slightly at the edges. He's twenty pounds overweight, has thinning hair and is old enough to be her father, but he has money, and because of that he *thinks* he's cool.

Her stomach turns. She knows he wants to strike up a conversation, but she'd rather eat a bowl of slugs, so she tries to ignore him by turning her back to him and staring out the window. Through the reflection in the glass, she sees him watching her. She focuses on the passing scenery, but her eyes keep returning to the stranger's reflection, and every time she returns, he's watching her. Heat warms her cheeks until the awkwardness becomes too much to take, and she turns back toward him.

"Haven't I met you before?" he asks. "You look familiar."

"*Seriously?* I'm sure we've never met." She adds an edge to her voice to discourage additional conversation, crosses her legs, and leans farther away from him.

He opens his mouth to ask what's sure to be another annoying question, when his phone rings. After a ten-minute debate over the hottest restaurants in town, he disconnects the call and grins at her. "What can I say? Someone always wants me." He waves his smartphone as proof of his awesomeness. "I can't believe he thinks *Jade Garden* is still an *in* place."

"Some people are just clueless." She smirks, hoping he'll get the message, but that's too much to wish for.

He grins knowingly, as if she's talking about everyone else on the planet and could not possibly be talking about someone as awesome as himself. "Listen, I'm meeting some friends at a karaoke bar. Why don't you come with me?"

"*Really?* Thanks for the generous offer but I'm meeting someone."

She glances back out the window but he continues talking anyway. "The karaoke bar is only two blocks away from the station and it's open all night. I do a great Elvis impersonation and we always have plenty of champagne."

Akari snorts. The image of this guy doing an Elvis impersonation is too ridiculous not to laugh. "I'm less than half your age and have no interest in hanging out with you and your loser buddies. It's late, and I'm just trying to get to Tokyo in peace."

"You're from a fishing village up north in the Tohoku region, right? I can tell by your accent." He leans in close towards her, his eyes intense and calculating.

Something about the way he says fishing village sounds odd, so she faces the window and refuses to budge.

18

Finally, he gets the message, huffs and fiddles with his phone.

The scenery turns from suburbs to city, and soon the train jolts to a sudden stop.

"Last station. Tokyo. Everyone off."

Thank goodness. Having boarded the train in Hachinohe eight hours earlier, she can't wait to get off, and the last hour was the worst. She could barely breathe with the creepy guy next to her stealing half her space.

She glances at him as other passengers rustle around them, but he seems oblivious that this is the last stop, mobile phone still pushed against his ear.

She sighs loudly and stretches like a cat.

Still no reaction.

When she shifts her weight to stand, his arrogant expression turns dangerous. "Sit. You're not going anywhere."

Akari's face burns. "If you bother me, I'll stuff that cell phone down your throat."

Without warning, he chops the edge of his hand into her stomach. The blow knocks the air from her lungs and topples her back down, gasping. Stars dance before her eyes.

He leans in close and she smells peppermint. His lips almost brush her cheek. "I know who you are, and what you are. You're coming with me, *Chosen.*"

A bead of sweat rolls down the side of his face and drips onto the seat. He pushes the tip of a switchblade against her side to keep her still while the train empties.

She doesn't dare call out for help. *How did they find me so soon?*

"The Seeker will be here in a minute. Don't move. It'll be easier for you this way." He strokes her cheek with the back of his free hand, as if they were intimate friends.

She recoils from his frigid touch, but there's no place for her to turn. Adrenaline floods her body—they can't take her. She has to escape before the Seeker comes.

Her voice sounds more confident than she feels. "And here I thought you were just a jerk."

He grunts and glances at a text message on his phone, which gives her the opportunity she needs.

She moves fast, knocking away the knife with one hand and with the other blasting him in the throat with a miniature Taser, which she had grabbed from the bag at her feet.

His eyes go wide and his body convulses as fifty thousand volts shoot through him. When the charge ends she shoves him off the seat with a thud, grabs the bag by her feet, and jumps to retrieve her backpack from the overhead luggage rack.

Creepy Guy moans and grabs one of her sneakers. "Come here, you wench! You're worth a lot of money—"

She kicks him in the face and blood gushes from his nose.

He releases her foot, wipes his face, and stares at his blood as if there's no way it could be his. "You little—"

Akari doesn't wait to hear what he says. She bolts off the train, her heart racing.

Creepy Guy scrambles to his feet behind her.

The clock on the neon board reads twelve forty-two in the morning. Dozens of people meander about, yet the vast concourse looks almost empty.

She surges forward while Creepy Guy staggers into the doorway after her, unsteady on his feet.

Two police officers chat with a lone cashier at a small kiosk. She spins the other way and sprints outside— police will only complicate things for her, and things are complicated enough already. They can't protect her anyway.

Creepy Guy runs after her, only a few steps behind.

She can almost feel his hands around her neck, so she pumps her legs faster, jumps over the curb, and weaves through traffic. A horn blares behind her and a colorful string of curses echo off the surrounding buildings. When she reaches the other side of the street, she glances over her shoulder.

Creepy Guy picks himself off the concrete, sneers at her, and limps after her, his expensive suit pants now torn and bloody.

She turns and runs faster than she's ever raced before. Cars and pedestrians blur past her, air comes in gulps, and sweat coats her body as she switches streets at random. When she thinks she's gone far enough, she stops and looks for signs of Creepy Guy.

The street is clear.

She lost him.

Akari slows her breathing, shifts her backpack on her shoulders, and really looks upon Tokyo for the first time. Tall glass buildings tower over her while bright neon lights promote everything from Coke to sushi bars.

Her skin suddenly turns clammy and her head swims as the buildings start to close in on her. She squints her eyes and they begin to move. She starts to assign them personalities, which of course is truly idiotic. Her breath comes in gasps as her legs wobble.

She bites her lower lip, closes her eyes, steadies her breathing, and silently curses herself for being so stupid. *Really stupid.* With Creepy Guy somewhere nearby, she doesn't have time to waste, and these buildings will not harm her. Eventually air comes smoothly, her strength returns, and the panic attack fades.

When she opens her eyes, the buildings have returned to their true form, although one particularly tall glass office tower catches her eye. It reminds her of a headless samurai warrior, and for a brief moment she almost slips back into the panic attack, but she shakes the image from her head.

She needs to find Ueno, or Old Tokyo as the locals call it. Having memorized an old map her grandmother had given her, she knows where she is and where she needs to go, so she moves quickly, alert for trouble on the nearly deserted streets. When she enters the outskirts of Old Tokyo, the neighborhood becomes decidedly less friendly with graffiti-marred buildings, trash littering the ground, and tight, winding streets. A row of restaurants, bars, and nightclubs are all still open, and music gusts onto the street in bursts whenever doors open.

Her destination appears in the middle of the chaos: *The Twisted Samurai Swords.*

The three-story building stands out from its glass neighbors— a plain, light blue stucco structure with a red door, clay roof, and slanted eves over the windows. A bronze plaque above the door shows two samurai swords with different handles and blades twisted around each other, enclosed in a circle. Underneath the sign a wooden board says, "The Twisted Samurai Swords—A Hostess Bar Established in 1810."

She smiles to herself. Grandmother didn't mention it was a Hostess Bar. *Does she know?* Answers wait for her inside, so she steels her nerves, walks up the stoop, and opens the door.

A breathtakingly beautiful woman stands in the dimly lit hallway. Her long black hair is spun in an odango bun and secured by a porcelain and jade comb. A shiny black belt cinches a tasteful, sleeveless black dress around her thin waist.

"I'm here to—"

The hostess lifts her hand and speaks in a slow, precise, aristocratic voice. "I know why you are here. Let me look at you for a moment. No talking."

Heat flushes Akari's face as the hostess gazes at her for a few appraising moments.

"You're pretty enough. You have a beautiful round face, pleasing features. Maybe a tad short, but your eyes are absolutely stunning. You can do a lot with eyes like that. I don't know why you've cut your hair so short—it doesn't reach your shoulders. Still, wigs can fix that. I hate using them because so much of what we do is illusion in the first place, so why add to the list, but in your case I would make an exception."

Then she frowns. "But you're too young. What are you, fifteen?"

"I'm sixteen, but I'm not here for a job as a hostess—"

"Of course you aren't, dear. We never *hire* hostesses. We *make* hostesses. It takes years of study to become a hostess. You'll have to come back when you're eighteen. You can apprentice then." She turns up her chin and waves her hand at Akari, dismissing her by flicking her long fingers toward the door.

Akari crosses her arms over her chest and sighs. "I'm here to see Madam Kiko. My grandmother sent me."

"Now is not a good time. Madam Kiko likes to mingle among the clients. You'll have to come back in the morning. She doesn't like to be disturbed while she's working."

"I can't come back later. She'll want to see me. Tell her that Akina Kato sent me, and that it's time."

A sparkle twinkles behind the hostess's eyes as she nods. "You should have said that in the beginning, dear. Follow me."

She locks the front door and glides up a staircase, her posture perfect, only two fingers sweeping against the cherry wood handrail. She reaches the second floor and stops in front of a blue door. "Go inside and Madam Kiko will join you shortly. Don't touch anything."

Akari steps into the small office, which is elegantly appointed with a round yellow and red Asian rug, a small oak desk that looks extremely old, and a samurai sword in a glass case that hangs on the long interior wall. Three bonsai trees sit on the desk with short incense sticks burning next to them. The smell of sandalwood wafts to her in a light, pleasant cloud. The office isn't what she expected, but then again, she really didn't know what to expect.

She swings her backpack off her shoulders and checks to make sure everything is still inside: two pairs of jeans, a few shirts and other items of clothing, her small bag with the origami creatures, a packet of paper, a sharp three-inch fishing knife, and the crystal hilt of a sword. She has no idea how the sword works, but even now she feels a dark presence, as if it's calling her, reminding her of a responsibility she'd rather forget.

Frowning, she removes her prize possession: a yellowed photograph curled at the edges. Three people smile in the picture: her mother, father, and grandmother. Only her grandmother is still around. Her mom died during childbirth, and the ocean swallowed her father when she turned six. She never thinks of him as dead; that would be too hard. Lost is much better. If he's lost, he might simply find his way home and return one day.

As she tucks the photo into her back pocket, the door opens and Madam Kiko enters. She's styled her hair in the same decorated odango bun as the hostess, but she uses a more expensive gold and emerald comb to secure it. Thin and short, she wears a traditional black robe with a floral band around the waist.

Akari's gaze returns to her face, and butterflies swirl in her stomach. *She looks like Grandmother.* Well, not exactly. Her grandmother has a darker tan and more wrinkles around her eyes and forehead, but other than that, this woman *is* her grandmother.

Madam Kiko smiles, her eyes pointed daggers.

"Who... are you?"

"I see my sister never mentioned me. It's not surprising, really, as I'm the black sheep in the family, and my role in the Order requires secrecy. The farther removed I was from you both benefited all of us, although I would have thought she would have said something before you left. I hope she doesn't still hold a grudge against me all these years later."

"Grudge?"

Kiko shrugs. "It's not important, just a misunderstanding with her husband before they were married."

Akari's mind spins. *So many lies.* What's one more? Why should she expect anything else? Now the roles are reversed. She knows the truth, or at least more of the truth than her grandmother and great aunt, and it's her turn to stay silent — the only merciful thing to do.

Kiko lifts her hand, palm up, arm steady. "I believe you have something for me."

Akari studies her great aunt's small, delicate hand. With each step she plunges toward an uncertain future where she'll have to be strong, stronger than she has ever been before. She slowly removes a small bronze token from her front pocket. It matches the placard outside on the wall — two different samurai swords twisted together and enclosed in a circle.

Kiko closes her hand around the coin. "It's unfair, isn't it?"

"What's unfair?"

"This whole situation, really. My sister doesn't understand that. You're thrown in the middle—so many lives at stake. The world's balance teeters and everything rests on your thin shoulders, but you are Chosen."

Kiko glides toward the glass case that contains the samurai sword, swings it from the wall, and reveals a wall safe behind. A few moments later she holds a small bamboo box in her palm, the twisted samurai swords engraved on the lid. "This is for you."

"Do you know what's inside?"

She shakes her head. "The Order has kept this secret for over two hundred years. No one is allowed to open it but the Chosen."

Akari takes the box and tucks it into her backpack. It doesn't weigh much, but it might as well be a heavy chain that wraps around her neck and chest, and squeezes the air from her lungs. "What should I do?"

Her great aunt gently grabs her by the shoulders. "You must do what's right. No one can help you now. It's up to you."

Akari nods, although she knows differently. Others will help—three other Chosen. "A Seeker knows I'm in the city. One of his followers tried to grab me from the train. It'll be dangerous for you here."

"Don't worry about me, dear. I assume Akino left your village when you did?"

"Yes, but I don't know where she went."

"Good, that's for the best. You should go now. It's not safe here."

Akari retraces her steps from the hostess bar and stops in the middle of an empty street under a flickering streetlamp. She retrieves the box from her bag and leans against the side of a rundown restaurant that's closed for the night.

What's inside? For two hundred years, this secret has been kept. Her hand trembles. She doesn't know what to expect—another strange crystal maybe, or a potion with information about the enemy, or more powers to help her defeat the monsters who want to enslave the world.

One swipe with her fingernail breaks the wax seal, and she opens the lid. She shakes the box and two dozen polished diamonds of varying sizes roll around. It's a small fortune—enough to run, to start over, away from her destiny.

She slides the box into her backpack and hears a bottle shatter down the alley. Her heart races as a shadow moves in her direction.

Kiko's words ring in her ears. *It's not safe.*

Has the Seeker found me already? Is the end here so soon?

More noises, but this time they come from in front of her. Two men enter the alley, both wearing jeans, one with a plain blue T-shirt and the other in a white tank top. Both have bulging muscles and look to be in their early twenties.

She spins and finds the original shadow closing in on her. The murky figure has a smooth dome for a head and wears a crooked grin on his ugly face.

She's trapped.

The two men in front of her stop twenty feet before her. Tank Top speaks first. "What's a pretty young thing like you doing out on our streets alone?"

Akari smiles and almost laughs out loud with relief. These are ordinary thugs, not the enemy she fears. Her pulse returns to normal. "*Your* streets? I must have missed the sign. I'll make you a deal. If you guys turn and leave me alone, I'll let you go unharmed."

Tank Top points to a tattoo of a fire-breathing dragon on his arm. "You see that, little girl? We're Yakuza. No one works these streets without our permission. You're going to have to pay a price."

"Right! You're no more Yakuza than I am."

The notorious gangsters never flaunt their intricate tattoos. These are ordinary, dimwitted, second-rate thugs who like to prey on girls.

Tank Top's eyes narrow and his face burns crimson. "I'll show you who's Yakuza."

"Don't say I didn't warn you." Akari shrugs and tightens the straps on her backpack to secure it on her shoulders. "It's going to be hard for you to explain to your buddies how a sixteen-year-old girl whopped you, but it's your call."

Baldy laughs from behind her. "I like her. She has fire. I can't wait until we break her."

Akari stretches her back and feels energy flow around her. She directs it to her arms and legs and a familiar power fills her body. "Well, let's get it over with then. I don't have all night."

Time slows.

Tank Top darts forward and aims a front kick at her chest, but she easily sidesteps him and sweeps his leg out from under him.

The second guy tenses to throw a looping punch, but she rams her elbow into his face, busts open his nose, and he collapses on the ground.

Tank Top struggles to get up, but she stomps down hard on his head and hears his jaw break.

When she whirls, Baldy stands frozen. "How'd you do that? No one moves that fast."

Akari shoots him a wicked grin. "I'm not done yet." She focuses her attention on the alley behind him, feels power channel from her body, and pictures flames. The air starts to crackle and spark, and small flames swirl in a circle.

Baldy's face turns ash-white. "You're a witch!" he shouts, then jumps through the crackled air and sprints away.

"I'm not a witch, you idiot. I'm...."

I'm what?

She kicks a bottle as the shimmering air and the meager flames she had managed to conjure vanish. "I've got to do better than that."

Before she moves on, an explosion rocks the night air and shakes the ground. She runs toward the blast.

As flames lick the outside of the Twisted Samurai Swords Hostess Bar, she pulls an airplane ticket from her pocket: *Tokyo to New York City JFK.*

She's made her decision.

The world turns gray and then black. I wake with a start and bolt upright in bed. Morning light streams through the thin drapes, and it takes me a moment to remember where I am. All the trashy hotels blend together, and we pulled into this one late after we left Roy's.

Troy stirs in the bed next to mine. "Are you okay, Jules?"

"I'm fine."

"Did you have another vision?"

I nod and rub sleep from my eyes. I won't be able to go back to sleep now, another morning ruined.

"Was it a good vision or a bad one?" He calls my dreams visions, believing they're sent to me by the Great Wind Spirit to help me sort through events.

I know they aren't dreams. These are weird glimpses into the minds and experiences of the other Chosen, but they probably have nothing to do with spirits. Still, I don't argue with him about it. If it makes him feel better to think the Wind Spirit sends me visions and she's on our side, I'm not going to ruin it for him. Besides, I don't *know* the Wind Spirit isn't sending me these images. It is possible.

"A good one, I think."

Now relaxed, he drops his head against a pillow and falls back asleep.

CHAPTER

I wrap my arms around Troy's waist as we ride his motorcycle, a royal blue 1980 Honda CX he found in a junkyard and restored after six months of hard work.

"Check out the skyline!" he shouts.

"Pull over."

He swings the bike onto the shoulder of the New Jersey Turnpike right after we pass a sign for the Lincoln Tunnel, and a steady stream of cars whiz past us. We pry off our helmets and my long hair falls freely down my back.

A slate sky, heavy with moisture, drapes over tall buildings and I feel oddly disappointed. Maybe it's the foreign looking city or the dreary sky, but a bout of homesickness rifles through me for the first time since we left Arizona.

My voice has a melancholy lilt to it. "It's not what I expected."

"It's not a great view and we're still far away. Once we get closer, the buildings will look much bigger."

"It's not that. They're plenty big enough. They just feel kind of... hollow — not as beautiful or inspiring as the red rocks back home."

The skyscrapers scream "look at me" like a toddler might shout after building a tower of Legos, right before a bigger kid comes over to knock them down.

Troy shifts the helmet in his hands. "Of course they can't compete with those. Those rock formations were created when the world started, when the First Man lived and life began. How could we build something to match that?"

"I guess we can't." I shrug. "It's just that New York always sparkles in the movies like it's the center of the universe and magic glistens off the skyscrapers."

I've always wanted to visit this city. I thought the skyline would make my jaw drop in awe. I wanted to see magic, as silly and childish as that sounds, and now there's none.

"We're not going to find magic here. This place gives me the chills." He shakes his head. "Why would so many people want to live on top of each other? Look at those apartment buildings. There's no connection to Mother Earth with all the concrete and glass."

He doesn't understand, but I do. Humans are herd animals. We like the company of others — not the grouchy next door neighbor who drinks too much, but energy surrounds us when we gather. Our hearts pump faster and our thoughts quicken.

"It looks awfully big. We have to find the Inn and we only have the symbol to go on." My stomach tightens. It's possible to feel alone in the middle of a big party or a crowded city or on the New Jersey Turnpike with cars whizzing by you. I have Troy with me, but I still feel alone and that frightens me. I can't shake the idea that I'm no longer part of the herd.

I know we need to find the Inn because the Alphians gave me that information. I drank a fluid that had secret bits of knowledge embedded into it. At times, the information bubbles up to the surface of my thoughts, as if I've read a book and remember parts of it at odd moments. It's frustrating because everything is so fragmented. For instance, I know we need to go to New York City and find the Inn that uses a certain symbol. The other Chosen are supposed to gather there and we'll meet an Alphian who's called a *Host*. He will help guide us, but I don't know what the Host looks like or what his role will be. All I know for certain is that the Inn is in this giant city and we've got to find it among the monstrous glass and steel buildings.

Troy grins. "No problem. I have an idea."

We jump on the bike, drive through the Lincoln Tunnel and emerge in the middle of the city as if we break the surface of a river. Skyscrapers are everywhere, and we're plunged into a vast canyon where the buildings are massive cliffs.

Troy somehow manages to weave his way through the crazy number of cars that all have minds of their own. Cabs in particular have no compunction about cutting us off, and they stop wherever they want. He has to jerk the bike hard to the right to avoid one that swerved in front of us to pick up a fare.

When he pulls the bike in front of *New Beginnings* headquarters on 44th Street and 11th Avenue, sweat coats my back. Tall glass doors mark the main entrance, and a mural depicting young adults of different races, sizes, and shapes that head inside the building flanks the front doors, where a few teenagers mingle.

The building reminds me of a high school. Above the entrance is a round powder blue sign with the name "New Beginnings" spelled around the edges. In the center of the logo is an open door with light streaming through it.

I hand Troy my helmet as he locks the bike next to three others. "Are you sure this is a good idea?"

"No, but Landon's always been cool. He's lived here for three years now, so if anyone's going to know what that symbol means, it's him."

Troy's cousin finished two tours as a Marine in Afghanistan. The last time he came back, he seemed different—not talk-to-imaginary-people different, but damaged in a noticeable way, as if some of his soul had been stripped from him. He refused to look people in the eyes, and he cringed at loud noises and shrank away from crowds. We were all surprised when he decided to move to New York.

I'm not sure seeing him is a good idea. "If he calls back home or tries to turn us in, we'll have problems. When was the last time you even talked to him?"

"Must be three years ago when he was discharged from the Marines. Aunt Jane says he loves working here."

I hesitate at the doors, and the wind flips strands of loose hair across my face.

"Come on. He's family. It'll be fine."

Troy tugs on my arm and we go inside. To the left is a common area with walls painted bright colors, a small sitting area set up around cube-shaped chairs, and three knots of teenagers who chat around the edges, smiling and laughing. We amble to the right, toward a security guard, a glass partition, and a metal detector.

"We'd like to see Landon Black Bear Asher," Troy tells the mountain-sized guard.

The guard slowly washes his eyes over us. We must have passed some test because he points at the metal detector. "You'll have to give me those bags and go through the detectors. We don't let visitors bring bags into the dorms."

Troy glances at me and I nod. *What else can we do?*

We stroll through the metal detector and hand the guard our bags—Troy's with our clothes and cash, and mine with the Seeker Slayer hidden inside. As I hand him my cinch bag, a cold chill settles in my bones and butterflies flutter in my stomach. It's foolish—we're not going to face any Deltites here—but I remember what happened the last time I left it behind.

The guard sticks our bags into cubbies and points to an office down the hall. "Let them know you want to see Landon. They'll ring him."

A young woman with dark skin, long dreadlocks, and bright caramel-colored eyes sits behind the desk. With her runner's build she could easily have been a track star.

We tell her we want to see Landon.

She doesn't ask our names but smiles at us, her eyes sizing us up with that same look the security guard gave us. We pass the unknown test again, because a moment later she sends us down a hallway with instructions to meet Landon in the third office on our left.

"What does he do again?" I ask Troy as we amble toward his office.

"They take in homeless kids—" Troy points to the logo on the wall and grins. "—and give them new beginnings."

"Oh." That explains the looks we've been getting. With the number of kids flowing through these doors they probably have to make quick assessments about them all the time. I'm sure most are harmless, but some must have deep scars by the time they get here. Those types of experiences can change a person.

We reach Landon's office and find the door open and him sitting behind a desk. He could be Troy's brother, with the same body type—wide, strong but not sculpted like workout junkies you'll find in gyms. His hair is crew cut short, and a few patches of gray mingle with his black hair, which surprises me because he can't be thirty yet.

When we walk in, his eyes lift from the computer screen and a broad smile lights his tanned face. "Holy cow! Look what the cat dragged in—Troy Buckhorn and Juliet Wildfire Stone." He slips around the desk and shakes Troy's hand. "It is good," he says.

Troy takes his hand and repeats the traditional Dine' greeting. "It is good."

Landon wraps him in a tight hug, and they look like two bears wrestling. Once he releases Troy, he looks at me and turns down his lips at the ends. "I'm sorry about Jake. Your grandfather was an inspired healer. He helped me a great deal."

My heart swells with pride. I know Sicheii helped many people, but I never asked him about it—not in any real detail. I wish I had. "Really? I didn't know that he helped you."

"I brought a few dark spirits back with me from Afghanistan. He taught me how to put my world back in balance. They still haunt me now and again, but I can deal with them."

My eyes moisten.

Landon squeezes my hand. "He's still with us. A spirit as strong as his could never disappear. He's watching over you from the shadow lands. You'll never be without his guidance so long as you open your spirit to his."

"That's what I'm worried about. He'll haunt me forever." We chuckle and the sadness passes. It doesn't fade completely, but it slips to the back of my mind.

"You two have certainly created quite a stir back home. Mom's called me three times. The whole Tribe's worried about you. They want me to lead a search."

I grin nervously at him. "I guess we made your job easier, but we don't want to be found just yet."

Landon's eyes sparkle. "We'll talk. How about lunch? There's a great pizza place down the block."

Troy rubs his stomach like he hasn't eaten in days. "Pizza sounds awfully good."

I roll my eyes.

"What?" he asks me.

"We just ate an hour ago."

He doesn't eat like our friend Marlon back home, who inhales food as if he's always starving, but Troy will never pass up fast food like pizza, tacos, or burgers.

He smirks at me. "It's an insult to turn down food from a member of the Tribe. I'm just being polite."

Landon leads us back to the front door, his shoulders swaying confidently, his head high and his back straight. He seems whole, which is much better than he looked the last time we met. A green, long sleeve T-shirt fits snug over his muscled frame, and beige cargo pants swish as he walks.

I follow a step behind as we walk through the empty hallway. "So, what's New Beginnings? What exactly goes on here?"

"We provide new starts for homeless kids. We give them food, a safe place to stay, medical care, addiction counseling, and education."

When we reach the metal detector, the security guard hands us our bags.

On the way out, Landon stops in front of a young man and woman who are in the middle of a quiet conversation near the front door. "Hey, John," he says as he clasps the young man on the shoulder. "Shouldn't you be in the interview workshop?"

John combs his hands through his long straight hair. "They rescheduled the class until later. Don't worry, I'm not skipping out."

"Good." Landon turns toward the young woman. "Amy, I heard you missed Group yesterday." He crosses his arms against his chest, his eyes narrow. "You've got to stick with the program."

"Do you know everything that goes on around here?" She shoots him a half-smile and puts her hands on her hips.

"Only the important stuff. What happened?"

"Job interview with CVS."

Landon arches one of his eyebrows upward. "How'd it go? Did you land the job?"

"We'll find out later today."

"Good." Landon winks at her, and we head out the door.

"Amy's going to get that job," he tells us when we hit the street.

"How do you know?" asks Troy as he speeds up to keep abreast of us.

Landon marches us down 44th. "The assistant manager at that CVS is one of my first kids. I called him yesterday to set it up."

"Does she know?"

"Nope. We all have secrets. That's okay, so long as they aren't harmful. Most of the time these kids just need to know someone cares about them and is paying attention to them. Plus, a kick in the rear every now and again comes in handy."

We reach 10th Avenue and Landon leads us into a small pizzeria. It's around two o'clock so the place is empty. As we stroll into the restaurant, a middle-aged guy with a round face and a gold necklace recognizes him and points to the back. "Your table is open. Do you want the usual?"

Landon looks at me. "Is pepperoni, sausage, and meatball good?"

There's no need to ask Troy. His tongue practically flops out of his mouth.

"You bet," I say.

I sit opposite Landon at the metal table in the back corner. "They seem to know you here."

"Sometimes I do initial intake sessions here. People open up after they have food in their bellies."

"Is that what you're doing with us?" I shoot him a pointed look. We're not homeless kids looking for a place to stay. He shouldn't use tricks on us.

He leans back in his chair and smirks. "Maybe, but I'm hungry and Anthony's has the best pizza in town."

Just then the waiter brings over a large pie and places it in front of us. Troy jumps in almost before the waiter leaves.

I grab a small piece and take a bite. Landon's right; the flavors explode in my mouth, the best pizza I've ever tasted by a wide margin. Nothing else should even be called pizza.

After we've all finished a slice, Landon asks, "So, what's going on? Why'd you guys run?"

Troy and I share a look. He'll never believe the truth, and he shouldn't be involved in this mess. I already feel bad about Troy. "We didn't run away *permanently*. There's just something we need to do here before we go back."

"And this *thing* is secret, right?" When we nod, he asks, "What can I do to help you with this super-secret-you-can't-tell-me-at-all thing?"

Troy stops shoveling pizza into his mouth long enough to say, "We need to find a place. We don't know the name, but it has a distinctive logo. We figure you might have seen it around."

Landon clasps his beefy hands together and places them on the table in front of him. "Okay, here's the deal. Trust is a two-way street. I'll help, but there are a few conditions. First, you need to check in with me every other day. I need to know you're safe.

Second, you've got to send some proof of life back home. You don't need to tell them where you are or what you're doing, but they shouldn't be worried that you've been abducted by aliens or worse."

I glance toward the front of the restaurant and spot a mom with a young daughter. Pink ribbons tie the girl's straight blonde hair into pigtails. She couldn't be older than five. The mom orders one slice and the girl jumps up and down. I envy them, their ignorance. They don't know about Deltites, or the Chosen, or the fate of the world.

I turn back toward Landon and nod my agreement, sealing our deal.

"All right, so what's this symbol look like?" Landon asks, grabbing his second slice of pizza.

"It'll be better if I draw it."

He hands me a pen and I start to sketch on a white paper plate.

"Do you guys need money or a place to stay?" he asks while I draw.

Troy mumbles as the words compete with space for his third slice of pizza. "No, but I left my motorcycle back by New Beginnings. Is it going to be safe there?"

Landon grins. "I'll put a NB sticker on it. You're part of the family now. We look after each other."

He sounds serious, and his eyes sparkle as if he's found a treasure he wants to share with us. New Beginnings is more than a job to him; it's become a family, a replacement for what he felt with the Marines before he fought and killed overseas.

His emotions flood through me in a heartbeat. I pick up intense emotions from others easier than reading thoughts. Often they just whip through me without me doing anything. I hate when that happens.

I take a deep breath and pass him the plate with my sketch of the logo on it. The logo combines all four of our symbols — the twisted arrows, samurai swords, muskets, and English long swords. A circle encloses them, separated into fourths by swooping curved teardrop-shaped lines. Each section has a different symbol, so if I squint, it resembles a weird wheel with spokes.

Landon studies it for a second and looks back at us. "That's curious. I've seen it before. It's the symbol of a small boutique hotel in the Village. It's kind of upscale. Is that what you want?"

"Sounds right." I take back the plate from him.

"There's one more condition." He crosses his arms and his voice turns stern. Whatever the condition, he won't negotiate with us.

"You have one week. If you can't complete your secret mission by then, you've got to come completely clean with me, and I get to decide if you stay or go home."

Troy frowns at me. We've never discussed how long this would take.

I consider it for the first time.

You don't need to see or touch something to be convinced that it's real. We learn facts in school we could never verify with our senses, and yet we know they're true. I'm certain Seekers are coming for me even if I don't have any physical proof of it. If we can't defeat them in a week, it'll be too late. They'll have found us.

"Deal." I reach out and shake his hand.

He writes an address on the paper plate and hands it to me. "How about I show you guys around the City tonight? I'm doing an outreach run. You'll see parts of the City they'll never show you on any other tour."

"Sure," Troy and I say at the same time.

"Good." Landon beams a bright smile at us. "The run starts at midnight. Meet me back at NB headquarters and don't be late."

I close my eyes and a sudden thunderclap rips open my skull. The pain is so intense it makes me dizzy, but the storm dissipates as suddenly as it came. When I open my eyes, I study Troy for a moment as he shovels the last bite of his third slice into his mouth. A faint aura surrounds him—a soft white light. Landon has one also, but his has small swirls of black around the edges. I shake my head and glance at the waiter, who has an aura also— light gray. The cook by the pizza oven is surrounded by gray light tinged with a muddled red as he pounds flat a new ball of dough.

I don't know what it means, but I realize with dread that my aberration traits have kicked up to seven.

When do I stop being human and become something else?

Has it happened already?

CHAPTER 5

We finish lunch, leave the pizzeria, and take the Number 1 subway train to West 4th Street. We stand in the middle without holding onto the metal poles, like surfing in a tin can deep underground, only instead of riding waves we're on rails that wail and make sudden turns we can't see.

The train stops unexpectedly with a screech of the brakes and I fly forward. Troy grabs me a moment before I career into a stuffy looking man wearing a business suit. He glares at us, but we laugh, and I feel light for the first time in days—almost like I used to be.

I wouldn't mind riding the subway all day, but when we reach our stop, we shuffle off and find a map of the surrounding neighborhood. A few minutes later, we stroll down a tree-lined street with townhouses on both sides. The Village feels totally different from Midtown where New Beginnings is located. A slower more measured pace replaces the tense frenetic midtown vibe that surrounded the homeless shelter. We pass mostly townhouses, but a few bars and restaurants fill out the neighborhood.

"How are we going to send word back home that we're all right?" Troy asks as we look at building numbers. "We don't want to leave any trail that could get our families in trouble."

"My father has a burner phone. He got it before we left just in case we needed to call him."

Troy stops. "A burner phone?"

"Yeah. It's a prepaid phone that no one can trace to him or us. We'll get one here. He learned a few things while doing time over the past 16 years."

The court convicted my father of manslaughter before I was born. Although innocent, he *did* sell drugs and had committed some terrible acts. He wrote me a letter once a week while away, but Mom hid them from me and made me believe he wanted nothing to do with me. She figured he would be a bad influence, and that I should have nothing to do with him, without ever asking my opinion, which I'm sure she would've disregarded anyway, doing whatever she wanted because she *always* knows what's best for me. I thought I had forgiven her, but my hands ball into fists just thinking about it.

We stop in front of 156 Perry Street, a six-story stone townhouse with a red door and a copper sign that hangs from a rusty metal bar. The sign is almost identical to my drawing.

Troy glances at me, a worried look on his face. He knows I'm conflicted.

Part of me wants to run, but I've already made the decision to follow this destiny to the end, and I can't go back now. Besides, they'll find us soon, and I'd rather be the hunter than the hunted.

"I hope they have room service." He shifts the duffel on his shoulders.

"Do you always think with your stomach? You've just eaten your second lunch."

He shrugs. "I'm like a Lamborghini: at my best when fully fueled."

I roll my eyes. "That's about all you have in common with a Lamborghini."

"Hey, no need to be nasty." He feigns a hurt look.

The wind gusts and I smell the city — part sweat, trash, and decaying food, but also part electric and part sweet from flowers in a window box and pastries from a nearby bakery, which creates an odd mixture. Now that my sense of smell is getting stronger, I breathe deeply and smell pansies from a house halfway down the black, and wrinkle my nose at a suspicious paper bag left on the corner that I'm sure has dog poop in it.

The wind rustles Troy's shirt. "The Great Wind Spirit has spoken. After you."

He's only half kidding. He finds signs in the smallest things: wind gusts, animals, clouds, and once in the weird shape of a taco.

Those are just coincidences to me, having no more meaning than the day of the week.

The crimson door takes a firm yank to open. The small lobby has black and white alternating tiles on the floor, mahogany paneling, and a small chandelier that hangs from the ceiling. A curved staircase to the right leads upward, and to the left sits a cherry desk with an old-fashioned reading lamp and an open guest registry.

An odd-looking man sits behind the desk, nose firmly planted inside a romance novel. When Troy shuts the door behind us, he glances over the edge of his book. His red hair and beard twist into tight curls. The big jowls on his fleshy face make him look doughy, and he has a sharp pointy nose, narrow hazel eyes, and thin blond eyebrows that point upward and form an arrow.

His expression morphs from mild annoyance to intrigue in a heartbeat, as if a switch has been flipped, and a new light shines behind otherwise dull eyes. He stands but it doesn't gain him much height. He's shorter than I am, maybe five-foot-four, with a few extra inches padding his middle. He wears a black collared shirt and black pants, and pulls on his beard with fingers that have highly polished nails. A gold ring on his right pinky with the Inn's symbol on it catches the light and sparkles. He smiles at me by turning up only the edges of his lips, as if unsure if he's happy or annoyed.

His voice sounds strangely high-pitched and bubbly like a carbonated drink. "My, my, my. I was going to tell you we were full. What a mistake that would have been! The Host would have been so cross with me. Oh my, my. I've narrowly avoided quite an unforgivable mess with that one."

I step closer to him. "You know who I am?"

He speaks quickly, as if his internal thoughts fizz out of his mouth without a filter. "What a question. Oh yes, that *is* a deep one, very deep really. How does someone *know* another person? I don't think we should dive into those waters just yet. Not just yet. Let's just say I was expecting you. Yes, that would be quite enough for now. You're the Twisted Arrows. Yes?"

I nod, because I can't think of what to say, and try to tune into his mind and unlock his secrets. I really don't like to do this—it feels wrong, like reading private emails, but he could know something important about me and the other Chosen. Information he might not be willing to share. I concentrate hard but get nothing; just white noise, which is odd, but it's not the first time I've drawn a blank. Some people are harder to read than others. I don't know why—either they don't have anything on their minds, or their brains work at a frequency outside of my ability to detect.

Some of the bubble fizzles from his voice when he turns toward Troy. "You, I was not expecting. Very handsome and all, but we have no rooms for rent. No rooms at all. I can call around and find you somewhere else in the City to stay. Maybe the East Village?"

Troy starts to snarl at him.

I step in between the two. "He's with me. He'll stay in my room."

He pauses for a second and bunches his eyebrows together. His uncertain expression changes into a sly smile that I don't like. "Of course, of course. It is your decision. If you think that's wise, then stay in your room he shall. Yes, there's plenty of space in the suite. Plenty. You are in charge, after all."

He pushes his hand toward me. "My name is Stuart. I'm the Innkeeper."

His grip is warm and mushy like freshly baked bread warm from the oven.

"Where's the Host? I'd like to meet him."

"The Host, your benefactor, your patron? Yes, I'm sure he's anxious to meet you. Very anxious, but he'll want the other three to arrive first and they're not here yet. One grand meeting for the first time. That would be his style, certainly."

Troy leans forward. "Do you know when the others will arrive?"

"Oh no. Sorry no. I know very little about the other Twisteds."

"*Twisteds?*" Troy scowls.

Stuart raises both of his hands to his cheeks and forms a circle with his mouth. "Did I say that out loud? I'm so sorry. Yes, very sorry. I meant no offense. I just know the symbols. Yes, just the four twisted objects. Let me show you up to your room. You're the first of your party to arrive. You'll be staying on the top floor in the Arrow Suite."

He leads us to an elevator on the back side of the staircase. When the elevator stops on the fifth floor, we disembark and he opens a door with the twisted arrows symbol carved into the wood. The room is a blizzard of white—walls, carpet, furniture—everything snow-white except two framed paintings of red rock formations that hang over the couch.

"I hope you will like your stay with us. Yes, I'm sure you will. I live on the first floor. If you require anything, just ring." He smiles with his full face, half bows as he shuffles backward, and closes the door.

Troy frowns. "There's something about *Stewie* I don't like."

I grin. "He seems harmless to me. Of course he did say you were handsome, which probably means he has some type of vision impairment. Maybe that's what you picked up on."

I expect Troy to crack a smile or laugh but the lines on his face stay serious. "How did he know you were a Chosen and not me?"

"Oh, well, that's obvious, isn't it? You're just a handsome, not quite Chosen type of guy."

He grins, but I freeze as my blood turns to cold slush. A leather journal sits on top of the four-poster bed by the pillows. It's the same type of journal that Sicheii gave me—old with cracked leather—although this time it has the twisted arrows symbol carved into the cover instead of the slanted rectangle for the Wind Spirit.

Troy follows my gaze. "Did you know there was another book?"

I shake my head and lift the leather object. My fingers tremble. It's sealed with wax that I cut away with my thumbnail.

A crystal vial inside contains a liquid, just like the last two "books" I discovered. I touch the crystal.

Nothing happens. The liquid doesn't turn red and the top of the vial doesn't disappear like it did with the other two. Without an opening, there's no way for me to drink the liquid inside and gain whatever knowledge it contains.

I glance at Troy, shrug, and slip the small glass bottle into my pocket.

"There's a note under the vial." He hands it to me.

The handwriting is a fancy cursive.

You are the Alpha. This responsibility and knowledge is for you alone. When you are ready, the vial will open and you will learn all you must know. Be brave, for the only chance to save your world and their kind lies within you.

The note dissolves into thin air.

Troy's breath brushes against my lips. "What did it say?"

"Nothing really. The vial will open when it's time, but we should keep this secret from the others."

I'm not sure why I don't tell him the whole truth, but the last phrase in the note cracks my heart.

It said *their kind,* not *your kind.*

CHAPTER 6

Blake meets his parents in the immense foyer, his shoulders folded and his hands stuffed into the front pockets of his khakis. He feels small, as if he's nothing more than a statue in a museum—an *insignificant* statue. The mansion has that effect on him.

A massive crystal chandelier hangs from the vaulted ceiling, and a black Steinway grand piano stands to his left. He assumes it works, though he can't remember anyone ever playing it. The music room has a Steinway of its own—that one definitely works.

He faces his parents with his back to the front door. He doesn't want to turn around, doesn't want to leave. Bad things wait for him out there, dangers he'd rather not face, and a future his active imagination could never have dreamed of only a few weeks ago. He might feel small, but he's safe inside the house.

He shudders at the thought of leaving. "I don't understand why you're throwing me out like the trash. Can't I just stay here?"

His mother's expression turns to stone and his father shakes his head. "We've been through this already. You are Chosen. It's time. You must fulfill your destiny."

Jiles and Rachel Richards, were crew stars at Harvard twenty years ago, and still look much the same as they did when they competed. Jiles with his wide shoulders, chiseled arms, and well-muscled legs could still lead a team. Perhaps he's a little thicker in the waist than he had been, but that would hardly slow him down. Rachel, a coxswain in college, hasn't changed since. Slim and petite, her steely voice could make hardened criminals jump to action.

Blake wonders for the millionth time how these physically perfect people could have created him. He's sure he was adopted, and even confronted his father about the possibility, but Jiles dragged out the photo album that clearly showed Rachel's pregnancy and everyone in the hospital when he was born. He even produced Blake's birth certificate when he continued to ask more questions.

Yet Blake still has doubts whenever he looks in the mirror. To be generous, he usually describes himself as lanky. Others might say he's rail thin. His eyes are small and black, his shoulders slim, and his feet way too big and always tripping him up. Unlike his parents' straight blond hair, his black curly locks threaten to frizz into an afro at any time. The situation becomes alarmingly desperate during the summer when he's forced to use handfuls of styling gel to tame the beast.

Summer is his least favorite season. He rarely goes outside, not because of his hair, although that would be reason enough, but summer is hot and sweaty and filled with bugs. A few cases of West Nile virus have already been reported in neighboring Massachusetts, just one state away from his home state of Maine.

It's only a matter of time before infected mosquitos find him, and West Nile is only one of many different types of diseases he could get—and not nearly the most dangerous. Malaria and Ebola are admittedly less likely, but how can he rule them out completely? Leprosy is a distinct possibility. His acne had vanished just two weeks ago, so it would be perfectly ironic for chunks of his face to fall off now. The world works that way. Win the lottery and a truck is sure to run you over.

"I don't understand all this talk about destiny." Blake's voice raises a pitch. "I thought my *destiny* was to assume control over Richards Medical Equipment one day. That's what you've always said. We're creating an empire, and I would become the next CEO."

Jiles stares at him with emerald eyes, as finally honed as scalpels. "That's later. Right now, you have a more important destiny. You must defeat the devil so the gates to heaven can stay open."

"We don't know who these other Chosen people are. Maybe they're the wrong sorts of people. How can I possibly go out there with all those common people and rely upon strangers?" Blake waves his arm toward the door and the numerous dangers *out there*.

His mother speaks in a chuckle, as if the words are laughed from her lips. "Wrong sort of people, dear? God wouldn't choose the wrong sort for something so important."

Blake refuses to look at her. As tough as his father is, his mother can crumple Jiles into a tinfoil ball and toss him to the floor with one flick of her wrist. His only chance is to turn his father around, and those odds, never high to start with, are fading fast.

Blake crosses his arms over his chest. "What if one of these Chosen is an Excelsior Man? I refuse to work with someone from Excelsior. That's unreasonable." Excelsior is the dreaded archrival of his own private prep school, Cordwell Academy, where young men from his family have attended for over one hundred years.

"I wouldn't worry about Excelsior." His father frowns. "It's time for you to go. Stop stalling."

"But don't you want to know where I need to go? I'm—"

"Stop that!" His mother screeches.

He cringes as her voice knifes into his back and carves a small path down his spine. He couldn't continue if he wanted; she's simply too powerful.

She continues in a softer tone. "We *want* to know, dear, but we *can't* know. That would put you in danger. What if the devil's minions find us? You're not to contact us until this is finished."

Blake swallows the last bit of hope he had left and realizes what he really knew all along—he's doomed. He's on his own, which probably means he's a goner. "Well, this is shabby treatment for your only son."

He picks up the handle of his carry-on luggage. He wants to bring two other full-sized bags, so he can be more prepared for the plethora of dangers he imagines, but his parents limited him to the carry-on and the laptop bag. He stuffed the carry-on with so many different medications, none of which he really needs, there isn't much room for anything else—except for the ridiculous crystal hilt with the blade that appears every time he touches the darn thing. He keeps hoping it will stop working, so he can prove he isn't chosen to do anything, but so far no luck.

Resigned to his fate, he rolls the bag toward the door, stops at the marble pedestal table, pulls out an anti-bacteria wipe from the box perched on top, and vigorously rubs his hands.

His father hands him the box. "We only keep this around for you. Joffrey will take you to the private airfield. You're to tell Carl where you want to go."

Blake frowns. "You know how much I hate flying in the private plane. It's like a bus with wings."

His father slaps him on the back. "What do you know about buses? You've never been on one."

"I've seen the stories on the internet. They're always getting into accidents. The bus driver either falls asleep or a truck T-bones them. Everyone dies." Blake sullenly glances at his father and sees nothing but certainty. No cracks have formed in the emeralds that stare back at him.

"I don't think Carl's going to fall asleep, and there are no flying trucks to crash into the plane. You have two credit cards that are linked to trust accounts. There should be enough funds for you to do whatever you require." Jiles grabs him by the shoulders. "I know you don't see it now, but you're stronger than you think. You've always been special. It's time you lived that out. Everything will go back to the way it was when you finish and come home, I promise."

"Well, right, *if* I come back." Blake spots the tiniest trace of moisture in his father's eyes and feels bad; his dad is only doing what he thinks is right, what he had been taught is the only way.

He glances at his mom, who looks like a drawn bow about to spring. He closes his eyes, feels the energy around him, and creates a sharp gust of wind that rustles his parents' perfect hair. When he opens his eyes, both of them are smiling. His ability to summon wind always brings a smile, and it does come in handy when he sails.

"You see?" His father opens the door. "You are Chosen."

Blake suspiciously eyes the front walkway to the black Bentley.

His father kisses him on the forehead and his mom gives him a quick hug. When they separate, she nudges him out the door, or at least that's what it seems like to him.

He sighs, scans for mosquitoes and creeps toward the car, moving forward as if the ground has been transformed into a frozen lake and he's unsure whether it will hold his weight.

Halfway to the car, he looks back toward the mansion for what he expects will be the last time.

His parents are gone, the door shut.

His eyes focus on a square piece of marble toward the right of the door. Two twisted muskets in a circle are carved into it— *The Order of the Twisted Muskets.* He has lived with that carving his whole life and never asked about it. Now he knows what it means and wishes he had never seen the symbol or learned of the secretive group.

He squeezes into the car and sinks into the soft leather seats.

"Juliet, are you okay? Where have you gone?" Troy stands over me.

I shake my head to clear away the vision of Blake. "I'm fine. I must have taken a little catnap."

I don't tell him about the vision. I'm not keeping secrets; it's just that I don't want to talk about it.

CHAPTER

I wash the City from my face, and a weird sensation whisks through my head, as if someone's tickling my brain with a feather.

Sicheii's weathered voice rings in my mind. "A Chosen needs help. Find him."

"*Argh!* You started all this." I mutter to myself because it's not really Sicheii's voice I hear. He's dead, gone forever.

The tickle becomes a super-annoying itch, so I dry my face, leave the bathroom, and swat Troy on the leg. "Come on, we've got to go."

He points to the *NCIS* rerun on TV. "I want to see who did it. It's almost over."

"One of the Chosen is close. We should find him. He needs our help."

Troy stretches and lopes toward the door. "How do you know he's in trouble?"

"I don't *know.* I just have this feeling that won't go away."

"Who are we looking for?"

We start down the stairs. "Beats me."

I've seen Blake and Akari in the dream visions. The third is a mystery and I have a feeling we need to find the mystery.

"Cool. We're hunting Spirit Walkers. Which way? The City's kinda big."

"*No kidding.*"

He shrugs. "A direction would be nice. I'm just saying."

"Out there somewhere." We stroll past Stuart, who's sitting at his desk. He hides his face behind a paperback as we pass, yet I can feel his eyes follow us. He gives me the creeps.

When we reach the street, I say, "Let's wander."

Troy smiles. "It's like you're dowsing for water, only you're looking for Spirit Walkers instead."

"Dowsing?"

"Sure. Your grandfather told me about it. Dowsers channel the water spirit. Usually they use two sticks that form a Y, hold them with only their thumbs and index fingers, and let the water spirit pull the sticks toward an underground spring. Maybe we should get some sticks." He starts to search the ground by a tree.

"Come on." I pull his arm. "Sticks aren't going to help. Hopefully, we can dowse quickly because I have a hunch he's in trouble." My pulse quickens, and I start to speed-walk, turning at corners that feel right. I can't lose a Chosen now, not before we've even met.

We reach 14th Street, which is wide and busy, jammed with men in business suits, mothers with strollers, and college students jogging. They're all rushing as if they're late to get somewhere important.

A stabbing pain burns through my head, as though someone's stuck a needle through my temple. I stop in front of a pub called The Blarney Stone and peer inside. A long wooden bar stretches to the right and tables to the left. A cluster of people stand at the far end of the bar watching a soccer match on the flat screen in the corner—a river of red shirts with one blue buoy floating in the middle.

The pain vanishes, and I turn toward Troy. "Don't ask me how I know, but this is the place."

"Great." He opens the door, and we drift into the bar.

No one pays any attention to us. They're all watching the soccer match between Manchester United and Chelsea. The bar obviously supports Manchester United—a Red Devils banner hangs behind the bartender along with two signed Manchester United jerseys in glass cases.

Everyone in the bar wears a red shirt except for the lone Chelsea supporter. He stands a few inches taller than those around him, with an old blue Chelsea jersey stretched over his wide shoulders. He's around my age, with sandy hair parted to one side, a strong jaw and blue-gray eyes. His nose, bent slightly to the right, probably didn't heal properly after being broken, which only adds to his rugged good looks. He leans against the bar with strong, well-muscled arms, and looks comfortable, as if he's spent a lot of time in pubs.

I nudge Troy as a pint of beer travels down the length of the bar and into the stranger's waiting hand. His eyes never leave the flat screen as he chugs the entire beer in one messy gulp.

Troy smirks. "Can you do that?"

"You've seen me use telekinesis before."

Troy chuckles. "No, I mean chug a beer that fast. It has to be his special ability."

I stomp down on his foot.

"Oww! That hurt." He shakes his leg.

"Don't be a baby."

"Are you sure he's in trouble. It doesn't seem like he needs our help."

"Wait for it."

Tied at one, they're in the 85th minute of the match. All eyes are glued on the flat screen; even the bartender hasn't looked our way. When a blue striker dashes past the defense, the bar collectively moans, and the energy turns volcanic.

The soccer ball finds the top right corner of the Manchester net.

The Chelsea supporter pumps his hands in the air, and shouts, "Goooooooaaal! Goooooooaaaal!" The glass he's holding liquefies and melts down his arm.

The rest of the place groans and starts cursing at him.

A wicked grin flickers across his face as he jumps onto the bar. He wobbles as he lands and starts chanting with slurred words and in an accent I just begin to understand when he starts his second chorus:

Carefree, wherever we may be,
We are the famous CFC,
And we don't give a crap,
Whoever you may be,
'Cos we are the famous CFC.

The bartender shouts at him, "Get down from there, boy! I knew I shouldn't have let a Chelscum Blue supporter in the bar."

Two beefy men stalk toward the Chosen. They look like brothers with identical scowls on their long faces. "We'll get him down and teach him a lesson. No one shows us up in our place."

Glass shatters, and a middle-aged guy in the back holds a broken bottle by the neck. He's all sharp angles and bones. His eyes pinch together and gleam dangerously as he elbows his way toward the front of the mob.

The bartender grabs a baseball bat.

The Chelsea fan stops chanting and bellows, "It'll take more than a dozen Manure Red Hooligans to take me down, mates!"

"There's fifteen of us, you git!" shouts someone from the back.

"Oh, that could be a problem." He slurs his words and hops off the bar. "Still I'm willing... to give it a... go." He lifts his hands into fists with his back to the bar.

The bartender moves behind him with the bat raised, and the two brothers poise to leap at him. The man with the broken bottle sidles next to them, his mind full of anger and hate. He wants to kill.

Troy and I dart forward. We jump in between the Chelsea fan and the broken beer bottle. I keep my eyes glued on the jagged glass.

The sneer on the man's face deepens. One of the brothers slaps his shoulder, and he doesn't let go. The man tries to shrug him off, but the other brother grabs his elbow.

Troy smiles at the bartender. "Thanks for keeping an eye on our cousin. He escaped from the psychiatric hospital today. We'd better take him back. They're looking for him." He lifts his hand to his temple and rotates his finger in a circle.

The bartender lowers the bat. "You'd better get him out of here or he's gonna leave in pieces."

Some of the anger dissipates from the mob. The two brothers pull the man with the bottle backward and the rest step to the side and create a clear path to the door.

I grab one of the Chosen's arms and Troy grabs the other.

"Wait a minute," he protests, but we hold him steady as we drag him toward the door. "The match isn't over yet."

"It is for you." I grab a beaten-up backpack from the end of the bar that I assume is his.

He shouts over his shoulder as we leave. "I'll be back for the next match. Save me a spot!"

Troy hails a cab and I push the Chosen into the back with us.

"What do you guys want? I'm not into any kinky stuff," he says.

"We're taking you to the Inn."

"Oh, you're one of the Freaky Four." He holds out his hand. "My name's Connor."

"I'm Juliet." I shake his hand.

"Hey, you guys aren't Manhole supporters are you? Cause I'm getting out if you are, and the world can piss off."

"We're from Arizona," says Troy, as if that answers the question.

"Oh." Connor smiles at me, closes his eyes, and drops his head on my shoulder. When the cab screeches to a stop in front of the Inn, we wrestle him out of the car, loop his arms over our shoulders and half drag, half lift him into the hotel.

Stuart pops up from his desk. "Oh my, my, my. You've found another one in your party. Mr. Long Sword. Yes, he most definitely is Mr. Long Sword."

"His name is Connor," I say as we drag him to the elevator.

"I'd ask what happened to him, but the smell gives him away. Yes, it certainly does." Stuart bats the air in front of his face and wrinkles his nose. "He's brought the entire brewery back with him, hasn't he now? Me, I never touch the stuff. Well, not never — I do have a weakness for a Pina Colada now and again, always before dinner and never more than two. I collect the umbrellas. I have a nice assortment now. Sometimes I imagine miniature people caught in a rainstorm." He flutters his fingers in the air seemingly making believe they're raindrops.

We leave the elevator and Stuart unlocks the door, the one with the twisted long swords carved into it. Connor's rooms look the same as mine, except pictures of the River Thames and Hampton Court Palace are hung on his bedroom wall instead of my red rock formations. We toss him on the bed, and I drop his rucksack on the floor.

He rolls over and starts snoring.

"Great." Troy scowls. "I hope we're not going to need him. He's useless."

I shoot him a half smile, half shrug. "Maybe he only drinks during soccer matches."

Troy shakes his head. "No one chugs like that without a ton of experience. Look at him. He's a hopeless drunk."

I know Troy's thinking about his father, a nasty drunk whom Troy has had to rescue from bars back home.

Still, I look at Connor and hope he's wrong. Just meeting another Chosen has lifted my spirits. Even though I know there are others out there like myself, now I've met one. They are real... and there are two more.

Connor melted that glass in his hand, which means he can liquefy solids. I can hear thoughts and possess animals. Akari creates fire, and Blake can harness the wind. Those abilities have to count for something.

The Deltites will have skills of their own, which will probably be stronger than ours, but still, a faint sense of hope flutters through me for the first time since I've started this journey.

I glance around the rooms and get the uneasy notion that something is missing, and then I realize he doesn't have another book. It would have been on his bed like it was for me.

I swallow hard, and the feeling of isolation returns.

I grab Troy's hand to chase it away.

CHAPTER 8

Troy and I reach New Beginnings headquarters five minutes before midnight.

Already out front, Landon leans against a white van with the NB logo on the side. He grins when he spots us. "So, did I send you to the place you wanted?"

I'm purposively vague. "You started us in the right direction, thanks."

He shoots me a piercing look. He wants to know more, but he doesn't ask. Our week has only started, so he's giving us time to tell him what we're up to when we're ready.

A man and woman, both in their early twenties, bound out of NB. The woman is the same one who manned the office earlier in the day. Her dreadlocks sway as she springs forward.

Landon introduces us. "I think you met Tara this afternoon in the office."

She smiles and we all shake hands.

The man has short black hair, huge shoulders, pitch-black eyes, and wears a black *Batman* T-shirt. Tattoos cover both his arms and neck, turning his body into a giant canvas. A hoop earring dangles from his left ear and a long cross hangs from the right.

He's terrifying. I can't imagine someone looking scarier, but when he smiles the illusion shatters, and he's all sugar. His voice is soft and filled with sweetness, sounding nothing like I would have guessed.

"My name's Frankie. Welcome to the family. Any friend of Black Bear's is a friend of mine." He extends a massive fist the size of an anvil, which we bump in turn. A distractingly white aura surrounds him like a cloak.

Landon opens the back door to the van. "Frankie's been in charge of our outreach program for five years now. Everyone on the street knows him."

Frankie and Tara sit up front, and I squeeze in the back between Landon and Troy, feeling a little like the inside of a taco.

"Not everyone, Bear, but we're making progress." Frankie starts the van with a rumble. "We're happy to have you guys on board. Let's do some good."

Tara turns to face us. "We're going to cruise around some of the projects in the Bronx. A lot of kids up there have no place to stay. They spend nights in stairwells or on park benches or at Uncle ACE's."

"What's Uncle ACE's?" asks Troy.

"Oh, that's right, you guys are newbies. The A, C, and E subway lines run all night. Kids will curl up on a bench. It's dangerous though—anyone can prey on them."

A chill whips through me. I remember the subway car from earlier in the day. *How can someone sleep in that?*

The van turns north on the West Side Highway. Skyscrapers with golden *Trump* signs tower over the road to our right.

My mouth must have dropped because Landon says, "New York City has the greatest concentration of millionaires in the US and, even with all that wealth there are well over 20,000 homeless youth in the City, and it's only getting worse."

The statistics overwhelm me and my face burns. "So many kids. We don't have a homeless problem back home."

"You'd be surprised. Homelessness has a way of sneaking by you unless you pay attention," Landon points out the window as we rumble north. "St. John the Divine is on 112th and Central Park West. You can't see it from here, but it's my favorite church in the City. I think it's the largest in the world, but a massive fire damaged it over a decade ago and the church is still under construction today. If you guys have time, you'll want to check it out." He hands Troy a thin paperback. "I brought this for you. It describes the Native American influences on this part of the country."

"Cool." Troy slips the book into his back pocket.

"We're going to three projects in the Bronx—Soundview, Milbrook, and Marble Hill," Tara tells us. "They're all basically the same. First stop is Marble Hill. Frankie used to live there."

"I did many things in Marble Hill, but very little living." He's not boasting. Sadness weighs down his words, as if he regrets how he spent his time there.

The van pulls to a stop on 230th Street in front of a towering brick apartment building that stretches fifteen stories high. We pile out and find other similar buildings that form a vast courtyard with a small park in the center.

Frankie frowns. "There's crime at these sites. People know us, so we're usually okay. Just make sure you guys stick with us. Don't go wandering off."

Troy and I happily agree, but I have to suppress a smile. Frankie is huge, and Landon can no doubt take care of himself, but I'm still stronger, faster, and more dangerous than the two of them combined.

Troy shoots me a sly grin and winks at me.

"So what do we do?" I ask.

"Tonight, we're just hanging out," answers Landon. "They're used to seeing us at these projects, so kids will stop over and see what's up. We're building trust. Sometimes they share the latest rumors, which helps us figure out what's going on and who needs help."

A group of three teenage guys notice us and saunter over. All three wear grungy T-shirts, baggy shorts, and baseball caps with wide, flat bills. The tallest of the three walks in front and smirks when he gets close. "Hey, it's the fresh start team."

Frankie's voice rises and falls with amusement. "Come on, Amare, you know better than that."

Amare sticks out his fist for a bump with Frankie and beams him a bright smile. "I'm just giving you some grief. Don't get all up in my face about it. How's life, Smoky and the Bear?"

"I quit smoking six months ago," says Frankie. "You should do the same."

Amare shrugs. "I'm not worried about dying from cancer. I'll never live that long." He glances at Troy and then at me. "Who's the new blood?"

Landon nods at us. "That's my cousin, Troy, and his friend, Juliet."

He studies Troy for a second. "Nice braid. How goes it, Little Cub?"

Troy stands taller and puffs out his chest. "Little Cub? I'm bigger than you."

"Yeah, but he's Black Bear, so you gotta be Little Cub."

Amare chuckles and so does Troy. We all fist bump and Amare introduces his two friends, Jalen and Pete.

"You guys want something to eat?" asks Tara. "I've got PB&J sandwiches in the van."

Jalen and Pete grab one, but Amare passes.

He pulls Frankie off to the side and whispers, but my hearing is super-sharp so I can hear what he says. "JJ has got some problems. He's sleeping in the stairwell at his mom's building. His stepdad tossed him out. I think he's ready for some help. Come back...."

I turn my attention to Pete and Jalen, who don't think anyone's watching them, so they're not wearing their tough guy masks. Despair and a certain hollowness play in the shadows of their eyes. I've seen it sometimes in really sick people or those addicted to drugs or booze; people who've lost hope that life might work out for them. It makes me angry and sad at the same time.

Frankie waves Landon over to join his conversation with Amare.

"What's up?"

Frankie's face pinches tight. "Amare saw that dude we've been warning people about — the tall albino with funny-colored eyes."

My heart jumps and the hair on the back of my neck become needles. He's describing a Deltite.

Amare nods. "He had two kids with him yesterday. Took them into a black Mercedes."

Landon's entire body tenses and the veins on his neck pulse. "Every time this guy shows up, kids go missing and they never come back. He keeps switching to different projects around the City, so we never know where he'll be next."

All the sweetness in Frankie's voice vanishes. "I'd like to meet up with him."

Landon hands Amare a card. "Next time you see him call me right away. And spread the word that he's no good."

"You got it." Amare waves Jalen and Pete over. "We've got to go. Big blast tonight in Building 4. We've got ladies to impress. I'm like candy—they all want a piece."

Frankie bends at the waist and stomps his foot in a full body laugh.

We stay at Marble Hill for another hour and then go to Soundview and then Millbrook. Similar scenes play out at the other two apartment projects. The kids are different sizes, races, and ages, but they share the same attitude—hard and callous on the outside, filled with pain and despair on the inside.

When we leave Millbrook and jump back in the van, Tara says, "We've got one last stop for the night. We like to end the run at Chelsea Piers. It's a little different from the projects. There's more LGBT homeless around and more adults, but still plenty of teens."

Landon adds, "They fixed up Chelsea Piers over five years ago. During the day tourists come and it's a fun place filled with basketball courts, soccer fields, and a driving range. At night it still turns rough."

The van stops on 25th Street and 10th Avenue across from a park. The City is never fully dark, not like home. Streetlights flicker and a few lights shine from businesses and apartments, even at three in the morning. However, the park is mostly dark and filled with shadows within shadows. I absorb energy from others around me—dozens of people are sleeping in the park. From the street it's impossible to tell so many call it home for the night. I wonder if we have parks like this back home.

A few people spot the van and wander over. They're moving slower than at the projects, possibly because it's so late, or maybe they're in worse shape.

Tara asks Troy to grab the rest of the sandwiches from the van while Landon and Frankie greet a few regulars.

I'm about to join them when a chill sets me off, which feels as though someone's hacking away at my brain with an ice pick. I double over and gasp. A voice screams inside my mind; it sounds like a long wail from a siren, but it's a voice.

A girl needs help.

I glance around the park, but it's too dark and I'm too far away to see her. Still, the call for help pulls me, so I start off in the direction I sense it's coming from, treading on grass, passing benches, and skirting an empty basketball court to my left.

I glance back and the van is barely visible, but the pleas for help scream louder. I spot a bench with shrubs on both sides. A small figure lies behind it, covered in a dark blanket. I kneel so my head is underneath the bench and see the other side. Two small eyes wide with fear stare back at me.

"My name is Juliet. I'm with New Beginnings. Do you need help?"

The girl trembles and shakes her head, but inside my mind her thoughts thunder. *Help me! He's going to come back for me!*

I've felt fear in my life—all types of fear—but her fear is so intense my legs almost buckle when faced with it. I can't let her confront this alone. "I know you're scared, but I have people with me who can help. They can take you to a safe place for the night."

It's hard to see her clearly, but her voice squeaks and sounds young. "I can't... he beats me... and worse." She stops talking and closes her eyes, but her thoughts scream louder in my head: *He's coming!*

I spin and spot a man marching toward us, his shoulders swinging aggressively. His crimson aura casts off enough light that I can make out his features. His thin body juts out at pointed angles. Stubble speckles his face, and his eyes are small, bloodshot orbs. He's wearing an army jacket and cargo pants. I can smell him from fifteen feet away—body odor and booze.

"Hey! What're you doing there? That's my spot!" He stomps toward me, each step pounding out an angry rhythm.

"I'm talking to my friend."

His body tenses as if he's about to explode, his fuse short. "Don't you talk to her! Get lost!" He reaches into his jacket pocket with his right hand.

I'll never leave him alone with this girl. I'll stand here all night if I have to, so I straighten my shoulders. "I just want to make sure she's okay."

"I'll teach you...."

Suddenly Landon, Frankie, Troy, and Tara are next to me.

Landon steps between us, his voice hard. "Is there a problem, friend?"

The stranger flicks his eyes between Landon and Frankie. "She's meddling where she doesn't belong."

The scared girl stands behind me.

"It's okay." I wave at her to come forward. "You don't have to stay here with him any longer."

Brilliant blue eyes stare at me, deep pools of pure water rippling with tears. Sweat mats her long hair and dirt streaks her forehead, but none of that can hide her beauty.

Tara touches her hand. "We can take you back to the center. It'll be safe there. We'll get you some food and sort through things in the morning."

The girl nods and looks down toward the ground. She can't look at the homeless man who has tormented her.

I glance back at him. I don't know his story or how he got this way, but he's no longer human. He's become a predator. I wonder if he can ever be changed back.

"You're not taking her! She's mine!" He yanks a knife from his pocket and lunges toward me. I step back and Landon grabs his wrist and twists.

The knife falls to the ground and Frankie shoves him hard in the chest. The man falls and Frankie hovers over him. "You'll leave this girl alone. If I hear otherwise, our next visit won't be so *friendly*." He crunches the man's fingers under his sneaker.

The man's anger is gone now. He mumbles something into his chest and looks away.

We surround the girl and take her back to the van. "Her name is Lilly. She's thirteen," I tell Tara, unsure how I know those things, yet I do.

Tara smiles at me and helps Lilly into the van.

Troy takes my hand as Landon and Frankie tower over us.

"I'm sorry I wandered away," I say. "I heard her and had to help."

I expect them to yell at me, but Frankie smiles and Landon says, "You did good, but next time tell one of us."

They drop us off in front of the Inn. My entire body aches from the long day, but I'm worried about Troy. He's been unusually quiet on the ride home, which can only mean one thing: he's angry with me.

"Some night," I say when we enter our rooms.

"I don't know what to do." Frustration burns in his eyes as he grinds his teeth. "I'm supposed to protect you, but I don't know how. I—"

I throw my arms around him and hold him close, my head burrowing in his chest. I'm so sorry I've made him feel this way. "I can't do any of this without you. You're my rock."

I kiss him on the cheek and let him hold me in his strong arms until the tension melts away from his body.

It's all I can do.

CHAPTER

My head sinks into the feather pillow. I'm exhausted, yet sleep only comes in fits. Most of the night I flail about, checking the alarm clock every fifteen minutes, hoping I had slept a little since the last time I looked. Twice I refill my glass with water, and once I stare out the window to watch an old man walk a dog at four in the morning.

I miss real sleep—a deep slumber that rejuvenates the body and soul. Sleep used to be one of my top five favorite activities, along with spending time with Troy, eating ice cream, watching TV, and playing lacrosse, not necessarily in that order—Troy can easily drop to the bottom of the list when he's being annoying. I haven't slept more than a few hours at a time since Sicheii died. Every time I try, my mind races in a million different places all at the same time. I can't figure out a way to slow my thoughts and it's driving me crazy.

When the sun finally rises, my head feels as if the skull has been peeled back and crows spent the night pecking at my brain. I

73

crack open my eyes and wince at the light. Strange energy pulses whip through my arms and legs, which burn as if they're set on fire. I've had a few migraines in the past, but this is more intense than any of the other ones, and a deep melancholy settles into my bones that I can't shake. I spend most of the day in bed with the lights off, my eyes closed and a pillow stuffed over my head.

Throughout the day, Troy busies himself by exploring the neighborhood and reading the book Landon gave him. He struggles with dyslexia, so reading is a real chore for him, but he absorbs anything Native American like a sponge, and attacks the book with more zeal than he's spent on any other book in years.

Time crawls along, but by late afternoon the pain breaks like a wave that crashes against the shore. I'm left a little dizzy, but my head is clear and my body has returned to normal.

I finally have the strength to get up and walk toward Troy, who sits on the couch.

He smiles at me. "Feeling better?"

"I'm hungry. That's a good sign."

"I bought some chicken soup for you from the local deli. The sign said it was homemade, but I saw giant tin cans in the back. I guess they never said whose home."

"Thanks." I plop on the couch, happy that the pain has disappeared as he hands me the soup and a plastic spoon. The soup's cold, but still nourishing. "Have you heard anything from Connor?"

"*Sir Drinks A Lot?*" He shakes his head. "Nope. Good chance he's on another bender."

"Give him a break. We don't know him yet."

"I know his kind, Jules. The more chances you give him, the more times he'll mess up."

"You gave the burglar back at the hotel another chance. Why not Connor?"

He purses his lips. "Drinking is different. How many times has my father gone sober for a week or two only to slip back? And drinking brings out the worst in him. Connor's going to be the same way."

I feel the start of another headache coming on. "You can't judge someone because you—"

Cathunk.

The sound comes from the hallway, followed a few seconds later by another *Cathunk.*

We stroll toward the door and hear Blake's voice. "I can't believe the elevator is out. That's very shoddy work for a hotel."

"Are you always like this?" It's Akari. I can understand what she's saying, but her words are wrapped in a thick Japanese accent.

Cathunk

"Like what?"

"Constantly complaining like a *two-year bebi*. It's annoying."

Cathunk.

"That's not the point. Hotels should be run a certain way—Ouch! You kicked me!"

"Sorry. Must be an accident."

Cathunk.

I grin and open the door.

Blake and Akari appear in the hallway with a red-faced Stuart huffing behind them.

A second later Connor opens his door. "What's all this bloody racket?"

His eyes look clear, but his tousled hair makes me think he just woke up. Slight traces of stubble have sprouted on his chin since yesterday.

Stuart grins. "Well, well, the entire group is here—all four Twisteds at once. This is good, extremely good. You're all invited

75

to dinner tonight. Eight o'clock sharp in the downstairs dining room."

"Will the Host be there?" I ask.

Stuart's blond eyebrows arch upward. "Oh yes, the Host.... He should certainly attend the dinner. Yes, now that all four of you are here, he'll want to get started right away. There is really no time to waste."

Blake leans his luggage against a wall. "What's the dress code for dinner?"

Akari snorts.

Connor chuckles. "I left my supper jacket behind, so I hope a T-shirt will be good enough. I promise to wear a clean one."

Stuart unlocks the doors with carvings of the Twisted Muskets and Samurai Swords etched into them. "Casual will be best. I'm certain you will all have a long night." He chuckles to himself as if he knows a secret joke. "Yes, yes, an extremely long night. I suggest you all get some rest before dinner, and don't be late. Oh, and please bring your swords. Yes, yes, you should carry them with you at all times now, I suspect."

We follow him with our eyes as he marches past us and down the staircase, mumbling to himself about how much he has to do before dinner.

Blake shakes his head and talks to no one in particular. "He's quite an odd fellow for a hotel manager."

"Right, *he's* certainly the odd one." Akari shifts her backpack on her shoulders.

"Let's face it, we're just a freak show." Connor rakes his hand through his sandy hair.

Akari bristles. "What do you mean... freak?"

Connor speaks in a single gust. "You know, weird, odd, strange, not all there, damaged, screwed-up, cracked! We're freaks."

76

"Who're you calling this... freak?"

"We're not exactly normal. You should have figured that out by now."

Akari's face reddens. "Call me this freak again. I dare you!" A full head shorter than Connor, she must weigh less than half as much as he does, yet she's undaunted and takes an angry step forward.

"I've never gotten into a dustup with a girl before, but I'm a feminist. Equal rights, I say. I'm willing, if you want to have a go at me."

Akari tenses like a coiled spring.

"This is a really bad idea," I say, but it's too late.

Akari springs halfway up the wall to my right, pushes off with both feet, and flings herself onto Connor's chest. They topple backward in a tangle. She lands an elbow to his head and twists on top of him. She brings her fist back, but he throws her off with a two-handed shove that sends her flying, and she lands hard on her back.

The few feet of clear space is my opportunity, so I jump in between them with my arms stretched wide, trying to keep them as far apart as possible. Energy flows from both of my outstretched hands, which freezes Akari and Connor in place. "I can't believe how stupid you're acting. We need to band together! Fighting amongst ourselves will only get us killed."

I can't hold them for longer than a few seconds, so I drop my arms and the power subsides. I turn to face Akari. "We're all freaks, but that's a good thing. We wouldn't stand a chance if we were normal."

Then I spin and face Connor. "*You* don't have to be such an *ass*."

Connor smiles, his face transforming into an oh-we-were-just-kidding-around expression, and sticks his hand past me toward

Akari. "I'm Connor. Sorry about the offense. I like you. You've got spunk."

She shakes his hand. "No harm done." A small smile creases her lips and her eyes brighten.

Blake rolls his luggage past us to his door. "Terrific, now that that's settled I suggest we get some rest before dinner like the manager guy said." He walks into his room and shuts the door behind him.

"It's been a long trip," says Akari as she opens her door. "I'll see you all at eight. *Sayonara.*"

Connor shrugs and disappears back into his room.

"That's quite a team you've got there," says Troy. "How are you going to stop them from killing each other long enough to face the dark spirits?"

"I'll have to think of something, but we won't have a lot of time together. Whatever is going to happen, it'll happen quickly."

Troy grabs the doorknob. "What do you think Stewie meant when he said we're going to have a long night?"

"I don't know, but I don't like it. He knows more than he's letting on. Why do we need to bring our swords to dinner?"

CHAPTER

I've never been a patient person. I'm not proud of it. I used to search my house for presents the week before my birthday, and I'd always find them. When I tried out for the lacrosse team at my old school, I stalked the coach for two days until he posted the list of kids who made the squad. He threatened to get a restraining order against me.

Since Stuart left us in the hallway, time has crept along like an inchworm with no particular destination in mind. Once the clock reaches eight, Troy and I race down the stairs, my string bag bouncing against my shoulder, the sword feeling heavy inside.

My insides twist into a pretzel as we approach the lobby. Who *is* the Host, and what information does he have? Will he tell us everything we need to know? Seconds away from meeting him, I realize that's a lot to ask. Maybe he's as clueless as we are.

What happens then?

I grab the pendant Sicheii gave me for protection. He called it a *Wind Catcher*. Made of flawless, blue sleeping beauty turquoise, it's a simple slanted rectangle with another slanted rectangle etched in sterling silver along the edges. The slanted rectangle is my tribe's symbol for the Great Wind Spirit. It's supposed to mean the Wind Spirit is within me and will protect me. I'm not convinced the Wind Spirit is real, or that she really cares that much about my safety even if she is. Still, the pendant reminds me of my grandfather, so I touch it now to know his strength and wisdom.

The pretzel tightens as we reach the lobby. Troy must sense my apprehension because he grabs my hand; his warmth and certainty make me feel better.

The lobby is empty, so we drift past Stuart's desk toward the hallway to the left, where I shove open a plain oak door with a brass sign that reads "Private Dining Room."

Already seated, Blake and Akari look up as we enter. They both smile and nod, but their anxious expressions tell me they're also eager to meet the Host. Akari wears a plain gray T-shirt, and Blake has on an expensive-looking navy polo shirt with a fancy logo that hangs on his thin frame.

A long rectangular table with eighteen chairs fills most of the room. The table is divided into fourths with each one of our symbols carved into the wood in the different boxes, and a crystal chandelier hangs over the center of the table, which provides the only light in the room.

The table is set for five people—*five* people. My spirits drop. We're five without the Host. *What does that mean?*

Blake and Akari face each other on the far end of the table, sitting in front of the boxes matching their signs.

We settle into the two empty chairs next to Akari, close to where the twisted arrows are carved. "No sign of the Host yet?" I ask them.

"Just us so far." Blake slides the menu toward me, which is printed on pale yellow linen paper with elaborate cursive words scrolled across it. There's something for each of us: New England Clam Chowder, assorted sushi pieces, grilled salmon, and bangers and mash.

My stomach growls, the only thing I've eaten all day being the cold soup Troy gave me. Just reading the menu makes my mouth water.

"We won't go hungry." Troy licks his lips.

"You guys haven't met this Host yet?" Akari asks.

"Not yet," answers Troy.

Blake points to a clock on the wall. "Well, he's already fifteen minutes late, isn't he? What could he possibly be doing that's more important than this?"

Akari rolls her eyes, and I shrug.

Just then the door flings open and bangs against the wall.

Bam!

Connor strolls in with a cat-that-ate-the-canary grin on his face, holding a half finished water bottle in his hand. "You haven't started the party without me, have you?" He saunters toward Blake and settles next to him. "I see the elusive Host hasn't joined us yet."

Troy huffs lightly. "Wow, nothing gets past you."

Connor leans forward, but before he can respond a waitress in her twenties strolls into the room holding a silver tray with five soup bowls. She's dressed in black, has a golden tan, a thin build, full lips, intelligent blue eyes, and is otherwise gorgeous. Her dirty blonde hair cascades into a waterfall of ringlets that ripple as she walks.

I've always wanted curly hair, but mine is pin straight. I tried to make it curly once, and it turned into a total disaster. Imagine frizzy snakes that puffed from my head at weird angles that would have embarrassed Medusa.

The waitress places a bowl in front of each of us. "My name is Sydney and I'll be your server for the evening. The Host is delayed. He sends his apologies and wants you to enjoy dinner. He'll join you when he's available."

Her husky voice smolders across the room like heat from red-hot pieces of coal. She beams a bright smile at us, but her eyes linger on Troy. He has that effect on women, even older women.

I immediately hate her and imagine strangling her as she leaves the dining room.

"Terrific." Blake looks at Sydney as she closes the door with a question in his eyes, but he doesn't say anything else.

Troy grabs a spoon. "It could be worse. He might've wanted us to wait until he showed up."

Everyone but Connor starts eating. He stares at Troy for a moment and drinks him in with an odd look on his face. "No offense, but I don't understand what you're doing here, mate. They've monkeyed around with our DNA and made us into...." He smiles at Akari. "Well... different. We've got some bloody obligation to save the planet and all, but you seem normal enough."

I don't like the tone in his voice, implying that Troy's not welcome. "He's with me." I add bite to my words to make sure he understands I'm serious. I glare at him to clarify, just in case he's a bit dumb.

He lifts up his hands palm out. "I'm just asking."

"I'm in the Order of the Twisted Arrows, so I've probably known about this longer than you guys." Troy shrugs as he shovels another spoonful of soup into his mouth.

"What's the story behind your Order?" asks Akari.

Troy leans back. "Juliet's grandfather told me an old Native American prophesy. Once humans forget how to live in harmony with Mother Earth, the world will regenerate and humans will vanish. The dark spirit, Coyote, thinks that time has come. He wants Mother Earth to return to her natural state, the way she was before First Man."

"Well, he's probably right. We're certainly messing up the planet. Climate change will affect everything and likely wipe us out," Blake says.

Troy smiles. "Hopefully not yet. The Great Wind Spirit protects us. She wants to give us another chance to remember the old ways. The two spirits are locked in a battle over Mother's Earth's future."

"Who are the bloody Deltites then?" Connor leans forward.

"That's easy. They're Coyote's pawns, doing his bidding."

When Troy finishes, Blake and then Akari explain the legends behind their Orders.

Akari's English is surprisingly good, but she stutters over some words. When she finishes, a reluctant Connor talks about the Order of the Twisted Long Swords.

He takes a swig from his water bottle. "My Order isn't all that different from yours. They believe Satan is about to return to Earth. It's our job to defeat his minions. *Blah, blah, blah.* If we don't win, the world turns to chaos and becomes ruled by Beelzebub himself. *Blah, blah, blah.*"

By the time he finishes, we've already eaten through the sushi and salmon. Sydney returns with the bangers and mash—a messy looking dish with two sausages on top of a pile of mashed potatoes. She smiles at Troy when she places a plate in front of him, and the fingers of her left hand brush against his shoulders.

I grip the armrest of my chair so hard my knuckles turn white. I have to resist the urge that swells inside of me to rip out her hair.

There's no reason for me to act this way. Troy and I are just best friends; he's had more than a few girlfriends over the past few years. We've never been anything more than friends, but her flirting irritates me — she acts as if I'm not even here.

"Why'd you say the stories are all the same?" says Akari. "They sound different to me."

"Not really." Connor spears one of his sausages. "They all use the local religion to create an *end of world* scenario. Either the Order keeps this secret and does as the Alphians require, or our world gets overrun by evil forces that will destroy it."

Connor's right; every story boils down to the same elements. I should have seen that right away; he's smarter than he looks.

He continues, "Of course, we know it's all wonky rubbish at this point."

Troy shifts forward in his seat and leans on his elbows. "None of these stories have to be wrong. The way I see it, everything is consistent. If you guys don't defeat these... Deltites, the world will fall apart and who-knows-what will come of us. The stories still work. The Deltites could just be Coyote's henchmen or the devil's minions or whatever."

Blake clanks his fork against his plate. "Well, I don't know why we have to be the ones to stop the Deltites in the first place. We have governments with militaries who're trained for this type of thing. What if we just go back to our homes and tell them we did whatever we're supposed to do?"

Akari rolls her eyes again.

Connor takes another pull from his water bottle. "Listen, I don't like being forced into this situation any better than you, but

84

I don't see as we have a choice. One way or another these guys need to be taught a lesson, or it's going to get a little awkward when they take over."

"If we don't hunt them," I say, "they'll hunt us. And trust me, you don't want to meet one on your own." I look up and find three faces staring back at me.

I wonder if I said something crazy when Akari whispers, "You've *seen* a Seeker?"

Now I realize why they're looking at me as if I have two heads. None of them have run into a Seeker.

I nod. "Right before I took the fusion from the third book, a Seeker found me. He kidnapped my mom, so I had no choice but to face him."

"What was he like?" Blake rubs his hands together as if he's chasing away a chill, and his eyes widen.

Memories flood back to me—Sicheii dying in the villa, his last words, and the expression on the Seeker's face when my sword plunged into his chest. I won't mention those details. That would be too hard, so I stick to the facts and speak in a numb voice. "He looked like the visions from the fusions—tall, thin, bald, beautiful. His blue eyes were specked with violet and burned right through me. We fought. He was incredibly strong, stronger than anyone I've ever met, but he underestimated me. He thought I was nothing, just a weak girl, so I caught him off guard and stabbed him with the sword."

Connor's eyes sparkle. There's newfound respect and maybe even a little admiration in those eyes that wasn't there before. "Brilliant, now we know they can die."

Awkward silence chills us for a minute.

I look down at my mostly empty plate and remember Sicheii—his sacrifices for me, his wisdom, the way he always blessed the food before eating it and left a small portion of his meal uneaten as an offering to the spirits. I miss him, his weirdness, his unique way of seeing the world, his horrible singing voice, and even his stories, which never seemed to make sense.

Troy probably senses my sadness, so he asks Akari, "So how did you and Blake meet up? Do you know each other from before?"

"Well, not exactly," Blake answers before Akari can speak. "I found her wandering around Perry Street and thought she might be one of us. If I hadn't said anything, she'd still be looking for the place."

Anger burns in Akari's eyes and her face turns pink. "I would've found its location without you. I knew it was here somewhere nearby. It felt like an invisible *Yokai* had shoved me toward the Inn."

"*Yokai?*" asks Blake.

Akari's face turns a slightly darker shade of pink. "Oh, I mean spirit."

"How did *you* know where to look?" Connor points his fork at Blake.

Blake smirks. "It's obvious, isn't it? I knew what the symbol looked like, so I searched the Internet for it. It took an advanced image recognition program, but I found the circle in an old *Village Voice* article. The story wasn't about the Inn, but it had a label that identified where the photo was taken. From there it was easy."

"Oh bollocks," says Connor.

"What's wrong?" asks Akari.

From the look on Connor's face I can tell we have the same idea, so I say, "If *you* could find it on the Internet, that means *they* can find it."

Blake shrugs. "Only if they know what to look for, and what are the chances of that?"

"Higher than I'd like," I say. "They know about the Twisted Arrows by now."

"They've also learned about the Samurai Swords." Akari pushes her plate away from her. "I just barely escaped a Seeker before I left Tokyo."

"Great. What a bloody cock-up." Connors scowls as he drains the last of his water bottle. "The sooner we get this over with, the better."

Just then Sydney—with the pretty smile and flirty ways—returns to take away our plates. "The Host has arrived. He'll be here shortly." She glances at Troy one last time and I swear she winks at him.

I focus my mind on the Host and ignore the flirty waitress for once. Finally we get to meet him. So much depends on him.

The dining room door creaks opens, and he stands in the hallway.

My jaw drops.

CHAPTER

Alex Gagarin inhales, and lilac scented air fills his lungs. Of all the many things he despises about this planet, he hates the stench worst of all. The fragrance of lilacs somewhat covers the stink, but he can still smell the offensive odor. He can't avoid it—it hovers in the air, sticks to his clothes, and worst of all, clings to the people around him. *Humans*, with their acidic body odor, reek horribly.

He frowns as he weaves his way among the exhibits. The prior owner of this estate used the vast underground structure as a garage for an army of exotic automobiles. Alex has replaced those cars with new displays, more exotic ones that he likes better.

Two Deltites march five feet behind him. Having just delivered bad news, they are weary of his explosive temper. "How could Damien be so stupid?"

He keeps his eyes focused in front of him as he examines a recent addition to his collection, a perfectly stuffed silverback male gorilla. His fingers comb through the coarse fur on the gorilla's shoulders. In life the animal had strength; now, only the illusion of strength remains.

Bailey answers him, her voice high-pitched and measured. "Damien was the weakest among us."

"Did he die with his sword in his hand?" Alex glances at Caleb, who shakes his head.

"We recovered the sword from the local police department."

"Good. He doesn't deserve to go to the next life as a warrior. Let the imbecile stew with the less deserving. Make sure you purify the sword before we let another use it. We don't want the stink of failure to remain on the weapon."

Caleb nods. "It will be done."

"He must have underestimated the hybrid," says Bailey. "Perhaps he thought he had turned her so we could use the information fused within her?"

"Maybe." Rage ripples through him. If he had gotten rid of Damien years earlier, this folly would never have happened. He should have chopped off his stupid weak head when Damien had first failed him—a dumb mistake Gagarin would not repeat.

He leaves the gorilla and ambles onward. It takes all his willpower to keep his gait steady as he stops in front of an African elephant. The animal's head lifts toward the ceiling; ivory tusks immense, fluorescent light glistening off the points. "Do you think he was convinced this hybrid is the Alpha?"

"Completely," Caleb answers. "Her name is Juliet Wildfire Stone. She was born in Arizona almost sixteen years ago. Nothing about her seems remarkable in the least, until now."

Gagarin stalks toward a giraffe. "Where's this Juliet Wildfire Stone now?"

He clenches his hands into fists as anger courses through him—anger at Damien's foolishness, anger that the Alpha has eluded them, anger at so many things. Thirty years he has spent on this stinking planet, stuck making plans on how to use these humans—thirty years of befriending them, learning their pathetic ways, living with them. Now, so close to the end, Damien acted like a fool and let the Alpha slip through his fingers! *Thirty stinking years!*

"We don't know where she is," answers Bailey. "She's vanished."

Gagarin speaks through gritted teeth. "Vanished? Really?" Energy pulses within him. He wants to explode, to hurt someone, but that would be weak and he can't appear weak to his subordinates, so he keeps control and continues through the exhibits.

After a long moment, the jagged edge in his voice subsides. "Tell me about the other hybrid—the one from Japan. Somehow she also snuck beyond our reach."

"They almost captured her on a train in Tokyo. She escaped before one of our people could get there, but we think she left Japan," says Bailey.

Gagarin stops in front of his favorite exhibit. He takes three deep breaths and steadies his trembling fists. "Two hybrids so close. After all these years they're scurrying from their hiding places like cockroaches. It must be time for them to gather." He chuckles. "What stupid, weak creatures. How could the Elders think they might defeat us?"

Bailey and Caleb stand tall with smooth hairless heads and pale skin that glistens in the harsh light. A light sheen of nervous sweat coats their faces.

Good. Let them fear me. For a second he imagines crushing Caleb's skull, his finger snapping bone, blood spurting from the wreckage. As his superior, it would be his right to end him if he so wished. The quick fantasy relaxes him.

All three wear loose-fitting white silk shirts and pants that flow as they move. Alex turns from the Deltites and touches the cheek of an adult male human, one of six different humans clustered together in his favorite exhibit. The youngest, a newborn, nestles in the arms of her mother.

He remembers fondly how he selected this family for his exhibit. He wanted the set to match, so he couldn't pick random humans—no, he needed a family. The media had dubbed the baby a *miracle child*. Having been born with a heart condition, she survived a dozen surgeries over six months before she was well enough to go home. They called her will to live *extraordinary*— only one in a million could survive those operations.

The news reports had intrigued him, so he visited the family when they brought the miracle child home. He watched them through a window. Joy filled the house. They had strung a "Welcome Home" banner across the living room, dozens of pink balloons floated in the air, and a giant stuffed panda bear sat in one of the chairs. The three siblings took turns holding the baby. The youngest daughter cried when she rocked her baby sister.

A thin smile graces his face as he recalls the details. They were easy to kill, weak, harmless really. He simply opened the door and froze the entire family with his mind—all except the miracle child. He lifted her so they could watch. He wanted to see something *extraordinary*, but as he squeezed her neck, she just wiggled, turned red, and expired. He took his time with the rest, going from youngest to oldest. By the time he turned to the father, the man had wanted to be killed. He begged Gagarin to end his life, tears streaming down the man's face. Gagarin hesitated. He thought about leaving him alive to live his life in agony, but the man had seen Gagarin's face.

"So much for the miracle baby." Gagarin touches the baby's cheek with the back of his hand. "These humans are the most advanced indigenous life form on this rotten planet. Given time and opportunity, they would either destroy the planet or evolve into something remarkable."

Bailey hands him two pieces of paper—one with the Twisted Arrows symbol on it, and the other with the Twisted Samurai Swords. "We did find these."

Gagarin smiles. "How poetic. In each case, two weapons are twisted together, but each weapon is different. One arrow for Alphians and another for humans, and the same design for the swords." He laughs now, a blood-curdling chortle. "How pleased the Elders must have been to come up with this *monstrosity.* They spoil our blood by mixing it with these beasts and then create symbols to glorify it. I can't wait until we shove these down their throats.

"Use the humans we pay, and have them monitor everyone close to this Juliet Wildfire Stone. I want them to capture every communication; eventually she'll slip up, And get our computer experts to search the Internet for these... symbols. There will be two others, no doubt, for the other two hybrids. The Elders can't help themselves. They will use these symbols somewhere else. It appeals to their warped sense of poetic symmetry too much to resist, and then we'll know their hiding place."

He hands the papers, wrinkled now from where he grabbed them, back to Bailey and strolls toward the far end of the structure. "How are you progressing on the experiments? Do we have a workable formula yet?"

Bailey matches his strides. "Almost. The fatality rate has dropped to fifty percent. It shouldn't take me long to reduce that number to a more manageable percentage so we won't lose that many humans."

So close now. So close.

Gagarin slides his hand into his pocket and traces the outline of the Hyper-Link Crystal. A crystal carver spent a year on it and fused the brainwaves of the Deltite leader into the structure. Even though the leader is on a different planet far from Earth, if Gagarin focuses on the crystal and pushes his mind into the structure, he would become linked with the leader and could communicate telepathically with him as if they shared the same space. Rare and valuable, he would only use the crystal for truly important news, news he desperately wants.

Maybe soon.

"The finalized formula is the last element I need before we start my plan." He glances at Bailey. "Have the survivors been following the instructions we give them through the cellular waves?"

Bailey grins. "Absolutely. The girl Caleb picked up yesterday killed another test subject without hesitation. She slit his throat with a kitchen knife and had no idea what she had done. The drug will make all humans follow our commands."

"Good. We don't need *all* these humans. If a quarter of them die off in the process, so be it. We'll still have more than enough for what I want. You have a week to do your best with the formula. Drop the fatality rate to twenty-five percent and then dump it into the reservoirs that feed into the drinking water. We'll do a test and see where we are."

"But millions of humans will die with such a high fatality rate." Caleb looks at him with questioning eyes, but when Gagarin glares back, he blinks nervously and shrinks backward.

"I don't care. It will only soften them up for the next stage of my plan. They'll blame it on some plague brought upon them by a divine power. One week and then we test the drug with the cellular signals." He slides closer to Caleb, feeling like a lit stick of dynamite, ready to explode. "Unless you want to challenge me. In that case we can settle the matter between us now."

Caleb averts his eyes downward, takes a long step back, and nods. "One week and we'll dump the formula into the water supply."

"Good." Gagarin resumes his stroll. When he reaches an unfinished exhibit, he stops.

Four empty pedestals wait for their charges.

He sweeps his hand against the tallest pedestal and glances down at the name carved into the wood — *Alpha*.

CHAPTER

The Host strolls through the doorway with Sydney a step behind.

People often surprise me. Take Frankie, for instance. At first he looked like a thug—nothing but a collection of muscles littered with tattoos, but the real Frankie is completely different from what I had imagined; his rough edges smoothed out with compassion and infectious sweetness.

I glance at Troy, who squints his eyes and shakes his head. I know *that* look. He's unhappy. He's always been better at reading people than me. Whenever someone new showed up at school, he'd size him or her up by the end of the first day. Usually, I'd say that wasn't fair, but his one word pronouncements—jerk, cool, smart— were always spot on. He has a sixth sense for these things, and he's clearly not happy with the Host, which puts me on edge.

Stuart sits at the far end of the long table while Sydney stands behind him. "Hello, Twisteds, I trust you've enjoyed dinner. Yes, yes, I'm certain you did."

I'm not sure what pisses me off more — that Stuart is the Host and kept that secret from me, or that Sydney appears to be entangled with us, which means she'll be spending time with Troy, smiling and winking and flirting with him.

"You're the bloody Host?" Connor sounds as confused as I am.

None of the visions I've had about Alphians included anyone who looks like Stuart. I assumed he was just a person who helped the Host — some quirky guy who likes romance novels and for some tragic reason decided to dye his eyebrows blond. I guess the ring with the Inn's symbol on it should have made me think twice about him, but Stuart the Host?

He's going to help us defeat the Deltites?

He nods. "I hope you're not disappointed. Were you expecting someone taller, thinner, and better looking, perhaps?" His eyes twinkle, but behind the surface they look menacing.

The hair on the back of my neck stands at attention. I've totally misjudged him.

Blake leans forward. "No offense, but all the dreams from the Fusions show a different type of Alphian. You're just not what we expected."

Stuart strokes his beard. "Yes, yes, I understand completely. Each Fusion could only contain so many... dreams... yes, let's use dreams for lack of a better word. The Elders didn't deem it necessary to include *my* kind in those dreams."

"Your kind?" Akari asks.

He leans back in his chair, looking at ease, comfortable even. "You see, there are two types of Alphians. Always have been. The tall, thin, hairless, fair-skinned Alphians that are quite beautiful, really. They're simply called Alphians, and then there are... my kind — shorter, hairy, with...." He pats his ample stomach. "Let's

96

just say a little rounder. We're commonly called the Uglies. It's simple—just Alphians and Uglies existing together.

"The Alphians rule Alpha. They certainly do and always have. None of the Elders has ever been an Ugly. Not one." He snorts. "What a thought, really. *An Ugly as an Elder.* Now that would certainly create a stir, but we're not meant to lead. No, no, it's our role to serve. We're not gifted with the same *abilities* as the Alphians. Generally not, although there have been exceptions, certainly, but what you see is what you get with my kind."

He pauses, calmly clasps his hands on the table, and watches us. It takes a moment for me to process what he has just told us. *There are two types of Alphians? Why would they send an Ugly to help us? It makes no sense. He doesn't have any abilities. How much help will he be?*

The others shoot questions at him as if they're a firing squad and he's bound and propped up against a wall.

He remains stone-faced; his mouth purses but stays closed.

The questions start to slow.

Blake asks, "Well, why don't you say something?"

Stuart leans on his elbows, his chin cupped in the palm of his hands. "So many questions. Yes, understandable, really. I'm sure I would have even more if our roles were reversed." He checks his wristwatch. "But we simply don't have time to answer them right now. Let me fill you in on the necessary bits, and hopefully we'll get to the other stuff later."

"Hopefully," mutters Akari.

Stuart ignores her and locks his eyes on me instead. "You should all understand the stakes of this little enterprise. Not only is Earth in play, but also the entire known universe is in jeopardy. Yes, yes, the whole ball of wax, as some might say." He lifts his head and laces his fingers together, and the light glints off his pinkie ring. "The Deltites believe they are the most advanced beings in the universe, and that as such, they deserve to rule over all other life forms. The Elders dismissed this way of thinking centuries ago and expelled them to the far reaches of the universe, hoping that they would be trapped and we'd never see them again.

"At this point, it's safe to say they were wrong about never seeing them again. Yes, safe indeed. I doubt they will make that mistake again. Yes, yes, that would be extremely unlikely. Still, here we are. Having grown in power, the Deltites have spread like weeds, causing destruction and enslaving entire planets in their wake. At least half a dozen planets are now ruled by Deltites. A totally manageable situation if the Elders act quickly. *If, if, if.*"

"So, *if* it's manageable, then why do you need us?" Blake asks.

"Fair question. First, the Elders are only now convening a Gathering to decide what to do. If they decide to battle the Deltites, it will take some time to prepare. And second, the Deltites *are* here. Earth *is* a high value target for them. If they control the planet, it would make things more difficult for the Elders to eventually defeat them."

"What can we do to stop them?" I ask.

"Time is all we need. Earth is a worthy acquisition, but it's one of three such targets. Perhaps it's the most valuable, but any one of the three will strengthen them. The Deltites have plans to take over all three, but they will only move against one at a time. They simply don't have the resources to take over all three at once. So, we're stuck in a game for time, time, time. If we eliminate the Deltite leader on Earth, the one they call the Prime Elector, it will delay them considerably, probably enough to make one of the other two targets more attractive, which will keep Earth safe for now."

A lump forms in my throat. "By eliminate, you mean kill?"

"Of course I do! This is war and during war casualties are expected. It simply cannot be helped. No, not helped." He strokes his beard, his eyebrows arch upward, and his eyes blaze with an intense light.

"But, if we kill this Prime Elector, won't the next... what do you call him?" Akari waves her hand for a second, frustrated until she remembers the words. "Yes, the second in command, continue with the plan? How much time would it buy us?"

Stuart smirks. It's an annoying expression, as if he's the kid in class who knows all the answers even before the teacher has covered the subject. "Sometimes I assume you know more about our society than you do. All Alphians are not equal. Four levels exist based upon abilities. Only a few are among the most powerful and considered Level One Alphians. And among them only a couple are powerful enough to be called *Elites*. Our Elders are always Elites. The Deltites, who cherish power over all other attributes, firmly believe in this hierarchical type of society.

"The Prime Elector will be an immensely powerful Elite. They would never attempt to take the planet without his authority or leadership. If he dies, they'll wait for a new Elite to replace him, and that will take some time. Hopefully, enough time for the Elders to act."

"Do you know who this bloody Prime Elector is?" Connor asks.

"Yes, I certainly do." Stuart checks his watch and frowns. "But you do not need that information at this time. No, most assuredly you do not. It would be counterproductive. We do not have much time. Apparently, our Inn is less secure than I thought. Now that they know some of the twisted symbols, I am sure they will be on to us in no time."

How does he know that they've discovered some of our symbols? He wasn't in the room when we talked about them. I glance at the ceiling and spot two fire detectors. Both look identical, but only one is needed. He's spying on us. And if he's listening to us here, I'm sure he has concealed other devices in our rooms. If we're on the same side, why spy on us?

A bell chimes and prompts Stuart to pull a digital stopwatch from his pocket and place it on the table in front of him. "Your first test has begun. You have four minutes to reach Central Park West and 72nd Street. Go through the entrance to the park and you'll find a flask under the first bench on your left. Grab the flask and take one gulp of the cure each. Yes, just one gulp is all that is needed, but make sure you get there before the four minutes are up."

"72nd Street is more than two miles from here. We'll never make it in time." Blake crosses his arms.

"If you tap into your enhanced strength and speed, you have plenty of time. Better hurry and drink the cure."

Akari bolts upward. She's one leap away from strangling Stuart. "Cure! Why do we need a cure?"

Stuart slides the stopwatch toward me. "Because you've all been poisoned, of course. If you fail to drink the cure in time, you will die."

"All but you, Troy," says Sydney sweetly, a smile on her lips.

CHAPTER 13

The room practically detonates as shrapnel flies everywhere and tempers explode.

Connor swipes his plate from the table, and it shatters against the wall.

Chairs crash to the floor as we surge toward Stuart.

We're all yelling at the same time, making it impossible to hear what's being shouted because the voices mix together to create an indecipherable scream.

The air around Stuart sparkles and light bends around him.

Akari is the first to reach him and tries to grab him, but her hand bashes against an invisible wall. She tries again, harder this time, but when she can't touch him she streams a torrent of Japanese curse words.

Stuart stands on his chair. The force field distorts his features and twists his face, which is totally freaky.

He speaks softly, so we quiet to hear him. "You should know

that Uglies commonly have one ability. We can create an energy field around us. It's like a turtle and his shell. Unfortunately we cannot hold it for too long. In my case, maybe five minutes or so. Yes, yes, but that is plenty of time under the circumstances. You will all perish in four minutes unless you take the cure. Less than four minutes now and counting. I suggest you get moving. Time is running and you cannot afford to waste any of it. Move you must."

I grab the stopwatch—three minutes and forty-seven seconds left. *He's right! We had better move fast.*

Troy's eyes blaze hot, but he pushes me toward the door.

"Let's go!" I bolt.

Connor, Akari, and Blake run a step behind me as we race from the Inn and plunge into the night. Connor sprints in front with long looping strides. Akari pumps her arms and legs just behind him, and Blake is off and running to my left.

Only a few pedestrians walk the streets at this time of night. The sky is dark, but streetlights and lights from apartments brighten our path. My feet pound the pavement as I struggle to keep up with Connor and suck air in gasps.

We sprint fast and dodge people as we go, but it won't be enough. We need a new gear. We need to tap into our enhanced abilities.

I open my mind to the energy around me. A tingling sensation ripples through my arms and legs, and they start to surge as if I've flipped a switch, and I dart forward.

I'm flying.

Obstacles blur past as I race incredibly fast—faster than cars, faster than anyone has ever run before. As the wind whips through my hair, a new emotion bubbles up inside of me. I stop worrying about the cure and the Seekers and the Prime Elector, and a joy-filled smile bursts on my face. For the first time, I'm happy I'm different. I start to scream.

Then Connor's next to me and he's also screaming. Akari and Blake are a few steps behind us and they howl into the night. Ours is a primal scream, full of life and energy and joy.

We reach a busy intersection with a red light, and I can't stop. Cars stream in front of me. A bus lumbers across the road. There's nowhere for me to go but in front of that bus. It's going to crush me. I'll be flattened against the windshield like a bug.

I close my eyes and leap, pushing off the ground with my right foot in full stride, and for a heartbeat I'm really flying as my body climbs into the air, my legs still churning. I pass over the top of the bus and land on the other side of the intersection. My right foot hits first and then my left. I stagger a step, but keep my balance and race on. I glance over my shoulder to see the others take flight with the same wide grin on their faces.

I turn north and really fire up the afterburners. The sidewalk is too congested to avoid pedestrians, so I hop over the curb, swerve onto the street, and burn past everything. Each time there's a red light I take flight and soar higher and farther. Central Park West is only a few heartbeats away, the first trees that mark the beginning of the park in sight. The sidewalk is empty now, so I jump back over the curb and peek at the stopwatch. We still have one minute twenty-two seconds and only 13 blocks left. I gulp air as my legs and arms pump faster than I could have ever imagined.

I reach the entrance on 72nd Street, swing to the right, enter the park, and screech to a stop at a park bench on my left. Diving underneath, I find a leather-covered flask with the Inn's symbol etched onto it. I tip it back and down a gulp. The syrupy liquid tastes like roses. When I look up, Connor jogs to a stop in front of me. I hand him the flask, and he takes a swig before passing it on to Akari.

"Woooow!" he shouts. "That was *absobloodylootely* amazing."

I glance at the stopwatch. "We still have thirty-seconds. Where's Blake?"

They both spin.

"I'm sure he was right behind me." Akari spins, but he's nowhere in sight.

My heart sinks. Something's wrong. There are twenty seconds left.

I grab the flask from Akari, streak back out of the park, and turn south on Central Park West. My body shakes with energy as auras flash on all around me, not just for people, but every creature. Their life forces burn in the night air like flares.

My legs pump fast. He has to be here somewhere. An internal countdown ticks in my head.

Fifteen seconds.

Details bombard me and my mind spins: a middle-aged married couple walk a miniature poodle off to my left; a homeless man slumps against a bench across the street; a group of four twenty-somethings laugh and point toward the park; I smell pizza.

Ten seconds.

I don't know if anyone can even see me; I may be moving too fast. Squirrels race in front of me, and two pigeons find crumbs by a mailbox. I see everything in such stark detail it's scary. A man who waits to cross the street has short black hair, a small scar on his chin and a cut on his cheek that looks old from shaving in the morning.

Eight seconds.

Where's Blake? How far back can he be? Then I see it: a brighter aura than the others two blocks away. It has to be him. I'm a ball of energy now and will myself faster.

Five seconds.

Blake's khakis are ripped, blood drips from his right shin, and a nasty scrape tears the skin on his hand and forearm. His eyes are wide and his aura swirls with colors as black mixes with the white.

Three seconds.

I thrust the flask at him.

Two seconds.

"Drink!"

He grabs the flask and tips it to his lips.

A firecracker explodes and shatters my head.

The stopwatch buzzes in my hand as Blake gulps the cure.

Is it too late?

The world twists and starts to gray. I fall and see nothing but black before my head hits the pavement.

CHAPTER

Sicheii smiles at me, his white hair pulled back in a low ponytail, his slate eyes twinkling. It's so good to see him.

I'm reminded of our secret trips to the gift shop next to his gallery. I was thirteen the last time we went. I'd give anything to go back with him now, just one last time.

The store sold mostly T-shirts and red rock souvenirs, but in the back they had an old glass freezer where they scooped homemade ice cream—four delicious flavors: chocolate, vanilla, chocolate chip, and strawberry. It was one of those small town places reserved only for locals, hidden from tourists.

I'd always get chocolate, and he'd usually choose vanilla, except for special days when he'd buy chocolate chip. Those times he'd shrug and explain how a part of me was in him and how some of him was in me. Back then I never really understood what he meant. Now I kind of get it.

"So have you decided to be the rock and not the river?" His

voice sounds soft and fuzzy around the edges. Rocks are strong and true to their inner nature. They don't bend and find the easiest path like rivers. He was always a rock, and he wants me to be the same.

"Yes, Sicheii. What choice do I have?"

"There's always a choice, Little Bird." He tips his head back and breathes deeply. "Do you smell that? Life floats on the wind and lives in everything around us."

Our surroundings come into focus. We're sitting on a grass field on the edge of a riverbank. The water rushes past us and laps against the shore. One log floats in the middle of the river, bobbing up and down in the rushing water. It looks lonely and out of place, as if it's one of a kind, lost in a watery world.

"What is this place?

"It's nowhere special and yet it is all things special. The river is more than just a river, as things generally are."

The river looks foreign, but I've seen it before—maybe not exactly in this form, but one that's similar.

My heart aches. I long for a simpler time, a time before Seekers and Prime Electors and before I knew I was a Chosen. That time never really existed—it was just an illusion—but that doesn't stop me from wanting it back. "I'm scared. I don't like the changes that are happening to me. I'm separated from everyone else. It's like I'm not human anymore."

He shoots me a pensive expression and nods. It's the look he gets whenever he's about to start one of his tales.

They used to annoy me. Now, I miss him so much, I don't even mind, so I sit up straighter and listen.

"You should have paid more attention to my stories." He arches his white eyebrows, but he's not angry. "What's human? When the world was new the First Man lived with all the animals:

the beaver, hawk, and wolf. He spoke with them and they lived in harmony together. Was the First Man human or something else, something greater? All living things are connected in spirit. Who cares if you have abilities that separate you from others? Your spirit is what counts. It's strong and connects with other creatures and the life around you. Maybe you're more human than these other people you so admire. Maybe you are closer to the First Man."

"They say... I'm the Alpha. What does that mean?" My voice cracks, and I fight back tears that form in the corner of my eyes. "Isn't it enough that I'm a Chosen? Why do I have to be still more different?"

Sicheii raises his arms out to his side. The wind gusts and blows his hair behind him like a kite's tail. "The Great Wind Spirit has big plans for you, Little Bird. Embrace your destiny. Be the rock."

I hate when he speaks in riddles. Most of the time I never understood what he meant. If he'd just speak plainly for once... but before he can answer any more of my questions, his face twists and morphs into Connor's face.

I try to hold onto Sicheii, to bring him back, but he's gone.

Connor's mouth is moving, yet I can't hear his voice. I focus on a small scar above his left eyebrow. It must have happened during a fight, maybe the same fight that broke his now slightly bent nose.

His eyes are carved with worry. I lose myself for a moment in them and find a depth I missed before—they're filled with compassion. They've been hurt before, and now they worry about me. Small violet flecks swirl in his blue-gray ocean.

Heat flushes my cheeks, and I begin to hear him as if he's talking from far away.

"Are you okay, Juliet? I thought we had lost you for a bit." He holds my shoulders and lifts me off the pavement, while Akari and Blake hover behind him. I smell traces of alcohol on his breath and remember the half-filled water bottle he brought with him to dinner.

"I'm fine." My voice sounds harsher than I expect. I push his arms away and sit up on my own. The world tilts, but steadies a moment later. When he lowers his hand, I grab it, and he pulls me to my feet.

Blake stands off to the side. His leg has stopped bleeding and he looks disheveled, but definitely not like he's about to drop dead from poison. The cure must have worked.

The auras that almost blinded me a moment ago have vanished, so I'm back to normal, or whatever version this is of normal.

"How long was I out?" I shake my head to chase away the cobwebs.

Blake answers. "I'd say fifteen minutes or so. Um... thanks for coming back for me."

"What happened to you anyway?"

His face reddens as he looks over his shoulder and down the street. "A mailbox got in the way."

"I hate when they jump out at you." I grin.

Connor adds, "You're a criminal now. Monkeying around with the post."

We chuckle at his expense and it feels good.

"I think that's the least of my problems." Blake smirks, so at least he's taking the ribbing well.

Akari glances at me. "When you left the park, you moved so fast we couldn't keep up with you... like a tsunami."

"We couldn't even see you. You were a blur." Connor shoots me a piercing gaze, as if he's studying me.

His expression worries me. I don't want them to think I'm different from them, so I shrug. "I'm sure I didn't go *that* fast. I knew we didn't have much time, so I gave it all I had. Either one of you would have done the same, if you had the flask."

"Right," mutters Connor, but he's not buying it. An odd expression still sticks to his face.

I want to change the subject. "How about you, Blake? Are you feeling all right? I was worried we had run out of time."

"Well, I'm not dead yet. Do you think he really poisoned us? I mean, maybe he just made that stuff up to encourage us. I bet we could have strolled to the park and we'd have been fine."

I remember his aura right before he drank the cure. His spirit had started to turn from white to gray and black. "That rat poisoned us. We all would have died if we didn't drink the cure in time. I'm sure of it."

"Well, what do we do now?" asks Blake.

"They're probably looking for us by the park bench." I want to head in the other direction, but Troy will be there with Stuart and Sydney. He'll worry like crazy if I don't show up. "Let's see what he wants us to do next."

We start to march north, and Connor walks close to my side. I try to focus on where we're going, but my eyes keep flashing toward him, which is super annoying. When his hand brushes against my arm, my skin burns from the accidental connection.

"Should we kill Stuart?" asks Akari.

I expect to see her grin, but her face is pure granite.

"Maybe. How hard could it be?" Connor waves his hand. "We're supposed to kill this Prime Elector. We can practice on that rat."

CHAPTER 15

Troy, Stuart, and Sydney bunch around the bench under which the flask had been hidden. Troy paces, each step punctuated by anger and tension, while Stuart relaxes on the bench with his legs crossed as if he has no worries in the world.

Sydney stands off to the side and studies Troy, a sly smile on her face. The top two buttons on her shirt are undone. They were fastened when we ate dinner.

What a tramp!

When Troy sees us, he stops pacing and the tension blows out of him. He tilts his head back, lifts his eyes toward the heavens, and stretches his arms to the side. He looks like Sicheii did in my dream. He quietly mutters, "Thank you, Great Wind Spirit."

I quicken my steps until his arms fold around me.

He holds me tight for a moment and whispers in my ear, "I was so worried about you."

What *do* I tell him—that everything is going to be all right? Blake almost died. One second later and we'd be carrying his lifeless corpse back to the park.

I won't lie to him, so I whisper, "I'm fine," brush my lips against his cheek, and push him away.

Stuart rises to his feet. "I am certainly pleased to find you all well. Yes, yes, pleased is a good word for it, but I'm confused why you didn't stay in the park."

Akari steps toward him and growls. "Blake had a trouble. Juliet brought the cure to him. He almost expired."

Stuart's eyes wash over Blake, and his lips turn into a disappointed frown. "That would have been a pity. Quite a pity for you to die so soon. We have much yet to do."

Connor grabs him by the shirt. "Maybe we should pitch you from a bridge. I'm sure I can find one in four minutes."

"Come now. That would be a poor choice, an extremely poor choice indeed. You need me. I'm the Host. Without me you stand no chance, and if you fail to kill the Prime Elector he *will* kill you. He's close as it is. Yes, yes, so close. We don't have time for all these threats. We have work to do."

Connor's hands tighten on his shirt, and Stuart's eyes widen in response.

I think Connor only wants to scare him, but the weasel is right. We need him. He's the Host, so he must know important information that'll help us.

I put my hand on Connor's back and feel the tension. "We can always kill him later if we want." I try to add levity to my voice, but the words sound flat. Part of me wants to help him toss Stuart from a bridge, but the rational part overrules the emotional for once.

The hard edge in Connor's face melts. "Okay, so long as all my options are still open." He shoves Stuart backward.

Stuart straightens his shirt. "So good we got that out of the way. Let's move along, as we have training to start. Yes, yes, training."

Blake limps to my side. "Well, I think I should see a doctor. My leg hurts. You'll have to go on without me."

Sydney clicks her tongue and shakes her head. "Don't be a baby. You're not even bleeding. You look fine to me."

Blake glares at her and then shoots laser beams at Stuart. "Did you really poison us? I could have died!"

Stuart tugs on his beard. "Died. Yes, certainly you could have died. Your life has been in mortal jeopardy since you were born and made a Chosen. That wasn't my decision. Others, yes others, chose for you. Not me. You need to confront this reality. You need to face your own mortality because it's so extremely close at every moment. The sooner you get used to it the better you'll react when you actually face a Seeker or the Prime Elector. We have no time, no time to dawdle."

Blake jabs an angry finger at him. "I don't know about the others, but my life was safe before this, before you tried to kill me."

"Really, Blake Richards, I don't think so." Stuart turns his head and his eyes linger on each of us for a second. "You've all been careless. Each one of you has been moments away from being discovered." He points at Blake. "Your family uses the Twisted Muskets as a play thing. It's not just carved into your house, but on your yacht and at Richards Company headquarters. Once the Deltites discover the Inn's symbol, they'll see the Twisted Muskets. How long before they knock on your door?"

Stuart points at Connor. "And you.... Have you ever wondered why your parents were racing in that auto so late at night? Why did they leave you, at the age of two, with the Vicar?

Not even a friend? Why indeed? They were running when they crashed. A Seeker was minutes away from discovering them. If they hadn't died in that crash, who knows what they might have told them."

Stuart waves at Akari and me. "You two narrowly escaped Seekers just a few days ago. Yes, yes, all your lives have been in danger since the very beginning. It's about time you realized it."

A thick and syrupy silence fills the air between us, as if we've all just failed an important test.

I glance at Connor, who looks distant as he grinds his teeth and clenches his hands until the knuckles have turned white.

All the Orders have been careless to some extent. It's only natural. Secrets can't be kept forever, but what strikes me as odd is how much Stuart knows about us. Has he been watching us, or has he been in contact with the different Orders?

Sicheii never mentioned an outsider—a Host. He would never have kept that from me. So how does Stuart know so much?

"I guess we'd better start this training then," says Akari, as she turns toward the park.

Stuart grabs her arm. "Where are you going?"

"Aren't were headed to the park to start our training."

He chuckles. "The park, yes, I can see how you might jump to that conclusion, but the park is not for us. It's way too public. No, no, I have another place in mind. It's a little musty, but it will serve our purposes much better than the park."

CHAPTER

It's not that I'm a control freak, but not knowing what's going to happen next sucks. Not every surprise is bad—a good twist in a movie is fun so long as your favorite character doesn't die, but real life is different. Almost every surprise is awful: the guy you like just asked out your best friend; a friend's parent loses a job; a relative comes down with a terminal illness; you're a Chosen and have to save the world. Good luck and look out for those Deltites who want to destroy you.

I crave certainty, a clear, lit path to follow, and solid ground to tread upon. I keep searching for that path, hoping it will light up at any moment. Instead, only shadows and cracks in the sidewalk wait to trip me up. *Must I always watch my step?*

My strides slow and become hesitant. Questions chip away at my confidence and weigh me down. Where's the Host taking us? How will we survive? Whom can I trust?

It feels like my first day at Bartens two years ago, only worse. So much more is at stake now.

We follow Stuart as he leads us from the park. Troy and I drop behind the others, and I reach for my wind catcher pendant. Just the touch of the cool turquoise bolsters my spirit, as if Sicheii is with me.

Troy, who knows me better than anyone, must sense my unease. He starts talking in an obvious effort to distract me. "Guess what they called the American Indians who lived on Manhattan?"

He likes when I have to guess at stuff. I find it generally annoying. "Suckers?"

"Manhattanoes."

"Manhattanoes? Come on, you're making that up."

He smiles. "Nope. It's in the book Landon gave me."

"What else does the book say?"

He frowns. "There's not one monument or park or sacred place dedicated to Native Americans on the whole island. It's like they never even existed. They tried to make a small park into a tiny reservation, but the City wouldn't go for it."

I shake my head. "Are you serious? A *Rez* on Manhattan. That would've been cool, but they would've screwed it up with a casino."

Stuart turns left on 75th Street and stops a few steps away from Central Park West. "We're here." He shoots us a cheesy moon pie grin, waves his arms, and bends at the waist as if he's proud of himself.

More shadows.

"What're you talking about?" asks Connor. "Have you gone mental? We're in the middle of the street."

Stuart twists his head in both directions to make sure no one is within eyesight, and points at a manhole cover. "Sydney, if you would be so kind?"

She pulls a crowbar from her bag and glances at Troy. "I could use a hand here."

Together they yank up the manhole cover with a collective grunt.

"Hurry now. We're going down into The Underground." Stuart points to the opening. "There's no reason to dawdle. Yes, yes, dawdling would be bad. We don't want to be seen."

"I'm not going down there!" Blake crosses his arms against his chest.

I'm sure he's never had to go into a dark and dirty place like this before. I can't blame him. It does look gross.

"Afraid to get your fancy shoes dirty?" Akari smirks at him.

"It has to be teeming with rats. Do you know how many diseases rats carry?" He doesn't wait for an answer and ticks them off with his fingers. "Well, there's the Plague, Hantavirus, Lasa Fever, Rat Bite Fever—"

"We have plenty of rats in my fishing village." Akari elbows him in the side. "Don't worry, I'll scare them away for you."

Stuart pushes Blake lightly in the back. "You'll only find domesticated city rats in The Underground. I assure you it's perfectly safe. Sydney will go first to prove it."

She glances at Troy, smiles, and plunges down the hole. For a moment, I imagine closing the cover and locking her down there, but I really don't want to be *that* person.

Akari climbs down after her, then Blake wrinkles his nose before he drops out of sight. Troy's next, which leaves Stuart, Connor, and me above ground.

Connor and I exchange a glance. I can tell what he's thinking: how can we trust Stuart?

Connor glares at him. "You go down first and then we'll follow. I'll roll the bloody cover back in place before I go down."

"Good, good. I'm happy to leave that task in your capable hands. Please hurry though." Stuart disappears down the hole.

"What do you think that tosser has down there for us? Some type of torture chamber?"

I smile. "That's very *medieval* of you. We're in New York, so whatever craziness he has in store for us is probably a little more modern. Still, there's only one way to find out."

A series of metal rungs are bolted into the concrete. White light flickers from below and bounces off a slimy film that covers the metal.

Stuart shouts, his voice echoing in the darkness. "Time's a-wasting!"

I take a deep breath and climb into the darkness. Fifty rungs later I reach the bottom where everyone waits for us.

Connor replaces the manhole cover with a clang and follows.

We're in a round concrete chamber barely large enough for us to stand without bumping into each other. Stuart shines a light against a wooden door. Silver letters spell *The Underground*, and underneath the name is the Inn's symbol carved into the wood. He shifts the beam to the doorknob, which has one of those locks attached to it where you have to plug in four numbers for the door to open. He presses the button marked 5 four times and pulls the door open.

Sydney flips a light switch, and overhead lights brighten a large room that resembles an old pub. The floor and walls are made from dark wood; large chunks of plaster have fallen from the ceiling. A stage stands on one end to our right, and a long wooden bar runs the entire length of the left side of the room. Half a dozen chairs, a few tables, and a full-sized refrigerator fill the rest of the room. A layer of dust covers everything.

"How can there be a pub in the sewer?" Blake looks baffled.

I can't blame him. The Underground wasn't what I had expected either.

"The sewer? Oh, we're not in the sewer. That would indeed be messy. No, definitely not the sewer. This space was originally excavated to become a subway station, but that project stalled. When prohibition started, the Order created a speakeasy in its stead." Stuart chuckles. "I'm told that for a dozen years The Underground was truly the best place *under the ground* to enjoy oneself."

"Prohibition?" asks Akari.

"During the 1920s it was illegal to make or consume alcoholic beverages in this country. This place was a secret oasis. The manhole cover was the back entrance used only in case of emergencies, or if the police interrupted the party. The main entrance connected to one of the buildings on the street, but that was walled off long ago." Stuart points to the stage. "Some of the best jazz musicians in the day played here. This place has quite a history. If the walls could talk they'd spill some secrets, but we have other uses for The Underground now. It's ideal to start your training."

Connor swings his legs over the bar and lands gracefully on the other side. "Any booze left?"

Stuart frowns. "No, and besides we're not here to imbibe spirits. A nasty habit that is, one you should consider refraining from until we're finished."

"Good luck with him," says Troy. "He's got a one-track mind."

Connor jumps back over the bar and shoots Troy a nasty stare. "There's nothing wrong with my mind, mate."

The two are about to face off, which would be totally moronic. To break the tension, I quickly ask Stuart, "What *are* we going to do here?"

The question works. We're all focused on him again.

"Swordplay certainly. Yes, yes, we need practice with the swords. First, push the furniture to the sides of the room so we have space to begin practicing. The swords are the only reliable weapons that can kill the Deltites. Although you've been fused with knowledge on how to wield the sword, actual experience will unlock all that knowledge and come in handy. Yes, handy indeed."

Akari and I reach for some chairs.

"Stop!" Stuart raises his hand. "Why use your hands when you can use your minds? Yes? Telekinetic abilities only. Start with the chairs and work your way up to the tables. Practice will strengthen your skills. Skills that might save your life."

I've only used my telekinetic ability on small things before, so the furniture will be a challenge. I focus on the chair closest to me, and it starts to rock. When I concentrate harder it rises a foot off the ground and flies against the far wall.

Crash!

Not what I had intended, but it still makes me smile. Using telekinesis feels a bit like working a robotic hand. I convert the energy around me into the power source. Not accustomed to the sensation yet, I'm not great at controlling my powers.

One chair slowly scrapes across the ground; sweat beads on Blake's forehead.

Another lurches unevenly through the air, and a third flies gracefully, completes a few loops, lands on its legs, and leans against the wall.

Connor winks at me. It seems stealing drinks at pubs has come in handy for him.

We gradually work our way to the tables. With practice I increase my control, but not perfectly. I shove a table with too much gusto and a leg snaps off against the far wall. Still, I make progress.

When the last table bumps against the far wall, I turn to face Stuart.

He's made himself comfortable on a stool by the bar, eating cheese and crackers with a full glass of water in his hand.

Troy and Sydney perch on the bar and let their feet dangle as they watch us. Sydney's thigh rubs up against Troy's leg. There's plenty of room so they don't have to sit so close.

I suppress the desire to screech.

Stuart joins us in the middle of the room. "Not good, not good. *Good* is definitely not the word I would use to describe your efforts, but it's a start. You definitely made progress toward the end. Some pieces of furniture still remain intact."

"It's not as easy as it looks," grumbles Akari.

"I guess not. Now take out your swords so we can see what we have." He steps back.

I remove my sword from my string bag that still hangs from my shoulders. When I grab the hilt, the blade appears. Energy floods through the sword and into my body as I connect to the sword in a way that goes beyond person and weapon. It feeds off of my energy and life force, magnifying my own abilities. The crystal blade pulses with my heartbeats.

"Yes, yes, that is something," says Stuart. "What an impressive sight! Four warriors with swords. Yes, yes, this would make any Seeker more than a little nervous, if I say so myself."

Each of the other blades shimmers with a faint pulse like mine. Connor swishes his in the air in a giant loop with a confident grin on his face.

Stuart claps his hands together. "Let's start the combat. First Blake and Akari. That's a good place to start, I think. Yes, let's see what happens. Try not to kill or maim each other. That would be bad." He turns toward Sydney. "You have the first-aid kit, right?"

She nods. "It's around here someplace."

"Are you crazy?" Blake's eyes narrow. "She could kill me with that thing."

Stuart tugs on his beard. "Yes, certainly she could. Of course you could kill her also, but that seems unlikely." His eyes glimmer and look as lethal as any of the blades. "What did you expect? *Wooden sticks?* No, the Fusion works with your sword, so we practice with the swords."

Akari swings her sword in a short, confident arc, her blade held steady, the weapon comfortable in her hand. "I'll try not to hurt you."

Blake shoots one last desperate look at Stuart.

He nods and says, "Get started. It's getting late. Use the knowledge the Fusion gave you. Start slowly and work your way to full speed."

Akari faces Blake, bows slightly at her waist and then starts to circle him. She steps forward and takes a slow sideswipe.

Blake easily deflects it.

When the blades connect they sound like glass breaking.

Blake swipes at her and she knocks the blow away.

They begin to pick up the pace and look more relaxed, and the sound of breaking glass fills the chamber.

Akari blocks a forward thrust by Blake, twirls and swings her sword by his side, stopping it just before she cuts him. They continue for a few more minutes, but Akari is obviously faster and more agile.

"Enough!" Stuart shouts, and the two separate. He shakes his head at Blake. "A rope is only as strong as all the fibers used to twist it together. You need to embrace this part of yourself and let the Fusion guide you. Stop fighting your special abilities before it's too late."

He waves at Blake to step back and then points at Connor. "Your turn. You fight with Akari."

Connor grins, takes out his phone and presses a button on the screen. Classic rock from The Who blares from the phone and echoes in the chamber. "All right, let's get it on." He wastes no time and darts forward with heavy strokes. Utilizing his length and strength, he beats Akari backward.

She's more agile, but his height gives him the advantage. She starts to sweat as he presses her toward the wall. She fakes a swing at his left side and spins back to her right, but he anticipates it and the point of his blade beats her to the spot and rips her shirt.

She scowls and charges, sending a flurry of strokes at him. For a moment her anger and the speed of her attack push him back.

He quickly regains his footing and confidence, using his strength to knock Akari's blade to her side, and stops the tip of his by her throat.

"Better! Next." Stuart glances at me.

The sword feels heavy in my hand. The last time I fought with it, Sicheii died and I killed a Seeker. Sweat coats my back. I'm thrown backward in time and can't help but remember how my blade had ripped into the Seeker's chest, and how blood bubbled from his mouth as life faded from his eyes.

Connor snaps me from the memory. "Ready? I'll try to go easy on you."

"Can we change the music?" I smirk at him. "How about some Taylor Swift?"

"Hey, winner gets to choose."

I smile, wave my sword in front, and bend my knees.

He creeps forward and tries a few lazy sideswipes that I have no problem deflecting. He's going easy on me to start, so I push forward with a few quick flips of my wrists—nothing too fast, but swift enough that he lumbers to parry them.

The Fusion starts to work. Even though I've only fought with the sword a few times, it feels familiar in my hand and my body knows the proper techniques. It goes on autopilot for a few minutes as I play defense.

I flash back to my fight with the Seeker a week earlier. He was so much stronger and faster until I used my abilities to enhance my strength and quicken my reflexes, until I used those abilities....

I step back from Connor and soak in the music and the energy around me. An electrical current zips through my body. Instantly, my arms and legs become as light as feathers and much stronger than before. The blade pulses faster. My other senses sharpen also.

A small stream of sweat drips down Connor's cheek.

I hear his heartbeat, fast and strong.

The muscles in his right hand tenses, and his eyes flash to my left, telegraphing his next move. He steps to my left.

I snap my sword out to the side ahead of him, catching him unprepared. My blade clashes hard against his, and he's left off balance. I spin back to my right and his back is unprotected, but I hesitate and pull back.

When he turns to face me, he's grinning. "I'm happy you're going to be a challenge. I guess I shouldn't go easy on you anymore."

"Bring your A-game. I can handle it."

He attacks with a blizzard of strokes that seemingly come at me from all sides and angles.

He's tapping into his own enhanced abilities.

He's moving faster and his strokes are stronger, but he's not fast enough.

I spin in a blur to cover his attacks, and press a few of my own. The sound of shattering glass pounds in my ears and mixes with a guitar riff. I could best him at any moment, but I don't want to.

He's surprisingly graceful for someone so tall and broad. He moves like a dancer, fluid and sure of himself. The violet specks in his eyes glow as his face pinches together in concentration, as he swipes for my legs.

I leap backward in plenty of time. I don't want to be stronger or faster than him—I don't want to be the Alpha—but I have a different gear than he does. It frightens me. I don't want them to see me as different, so I slow may blade and fall for an obvious feint, leaving my body unprotected.

He brings the tip of his sword to my chest.

I lower my hand, and my heart is thumping as air comes in gasps. "I guess... you won."

He's breathing hard also. "More like a tie, but that was *fun*."

The door slams shut and we turn.

Troy turns the music off. "Stuart and Sydney left. I guess that's it for tonight."

Blake limps to the bar. "Well, my leg still hurts. Where's that first-aid kit they were talking about?"

It's been a long night and I'm happy it's over. I step toward the door, but a wave of nausea washes over me and my head spins. A Molotov Cocktail explodes in my cranium and bursts into flames. I fall to my knees, the pain intense. I'm worried I'm going to throw-up those bangers and mash all over the place, and then a vision flashes in my mind. It's fuzzy, a bit out of focus, but it sends a tremor of fear racing through my body.

I blink and concentrate harder on the image, trying to force it to clear.

A familiar face begins to form, and I feel a call for help—a terror-filled plea, mouth wide open, eyes bursting, heart exploding.

It's Lilly.

CHAPTER

Obligation is a weird concept when it happens between two people who barely know each other. I understand when the bond exists between friends or family, but sometimes it happens between strangers. A man punches a woman in the middle of a busy street, and somebody usually feels obligated to help even if the next punch is likely to be thrown his or her way.

I feel obligated to help Lilly. Yes, last night was a spur of the moment situation, but we created a bond, which is why I can see her face and feel her terror right now. She's in mind- numbing, can't-move, oh-my-God terror, and I have to help her.

It's probably not a smart thing, this bond I sense. *Do I really need to be responsible for a thirteen-year-old girl when so much else is at stake?* Still, I'm more emotional than intelligent. I protect people I care about, and even though I've only spent a few minutes with Lilly, I care about her.

My vision clears and with it goes Lilly's terror and my pain and nausea.

Both Troy and Connor hover close to me. Oddly, their faces are etched with the same concerned expression.

"Are you all right?" Troy reaches for my arm.

Heat flushes my face. That's the second time I've gone wonky tonight. Some Alpha I am; maybe I'm the weak fiber in the rope.

"I'm fine, but I've got to stop making a habit out of doing that." My smile chases away their worried expressions, and then I remember my vision. "Troy, we have a problem. Lilly's in trouble."

"The girl from the other night? She should be at New Beginnings."

"She's scared. Something's happened to her."

Blake limps over. "Well, can someone fill us in? What's going on and who's this Lilly person? Why are we worried about her?"

I explain what happened last night with New Beginnings and how we saved Lilly from the creepy dude at Chelsea Park. I end by telling them about my vision and the connection I've formed with her.

Connor shifts on his feet. "So... you can see into other people's minds?"

He's struggling with the implications of my ability, so I shrug and try to play it cool. "Sometimes I can see a vision. I bet you can too. It only works with a person I've made a connection with."

I'm not going to tell them that I can read minds. First, their minds are blanks. For some reason I can't read any of them or Stuart, and second, my gut tells me to keep it quiet. I can't put my reluctance into words, but being too different from them feels like a bad idea. Even though I know better, I tell myself it's not a lie — it's just that no one has asked me about it.

Akari's eyes smolder. "So you think this creepy guy has her again?"

"Could be. All I know is that she's in trouble."

"Let's call Landon and see if she's with New Beginnings." Troy dials Landon's number on his cell and puts it on speaker.

Landon answers on the second ring. "Landon here."

He sounds wired, as if he's hoping for good news.

"It's Troy."

His voice slows. "Are you guys all right?"

"Yes, but that's not why I'm calling. We were wondering if the girl from last night is still with you. I think her name is Lilly."

Landon pauses, which gives him away. He's worried about her. "Do you know something?"

"No, nothing. Juliet just got a funny feeling that she might be in trouble."

He sighs. "I'm out right now with Tara and Frankie looking for her. She left the building a few hours ago and no one's seen her since. I'm worried she might've been taken."

I clench my hands into clubs. "Who took her? Do you think that guy from the park did it?"

"No, Juliet. We checked him out. Frankie and I made sure he knows how serious we are, but he doesn't know anything. Gangs make a habit of snatching runaways. They hold them against their will for a spell until they brainwash them into joining the gang."

"What can we do?" asks Troy.

"It's late. Go to bed. She might just turn up. You never know with new runaways. If we haven't found her by tomorrow, maybe you guys can ask around and canvas some streets for us. I've got to go."

Click.

The fuzzy image from Lilly's mind could have been a knife. Someone is threatening her. She's so young and scared.

A pain jabs me in the gut as if someone stabbed me with a stiletto and is twisting the blade.

"Well, it's possible she'll turn up tomorrow like he says." Blake shrugs. "Where—"

I ignore him. I have to leave, so I march toward the door and shout over my shoulder, "I'm going to find her! I've got to help her. You guys can come along if you want."

When I shove the door open with my mind, it shatters in a burst of splinters before me.

CHAPTER

The wind swirls, and I take a deep breath. This City air is different from the air back home. A trace of moisture clings to it as if it hasn't fully decided whether it should rain. I miss the dry fresh scent from back home, but there's no time for these thoughts, so I push aside the creeping sense of melancholy that threatens to fill me as everyone else clatters up the ladder.

Connor's the last one up, and rolls the manhole cover back into place. "So, let's get cracking. We've got a girl to save and some bad guys to pummel."

"I'm serious. You guys don't have to help. It could be dangerous."

Akari plants her hands on her hips. "More dangerous than a group of superhuman aliens who want to take over the world, enslave everyone, and conquer the rest of the universe? I'm in."

Blake nods. "Okay, let's find this girl. Where do we look?"

"Leave that to me. If I concentrate on her and start walking, we'll eventually find her."

"Like psychic GPS?" Blake stares at me wide-eyed.

"Kinda?" I shrug

Connor bows low and sweeps his arm before me in an exaggerated flourish. "Lead the way."

I close my eyes and picture Lilly's face, her brilliant blue eyes, her round cheeks, and her blonde hair. When I open them, I'm facing west. It feels like the right direction so I start in a brisk walk.

Troy strides along beside me, and the others follow a step behind.

After a block, Akari asks in a thick accent, "Why do you think the Alphians made a selection of us? I mean with so many people to pick from, why make us the special ones?"

"I'm not sure about you guys, but it's obvious why I was chosen." Connor grins.

"Why?" Akari takes the bait.

"My brilliant good lucks." He grins a crooked half-smile that means he's only kidding.

"*Right,*" mutters Troy.

"I have my charms if the beer is flowing and the lights are low."

"Very low," I say, and we all laugh.

"Seriously." Akari's boots clatter against the street. "How'd they even know we would be born?"

"Assuming they're this advanced race." Blake huffs from behind me. "They probably used genetic testing and sophisticated statistical analyses. That way they'd know what types of genes we would have and they could calculate the odds that an eligible baby would be available when the time was right."

"That or there's something else going on." Troy turns and stops, his voice serious. "Maybe the stories behind our Orders aren't all wrong. Maybe spirits are in play that can see into the future."

Connor shakes his head. "Bloody spirits sound far-fetched."

"It's possible." Akari nods. "My grandmother believes our ancestors visit us after they die, sometimes in dreams and other times in visions."

I shove Troy playfully in his chest and he spins forward. "Spirits or no, we need to hurry."

We walk in silence for a few minutes. Maybe the others contemplate spirits or God or whatever they believe in. I have my own doubts about spirits, but I can't dismiss what Troy said. He *could* be right. Sicheii certainly was convinced they're real.

At almost one in the morning, cars still drive by, and we pass small knots of people. Some are loud and act as if they've enjoyed a few too many drinks. Others scoot past quietly, eyes downcast, looking like they just want to go home after a long night of work.

Blake breaks the silence. "That Stuart fella isn't what I pictured. He looks nothing like the Alphians from those dreams the fusions gave me. All those Alphians were tall, thin and hairless."

"Did you see that look on his face when he explained about the Uglies and the rest of the Alphians," Troy says. "I know that look. It's the same one some Native Americans have on the *Rez* when they describe white men. On the outside it's pleasant, but scratch just under the surface and there's nothing but pure hatred."

Now that Troy mentions it, I know he's right. Uglies and Alphians living together, the Uglies subservient, almost slaves to the tall and beautiful looking Alphians.... It's hard to go through life with that giant chip on your shoulders. A weight like that can bend the strongest back. I know. I wilt sometimes from the discrimination I've felt back home, and Troy's so sensitive to the slights, he's quick to react to the smallest snubs, his nerves rubbed raw after a lifetime of being told he's inferior, not just in words, but in actions and looks and whispers, too, which are way worse.

"He can sod off. I don't care about his *situation*. All we need is the name of the Prime Elector." Connor kicks a bottle that breaks against a metal trashcan. "As much as I dislike the wanker, we need him until he gives us that name."

"Maybe he doesn't know. Maybe that's why he didn't tell us at dinner," says Akari.

Could Stuart have lied about that?

He doesn't strike me as the most honest type of person; more of an ends-justify-the-means guy, so he'd lie to get us to do the things he wants. Yet at dinner, I got the impression that he spoke truthfully about knowing the identity of the Prime Elector.

Still, that's what I *wanted* to believe, and I know how easy it is to convince people of the things they *want* to believe.

I don't have much time to ponder it because a tingle climbs up my spine. We're close, so I stop in front of a rundown four-story brick warehouse. "She's inside."

"Where are we?" Akari turns her head, and her eyes dance in a nervous circle as she shudders.

I wonder if she's having another one of those panic attacks she had in Tokyo. She gulps air and her body trembles, but no one else notices, so I slide away from her to give her space.

"We're in the Meatpacking District." Troy points to the building's facade. "You can see cattle and pigs carved into the top of the building. The City used to have a number of slaughterhouses around here next to those abandoned train tracks." He waves at tracks on the other side of the building.

"How do you know so much about it?" I ask him.

He beams one of his heart-melting smiles. "The book Landon gave me has a map and some info about the different parts of the City. We passed the Village to get here. The Inn is only a few blocks that way." He points east.

"What now?" asks Blake. "Should we call the police?"

I shake my head. "What would we tell them? I have a premonition that bad people are holding an innocent girl in the building? Besides, it might take too long. Who knows what they're doing and when they'll move her."

"So we go in and teach these blokes a thing or two about manners." Connor rolls his head and stretches his shoulders, his eyes gleaming with mischief.

What we're about to do is serious. I remember what my father told me before I set out to rescue my mother from the Seeker. He said I had to be *all-in*. They need to understand the same message before we blunder ahead.

"Listen, these guys are going to be dangerous. They're probably armed. None of you have to do this. You don't even know this girl, but if you're in, you've got to be willing to do whatever it takes. That might mean getting your hands dirty. We've got to assume anyone we come across will be happy to hurt us."

They all nod, although Blake looks two shades paler than usual.

I glance at the abandoned building and feel negative energy flow from it. It seeps through the bricks like a foul smelling fog rolling over a lake.

CHAPTER

We circle the building, careful to stay in the shadows. The main door is made of heavy steel. It's coated with dust and appears not to have budged in decades. We're not getting in that way.

The back of the building faces the railroad tracks and the river. Three steel bay doors are shut tight. They roll upward, but I imagine they'll make a loud high-pitched squeal if we open them.

There must be some other way inside.

Troy points to the corner of the building, his voice a whisper. "There's a small door over there." It's barely visible in the moonlight. "That must be how they get in. Let's check it out."

We race along the building.

Troy studies the ground. "See those scuff marks? They look fresh. A few people have recently used this door."

I close my eyes, concentrate on the inside of the building, and comb over the space with my mind. Every animal has a life force or spirit, as Troy would say. "No one appears to be on the first floor. Lilly is on the second. I'm sure a cluster of other people hang near her."

"Do you know how many?" Blake's face wrinkles with doubt.

I shrug. "We're too far away for me to be certain, and I can't tell if they're all bad."

"Well, how do you know Lilly's one of them?" Blake nervously shifts on his feet.

"Once I've met someone, my mind registers their unique spirit. I don't know how it works exactly, but I can see a face when I sense the person's energy. If I haven't met the person, all I see is a fuzzy image like a photograph that's way out of focus. The others in the building are all strangers, but Lilly's definitely in there."

Connor grins. "Good. I'm happy these creeps are with her. What fun would we have if she were alone? Who'd we get to hurt?"

Blake sighs. "Right, this is *way* more fun."

"You can still back out if you've changed your mind," I tell him. If he wants to come he'll have to be committed.

"No, I'm in. I'll be behind you every step of the way," he says, and I shoot him a look. "Well, someone has to be last."

The moonlight casts a silver hue against his face, but determination flares in his eyes. Maybe he doesn't want to be left out, or maybe he really wants to help Lilly. It doesn't matter; either way he's in.

I try the doorknob and it's locked. "Troy, do you think you can pick it?"

Troy checks out the lock. He's picked a few for us over the years—nothing too serious: the school, my grandfather's gallery, and once we snuck into the general store for a few late night ices. We both felt guilty, so we left ten dollars in the store before we left.

He reaches into his pocket and removes a key chain he always carries with him. One of the attachments is an Allen wrench and another is a small flat screwdriver.

Troy's always been mechanical; he just sees how things work. The day after his sixth birthday he showed up at my house with a wide grin and a bike he cobbled together from scraps he found at the dump. The mismatched wheels wobbled and the handlebars stretched so high he had to strain to reach them, but the bike held together.

Sicheii and I had helped him paint flames on the sides and everyone thought it was the coolest thing. He raced around the neighborhood for a year until he built a makeshift ramp and tried to jump over a fence in the park. He didn't come close to clearing it. He couldn't fix the bike, but he laughed it off just the same. That's the other thing about Troy; he's always pushing limits, and sometimes they push back.

These memories flash through my mind as he fiddles with the lock for a few minutes. "This one has a deadbolt from inside. I can't pick it."

'We could break it down," suggests Akari. "It shouldn't be a problem. One good kick and it'll give way."

She backs up and measures the distance to the door, so I step in the way. "I know you can knock it down, but I'd really like to surprise them. You might be able to set it on fire instead, but it's metal. Of course, Connor could just liquefy the doorknob. Then we'd be able to stroll right through without any noise."

Connor smirks. "I've never done anything like that before."

"I saw you at the pub the other day. You liquefied that glass in your hand."

"Never sober, anyway." He shrugs. "When I've tossed back a few, it just happens."

"It's a little late to find an open liquor store, so you'll have to use your imagination and try to focus on the doorknob." I squeeze his arm and lock onto his eyes. "You can do this."

"You sure you don't have a nip of something on you?" He shoots me a sly grin.

I tap my foot and place my hands on my hips. He has to believe in himself and stop using alcohol as a crutch. I'm sure he can do this if he sets his mind to it. "Stop fooling around. You don't need a drink."

"Okay, you don't have to glare at me. I didn't think you'd have anything, but it was worth a try."

He grabs the doorknob and closes his eyes. Five seconds pass, then ten, and the air crackles. Twenty seconds and he's sweating and the knuckles on his hand turn white. Thirty seconds and his whole body shakes. I'm about to tell him to give up, but when he gets to fifty seconds, electricity fills the air and the doorknob melts away, gushing to the floor.

Blake stands too close and the liquid splashes on his shoes. "Great. These are Ferragamos."

I slap Connor on the back. "Excellent work. And you didn't have to drink to do it."

Connor grins and shakes his hand as if it smarts from a shock. "No, but a pint would've made it easier."

"That's odd," says Troy as he bends low and touches the liquid that had just been the doorknob.

"You're going to have to be more specific," says Connor. "There's plenty of odd going around."

Troy straightens. "The liquid is cool to the touch. It should be hot."

"Oh, I thought you were talking about Blake. He's odd." Connor smiles. "It's always cool whenever I change something to liquid."

I push the door and it swings open and creaks a little on rusty hinges. Moonlight streams through dirt-encrusted windows and bathes the floor in just enough light to make out shapes in the darkness.

Inside the building is a vast open space. A large elevator big enough to hold two cars sits in the middle with a metal cage for doors. Dirt, dust, and debris litter the rough concrete ground. Smashed glass glitters along the edges of the room as if people commonly toss bottles against the walls.

We step inside and Blake shuts the door behind us.

"It's not what I thought a slaughterhouse would look like," says Akari.

Blake crunches glass under his foot as he steps past me. "They probably stopped slaughtering animals here fifty years ago. It looks like they converted it to warehouse space, but once the railroad stopped running, it must have lost its value."

He's stopped limping; I wonder if he even notices.

I whisper, "As far as I can tell, everyone is on the far side of the building on the second floor. It looks like there are two staircases, one on this end and the other at the far end where they are."

"We should split up." Connor grabs Blake by the neck. "I'll take captain courageous here and go up the staircase at the far end. This way he can make sure I don't lose my nerve. You guys go up here —"

"When we get to the second floor we'll go first." I nod toward the stairs. "This way we can distract them. Once they're focused on us, you guys can slip in from behind and make sure Lilly is safe."

Connor grins. "As fine a plan as we're going to get. Come on, let's go." He pulls Blake with him.

140

Troy, Akari, and I creep our way up the front staircase. When we arrive on the second floor, I slide open the door a few inches and sneak a glimpse. This floor has the same layout as the first, open with a wide elevator shaft in the middle. A battery-operated lamp brightens the far end of the building. A punk song beats a loud and annoying rhythm that ripples toward us. I can't see anyone clearly from here, which means they can't see us.

I turn to face Akari and Troy. "The elevator shaft blocks the middle of the floor. Let's sneak our way behind it. From there we should be able to see what's up."

They nod, so I open the door just wide enough to slip through and stalk my way toward the elevator shaft, dancing around bottles and anything that might crunch under my feet. My heart pounds and I breathe through my mouth.

Troy and Akari follow close behind.

At the elevator doors, I flatten my back against the cage.

The music is loud, but I can hear a few angry male voices mixed in. "Where'd you get that other ace for three of a kind!"

"What're you saying?"

Good. They're playing cards, which means they won't notice us. I crouch to the floor and peek my head from behind the elevators. Six guys sit in a rough circle on the floor, a pile of chips in the center. Smoke swirls above them as lit cigarettes dangle from two of the card players' mouths. More than a dozen beer bottles are scattered around them, but my attention is drawn behind the card players.

Three girls lay on old mattresses against the far wall, their hands tied to metal beams.

I've seen enough. "We need to make sure none of the guys can get to those girls. The girls are only twenty feet back from these creeps. They appear to be sleeping, or drugged."

"Let's draw them out," suggests Troy. "If they hear some noise over here, perhaps they'll come and investigate and leave the girls behind."

I nod. "I like it. What should we use for a diversion?"

"I'll create a fire by the staircase," says Akari. "When they come running, we'll surprise them from behind. While we clobber them, Connor and Blake should be able to make sure the girls are safe."

"Awesome." I nod and wait for Akari to do her thing.

The air starts to shimmer. First sparks pop and then a fireball erupts, an angry-looking thing the size of a Volkswagen Beetle.

A loud voice shouts from the other end of the room. "What the.... Look at that!"

As the fire rages and spreads along the wall, Akari beams a toothy grin.

"Grab a blanket!" one of the thugs yells. "We've got to put it out."

Loud squeaking sneakers race along the floor, kicking bottles and junk as they go.

As they get louder, so does the sound of my beating heart. It feels as if it might burst from my chest.

Four guys race past us, their attention fixed on the fire.

I spring forward, Akari a step behind me, Troy a few paces slower.

The slowest guy must have heard us because he stops and turns.

Before he can shout, I hit him with a hard chop to his throat and sweep his legs out from under him. He hits the ground hard and I kick him in the head. I move so fast it barely slows me down.

The Fusion has not only instructed me on swordplay, but also given me knowledge of advanced fighting techniques.

The other three guys spin to face us.

Akari sprints forward and launches herself in a flying bicycle kick.

The short chubby guy she hits has no chance. He's flattened.

I glance at Troy to make sure he's safe.

He tackles the man holding the blanket and rides him to the floor hard.

I turn to face the last guy, but it's too late.

He uses my distraction to rush me. He's solid and we both crash to the ground, and the wind is knocked out of my lungs. He's the first to stand and kicks me hard in the ribs. He must have steel-tipped boots because I see stars. When he tries a second kick, I grab his foot and twist, which sends him sprawling to the floor.

I roll away from him, wince at the pain in my ribs and struggle to my feet. By the time I'm steady he's also upright and facing me.

He's holding a six-inch blade and has a sneer plastered across his face. "I don't know who you are, but you messed up good. I'm going to carve my name into your face."

"Right." I stare him down.

His hand shakes a little. He was probably expecting me to run, but when he realizes that I'm not afraid, he dashes forward and swings the blade in a small arc.

My entire body feels electrified, and I can barely sense my limbs. I'm a ball of energy. I step forward, grab his wrist and smash his arm down on my knee. Bones break, the knife clatters against the concrete, and he yelps like a dog.

"I guess you messed with the wrong girl this time."

His eyebrows arch upward in disbelief, and his mouth gapes open in a circle. "How—"

"Like this." I throw a roundhouse, and he's knocked unconscious before he hits the floor.

I check on Troy and stop cold.

Blood drips from his nose, but the guy he tackled doesn't stir under the blanket.

The blood doesn't bother me; it's the worried look in his eyes that makes my heart jump.

I turn and my body hardens to stone.

CHAPTER 20

Connor holds his arms straight up over his head, palms out in surrender. Blake stands near the radio with one gang member knocked out by his feet.

A tall, greasy-haired, twenty-something guy has wrapped his left arm around Lilly's neck and presses a knife against her throat with his right hand. His wild eyes dance around the room. "Who are you guys?"

Connor speaks in a smooth, disarming voice. "We're a bunch of nobodies, but you really don't want to wind us up. Don't panic and wet yourself. Release the girl and we'll let you leave. Otherwise, you've made a really bad choice and we'll get angry. I won't be so friendly then."

I march toward them.

Lilly's eyes pulse with panic and her body hangs limply in the bad guy's arms. A new welt has appeared on her left cheek. They must have beaten her. If he stabs her with that knife....

I start to see red. All I can focus on is that welt and the knife.

"I've never seen anything like that before." He turns toward me. "What're you... witches or vampires?" His arm tightens around Lilly's neck and he stares at me. "Stay where you are."

I freeze.

He's hurting her.

She pulls at him and gasps for air. She's too weak to budge his arm and her face turns purple.

I can't let him hurt her, and he's too far away for me to grab him, so I reach out with my mind; bright blue energy bands whip from my body and twist around his arm. I've mentally created these connections. I'm sure no one else can see them, yet they feel real to me.

The link is different from the telekinesis I used back at The Underground — more solid, sturdier, more real. I'm using Greasy Hair's own electricity to connect with him. I yank on the bonds and loosen his hold on Lilly's neck. Then I summon more mental bindings that wrap around his body and hold him in place. He's practically mummified in blue energy.

Now that he can't move, I march toward him. "Don't be an idiot. There's no such thing as witches or vampires. We're way worse. We're Chosen."

His eyebrows arch upward and his eyes explode in their sockets. "What're you doing to me? Let me go!" He struggles against my energy but it's useless. He's locked in place, mine to do with as I please.

I stalk toward him. "Let you go? Are you *serious*?"

Connor says something, but he sounds distant, as if speaking under water.

My concentration is so intense I only see and hear the violent, greasy-haired, Lilly-abusing cretin. Everything else fades away. I stop a few feet in front of him and mentally yank on the streaks of energy that hold his arm. I pull hard, freeing Lilly and dislocating his elbow.

Connor catches her before she hits the floor.

Terror laces his words. "She wanted to... join us. What're you... doing? Why can't I move?"

His fright only strengthens the bonds I use to hold him. Energy flows between us and I twist his hand and point the knife at his face. The tip glistens.

He struggles to throw it away, but he can't. He's totally wrapped in blue light now.

I can make him do anything.

"Stop it! Please! I'll do whatever you want!"

I bear down, concentrate harder, and push the knife against his throat. I'm shaking. One more push and the blade will slice deep into his skin and cut his carotid artery.

"Please! No!"

"You don't have any problem hitting girls. Why shouldn't I cut you?"

Tears roll down his face. There's nothing he can do.

He doesn't deserve to live. He's used dozens of girls.

I close my eyes to give myself a moment to think, and a blast of white-hot pain sears my head.

When I open my eyes, I'm no longer in the abandoned slaughterhouse facing the greasy-haired creep. The air smells fresh, the sun is bright, and my hands and legs cling to the side of a cliff.

Sicheii climbs next to me.

I'm little, and my arms and legs will only reach so far—probably no more than ten years old. Sicheii taught me how to rock climb when I turned ten.

He smiles at me, and the wind blows his long white hair.

I glance above me and can't see the top of the cliff. "How much farther to the top? I'm tired." My voice sounds young, at least an octave higher than it is now.

"Does the fish wonder when it will reach the river's end, or does the hawk ask how high it might fly before it runs out of air?"

Great, another riddle. "Why does it have to be so hard?"

"The greater the destiny, the harder the journey. And your destiny is indeed great."

I climb the craggy rock face and reach for handholds and footholds, but they become more infrequent. I search and can't see any more. "What now? The path is gone. How do I climb to the top?"

His bushy eyebrows arch upward. "You'll have to find your own way."

"What should I do with the sleezeball?"

"What do you think you should do?"

"He doesn't deserve to live."

His voice sounds disappointed, as if I've forgotten an important lesson he taught me. "People can change. Every spirit can be redeemed. You can't rob him of that chance. It's not the way of our people."

"But you changed me! I'm not a member of the Tribe anymore. I'm a Chosen."

"You are my granddaughter. You will always be a member of the Tribe." Sicheii's eyes appear sad as he glances downward and into the ravine far below. He's thinking about falling and leaving me.

"Don't go!"

He shoots me a look he's given me a million times. Love glistens in his eyes; pride and a little mischief fight for room also. It's the same expression he had right before he died.

"You will find your way."

"No!"

He lets go of the cliff and falls backward with his arms at his side.

"No!" I glance down, but he's gone.

A red-shouldered hawk shrieks and beats its wings. His spirit guide was a red-shouldered hawk.

I don't really believe in spirits or animal guides like Troy, but I follow the bird as it soars toward the sun. I guess I've sort of adopted his spirit animal.

He's left me again and the pain is as intense as it was when he died a week ago.

The dream breaks, and I'm back in the abandoned slaughterhouse. Tears blur my vision and sting my eyes.

The tip of the knife has broken Greasy Hair's flesh. A trickle of blood drips down his neck and stains his T-shirt.

My body shakes.

Connor bashes a bottle against his head. The knife falls harmlessly off to the side, and the monster falls unconscious to the ground.

The energy bands vanish.

Connor shoots me an anxious look. "Are you okay?"

Before I can answer, a whoosh roars from behind me. Flames cover the far wall and lurch toward us. A wave of intense heat blasts me in the face. One of the broken bottles must have had alcohol in it and accelerated the fire. In a few seconds the entire building will go up. We'll be lucky to grab the girls and race down the back staircase in time.

I look at Akari and she shrugs. "I can't control it."

Fifty feet from us, Troy stands close to the fire—too close. The flames, fueled by garbage strewn in the middle of the floor, branch from the wall and cut in front of him, separating him from us.

He's trapped behind the flames.

My head spins. The fire will engulf him in a few seconds. My heart sinks as if I'm in a free fall. I can't get to him in time. Even if I do, how can I save him? Still, I have to try. Just as I'm about to race toward him, a strong wind gusts past me and beats back the flames.

The wind turns into a gale and windows explode in showers of glass.

The flames bend and then shrink until they're completely blown out.

I exhale.

I gaze out the window and think about my dream with Sicheii. He used to tell me to study my daydreams to discover secret meanings hidden within them. He thought our ancestors communicate with us through dreams. I've never looked for messages in my dreams before, but *he* was in this dream. If anyone can reach me from beyond the grave and send me important messages, it'll be him. However, even after I rewind the dream a half dozen times, I still don't have a clue what he wants or what I should do next.

Connor moves next to me and follows my eyes out the window. He doesn't say anything; he lets me think for a moment, which I appreciate.

After a few minutes of twisting and turning my daydream into knots, I give up, sigh, and turn toward him. "So why didn't you let me kill that dirtbag?"

He shoots me a half-grin, half-smirk that on most people would look annoying, but works on him. "I figured if you really wanted him dead you wouldn't have hesitated. If you still want to kill him, I'll drag the wanker over and we can pitch him from the window." He looks down. "It might not be far enough to do the job, unless he goes head first."

I chuckle. "Head first would probably do it." I take a deep breath. "So *why* did you stop me?"

He reaches for my hand and his face turns serious. His eyes have real depth to them, and his touch singes my skin. "You can't make a decision like that in the spur of the moment. It'll haunt you. I know." He sweeps a few loose hairs away from my forehead, and his fingers graze my cheek. He's strong and gentle at the same time.

"Have you ever had to kill someone?"

That grin-smirk returns; he shrugs, runs his hands through his shaggy hair, turns, and walks over to Troy, who's talking to the girls by the mattresses.

Akari binds the hands and feet of the gang members with shoelaces. When she finishes, she yells *"bakayaro,"* grunts, and kicks each one in the stomach. I don't know what it means, but I'm sure it's not a compliment.

I smile and glance at Blake, who leans against a wall with a faraway look on his face, so I amble over to him. "Hey, that was some neat work with the wind."

He doesn't look up. He heard me because he nods his head, so I stand silently and wait. Silence is a great way to get people to talk. Most people can't stand quiet stretches and will start to speak just to chase them away.

After a few minutes, he smiles and turns toward me. "I can't believe we did that. I can't believe *I* did that."

This is the first time I've seen him smile. I don't mean a grin or a forced smile on his face, but a genuine, wow-I'm-happy type of smile. It lights up his face and adds life to his thin features.

"I'm not surprised. You're Chosen for a reason."

He grins from ear to ear. "Come on, now. You're not even a little surprised?"

We both chuckle. "Well, a little, but you came up big when we needed it. That was awesome."

"To be honest, I didn't know I had it in me. Well, I mean my parents have always been the heroic type—champion athletes, fearless. It's all really annoying. I've always been a disappointment to them, afraid that I'd fail." He sighs. "I wish they could have seen me. It might have made up for all those times when I finished last in track."

We're molded by our experiences. The ones we live through when we're young have more impact on us than those we experience later in life. Getting picked last for the soccer team when you're five sticks with you. If it happens a few times, you no longer believe you can play sports. Overhear your parents talk about how disappointed they are in you when you're six, and you lose all confidence in yourself.

I know Blake battles his own demons. We all have them.

I'm happy he's overcome this one, at least for tonight, so I clap him on the back. "You don't need to worry about finishing last anymore. You're officially a badass."

CHAPTER

Connor shuts off the radio and we gather by the girls who sit zombie-like on the mattresses. "You guys should go back to the Inn," I say. "We'll take care of the girls. Troy and I will call his cousin at New Beginnings. When they get here, we'll make up a story."

"I don't fancy leaving you alone before your friends show up." Connor crosses his arms against his chest.

"I'm not alone. Troy's with me and Akari has done a darn good job tying them up."

Two thugs toward the far wall start to stir, but their hands and feet are bound tight. They wiggle like fish on hooks, but all they can do is spout long strings of colorful curse words.

"We can handle them."

"They're not going anywhere. I used knots the fishermen back home taught me." Akari grins.

Connor glances at Troy and then at me. "All right. You two

can clean up this mess without us then. Maybe we'll find someone else to save on the way back to the Inn."

Connor, Blake, and Akari saunter down the staircase and out of sight.

Troy grabs his phone, presses the speaker button, and dials Landon, who answers on the third ring, his voice gravely. "No, Troy, we haven't found her yet. We're about to call it a night."

"We did. She's in an abandoned warehouse on 11th Avenue and 12th Street."

Landon's voice jumps. "Don't do anything until we get there! We're only five minutes away."

"Too late," says Troy.

"What do you mean too late? These could be dangerous people we're dealing with. You guys didn't do something stupid, did you?"

"It turns out they're not as dangerous as you might think. Make sure you bring the van. Lilly isn't alone. Two other girls are with her. We're on the second floor, and use the door in the back that faces the river. The doorknob," he looks at me and I shrug, "is missing."

The white NB van pulls up exactly five minutes later. Landon piles out of the vehicle with Frankie and Tara on his heels. Within seconds he bounds up the stairs and is the first to plow through the door.

When he sees us, he slows and whistles. "What in the world happened here? This place looks like a war zone."

Tara rushes past us and over to the girls, while Frankie grins next to Landon. "You didn't tell me Little Bear and Juliet were *Special Forces*."

"I didn't know," says Landon.

Frankie scans the floor. "They took out six hoods. That's a lot."

Landon squints at Troy. "You've got dried blood on your face. Someone must have gotten a punch in."

Frankie waves his hand in front of his face and wrinkles his nose. "Why does it smell like smoke in here? Was there a fire?"

Troy and I shrug.

Tara scoots over to join us, her lips turned down. "All the girls are drugged. A few have bruises, but they all seem like they've just recently been taken. Hopefully we found them in time, before real harm has been done."

"That's as good as we could have hoped for." Landon looks at us with bunched eyebrows and narrow eyes. "All right, start talking. Tell us what happened. You two didn't do this on your own."

"We had a little help," Troy says, "but that's not important. We found Lilly and stopped these guys, which is the only thing that really counts."

"Help from whom?" Frankie steps toward us.

I figure it's my turn to contribute. "That's a strange story. We couldn't sleep knowing Lilly was in trouble, so we thought we'd walk the streets. You know, get some fresh air. We headed toward the river and ran into this group of guys who were just hanging out on a stoop. Must have been a dozen of them, right Troy?"

Troy nods, a cheesy grin on his face.

"We asked if they had seen Lilly and they brought us over here. When we told them what you suspected had happened to her, they were eager to help. We crashed the party and next thing I know, they're gone and we're calling you." I beam a bright smile, twist on the spot, and look toward my feet.

Frankie snorts and peers out the window. "Can you see that, Bear?"

"Yeah, I see it."

"What's out there?" I look at the windows.

"Pigs zipping by the windows, flapping big pig wings." Frankie chuckles a deep rumble and looks back at me. "Man, you're one bad liar. That's a load of bunk. Next time let Troy spin the tale. He couldn't do any worse. No one's gonna believe that story."

"And if we ask the girls, what are they going to say?" Landon glances at us.

"They look out of it to me," I smirk.

Tara puts her hand on Landon's shoulder. "She's right. They're in no shape to be reliable witnesses."

Troy sweeps his arm toward the girls. "We saved three lives. Who cares about the details?"

Frankie puts one beefy hand on my shoulder and the other on Troy's and pulls us together. We're mashed into a giant bear hug that squeezes the air out of me. "You're right. Whatever happened here, you guys are heroes. You did good. Just call us next time. Guys like these are dangerous. You and your... unknown friends from the stoop might not be so lucky next time."

He releases us from the giant three-person hug and I sputter, "What are we going to do now?"

"Let's call Susan," Tara suggests. "She can use a good bust like this, and she'll wash over some of the... details for us."

"Let me guess. Susan is another one of your graduates," I say.

"We have a few friends on the NYPD," says Landon. "Just because this worked out okay, doesn't mean you two are off the hook with me. We're going to have a discussion about this. You can't count on dumb luck. These streets can be dangerous."

Frankie winks at us. "Let's save that for another time, Bear. We should call Susan and get these girls back to the center. They've spent way too much time here already."

Greasy Hair moans and sits up. Shoelaces bind his hands and feet, but his mouth is free to yap. "Don't let her near me. She's a witch!"

We all stare at him, terror clearly scribbled in the corner of his eyes.

"What's he prattling about?" Tara looks back at me.

"She's a cracked witch or a chosen vampire or something like that! Keep her away from me!" He frantically kicks the ground with his feet and shuffles backward.

All eyes turn toward me, so I grin. "You see what drugs do to you? We should take a video of this guy and use it in the infomercials they play at school, Troy."

"Yeah, we could call it, 'This is your brain on drugs.' They'd love it."

Frankie shoots me an amused grin. "I think you'd better get a move on. We'll tell Susan that we found these dudes from a tip on the street. Arrests should be easy. There's plenty of evidence of drug use and these girls are obvious kidnapping victims."

He doesn't need to tell us twice, so we scoot down the stairs and back out onto 11th Avenue.

Troy stops me with a tug on the arm. "So what did Connor say to you in there? You guys were alone for a while."

I study his face in the darkness. I'm not sure what I want to find. I look for signs that he's jealous, but none exist. I'm not even sure if I want him to be jealous. We've never had that type of relationship. Since Sicheii died, I don't think about him like that so much anymore. Still, a little jealousy would by nice.

"We didn't talk about much. He offered to toss that guy from the window if I wanted." I shrug, but there was more to the conversation than that and more than the spoken words. I still feel his fingers stroke my cheek and how he swept the hair from my eyes. I try hard to prevent it, but heat flushes my face anyway.

Troy frowns. "Be careful with him. He's a drunk and he'll let you down."

"I don't want to talk about it." I turn and spot a 24-hour deli wedged between two larger stores in the middle of the block. "I'm starving. Let's get something to eat."

I buy a ham and cheese sandwich, some chips and a giant bottle of Arizona Iced Tea.

Troy can't help himself, so he gets a sketchy burrito that looks a few days old.

"Are you *serious*? You're going to eat that?" I ask him.

He takes a massive bite. Grease runs down his cheek. "Not terrible," he mumbles.

"Right." I munch down my sandwich in record time.

"Stewie lives on the first floor of the Inn, right?"

"That's what he told us."

"Good. I'm going to sneak into his apartment. There's more that he's not telling us. I'm sure of it."

"That doesn't sound like a great idea," I say, but I can tell that he's made up his mind.

CHAPTER

My eyelids open, only a few hours after I crawled into bed. The first rays of morning light beam through the windows and pierce my consciousness better than any alarm clock I've ever owned. I groan, stuff a pillow over my head, and try to lie still, keep my eyes shut, and go back to sleep, but it's useless. Faces and thoughts swirl in my mind. The harder I try to sleep, the faster they twist, until they whirl into a vortex that threatens to suck me down into some dark pit.

That pit scares me.

I stretch and tiptoe around the suite.

Troy snores on the couch with his face mashed against a cushion, one leg hung over the side, and his right arm flopped on top of his head. He'll sleep for hours, and I don't want to wake him. One of us should get some rest.

He left the book Landon gave him on the cocktail table. I snatch it and jump back on the bed. Sydney's name is written in red ink on the inside cover with her cell phone number scrawled underneath it. *When did she write that?* I grip the cover harder and smolder at the perfectly cute loopy letters she used to sign her name.

What's her role with us? How does she figure in? Stuart, I understand. He's the Host and although he's quirky and a bit rough, at least he makes sense. He's here to help us defeat the Deltites. He doesn't want them to take over the universe. Fine, I can put him into a mental folder. He might not care about us or about Earth even, but he does care about stopping the Deltites and that's probably good enough.

Sydney, on the other hand, is not a Chosen and she doesn't fit the mold of a secret keeper. Not like Sicheii, and from what I've gathered from the other Chosen, not like those in charge of their Orders. She's too young, for starters, and I can't picture her self-sacrificing for the good of others. She's too beautiful with perfect ringlets, full lips, a golden tan, and a small cute nose. She reminds me of the girls back at my fancy private school.

It might just be pettiness — I'm certainly not above pettiness — but I'll fetter better once I understand why she's helping us. *Maybe Stuart showers her with money?* That could explain her involvement, but money only goes so far. Once things become dodgy and her life's on the line, she'll bolt. Money can't buy loyalty.

Not like Troy. He'll stay with me until the end, if I let him.

I turn the page, doing my best to ignore the offensive Sydney signature and phone number, and start reading. The two-hundred-and-fifty-page paperback takes me twenty minutes to finish. It used to take me forever to get through a book, but now the words whip past me and, even weirder, I'm able to remember every one. Odd facts spring to my mind: approximately 500

Native Americans lived on Manhattan when they sold it to the Dutch; approximately 500 Native Americans live on Manhattan today.

While the particular Tribe who populated the island was called Manhattanoes like Troy said, they were part of the broader Legunes people. The Manhattanoes used the island mostly for sheep and goats and a few crops. It didn't have much value to them since the land wasn't particularly fertile. Only after the Dutch settled the island and it became useful as a port did Manhattan's true value come to light.

All these facts flash through my mind as I put down the paperback. I consider adding speed-reading as another aberrant trait, but we've all seen those commercials where people learn how to whip through books—not as fast as I raced through this one, but close enough. I don't want to add to my aberrant traits, as the number is getting perilously close to ten. Somehow I just know that once those traits reach double digits, I won't be able to fool myself into believing I'm still normal.

As if I can do so now.

Needing to waste more time, I grab all the books off the bookshelf on the far wall and pile them on the bed. It makes quite an eclectic collection: eight worn romantic paperbacks that Stuart has no doubt read, six encyclopedias that cover the entire alphabet, two thrillers, and one book about World War Two. Nothing I'd choose to read under normal circumstances, but that's all there is, so I prop up two of the pillows against the headboard and work my way through them.

By the time I start the sixth romance novel, I can read it by flipping the pages. I don't even have to pause and look at the words anymore; my mind registers them in a stream of data. It takes me only five minutes to finish an entire book. I stare at the last two romance books I haven't read, but decide against zipping through them. I keep inserting Troy and Connor into the stories, and my head has started to hurt.

I shove the books off to the side and think about Connor: the deep wells behind his eyes, his slightly bent nose, the way his touch is both strong and gentle at the same time. There's so much more to him than his drinking and his cocky attitude.

I'm sure Troy would see it, if he let himself. They're not that different once you peel back the surface. *Argh!*

Desperate to chase Connor and Troy from my mind, I meander my way through the encyclopedias. They take longer to read, as I have to stop and scan the entire page before going on to the next. I don't mind. At least it eats up time.

Eventually Sydney knocks on the door and calls out. "Wake up. We've got places to go! Everybody rise and shine and meet me downstairs in fifteen minutes!"

I groan. Sydney is the last person with whom I want to spend the day.

Troy rolls over, flops off the couch, and falls to the floor. "What's going on? Fire or something?" He shakes the sleep from his eyes.

"Your *girlfriend*, Sydney, wants us downstairs in fifteen minutes." The edge in my voice irritates even me. It's too late to correct it now, but luckily Troy acts as if he didn't hear it.

"Oh." He squints at the clock on the wall. It's eight thirty. "I feel like I just went to sleep." He stretches and points to the pile of books on my bed. "Some light reading?" He looks at me, a worried expression chiseled into his face. "Still having problems sleeping."

"Why sleep when there are so many tantalizing encyclopedias to read? I may never close my eyes again."

"Just don't start spouting off facts like our friend Marlon back home. No one likes a showoff." He pads his way to the bathroom to get ready.

We leave the Inn seventeen minutes later. To my surprise, Blake, Akari, and Connor are all waiting with Sydney. I wonder if they have problems sleeping as well.

She checks her watch and frowns.

"Where's Stuart?" I ask.

"He's not coming with us," says Blake. "Apparently he has *better* things to do."

"Where are we going?"

Sydney points to the Zip Car behind her. "We're all headed for an outing to the Bronx Zoo for some team building. It's my favorite place in New York."

Blake moans. "Well, I don't want to go. It'll be crowded, and do you know how many diseases kids carry with them? They're little germ magnets, sneezing and coughing all over the place."

Sydney opens the passenger door. "You're not going to get sick."

Troy rubs his stomach. "If you don't mind, I'd like to stay behind. That burrito I ate last night is staging a revolution in my stomach."

Sydney frowns. "I was hoping you'd squeeze in next to me, but if you're sick you should stay here."

"I'm sick too," whines Blake.

"Get in the car." Akari shoves him in the back.

I glance at Troy, who winks at me. He's not ill. He wants to sneak around Stuart's apartment.

Uneasiness washes over me.

I mouth 'Be careful' before squeezing into the Zip Car.

CHAPTER

Sydney turns off the Bronx River Parkway and pulls into a crowded parking lot on the east side of the zoo. We unfold ourselves from the small car and follow her as she bounces toward the park entrance, her curly ringlet-infused hair flowing behind her like a cloud.

I wonder how long it took her to make it so perfect. My straight black hair hangs lifeless in comparison, like overcooked spaghetti.

"I've never been to a zoo before." Akari looks excited, and for once we're just normal teenagers out for a day of fun.

"Well, zoos are horrible, smelly places." Blake trudges behind us. "Snotty kids run around spewing germs everywhere, and the animals probably have exotic diseases that no one knows how to cure when we catch them."

"That's rubbish. London has a cracking good zoo. I've never heard of anyone getting sick." Connor tucks a water bottle into his back pocket.

I look at it suspiciously. *Does he need to drink booze just to visit the zoo?*

Sydney pays for our admittance and we stroll through the gates. A golden sun hangs high above us, an island in a rich blue ocean that's interrupted by only a handful of white puffy beaches.

We pass a stream on the right and reach the first animal exhibit—the bison. Four clusters of animals gather in far-flung groups in a large pasture. One grand, majestic creature stands not more than fifty feet from us, his head up as he studies onlookers with a wary gleam in his eyes.

We approach a wooden stockade-style fence and peer at the lone animal.

"It looks like a cow with a furry head and neck," says Blake, obviously unimpressed.

"It's got to be twice the size of any bloody cows I've seen," says Connor. "I'd like to see you try and milk that thing."

I lean against the fence. "The bison is my favorite animal. They were like an early version of Walmarts for Native Americans. We used every bit of the meat for food, the skins for clothing and blankets, and the bones for tools and weapons. The bladders were used for canteens and the horns became spoons. We even made bowls out of the skins from their heads."

Connor slides next to me and grips the top of the fence, his fingers brushing against mine.

Heat sears my skin and flows between us where his pinky touches me. Ridiculous, I know, but I can't help but wonder if he does it on purpose or even notices the connection. Still, my hand is frozen in place.

"Aren't they almost extinct?" Blake stands behind us.

"Almost." I pull my thoughts away from Connor's hand and glance at Blake. "Once hunters showed up with rifles, they killed off the herds. The bison never stood a chance. Now they're protected and making a comeback."

A few years ago, Sicheii told me a story about the vast herds that roamed the plains and the symbiotic relationship between the people and the animals. A sad look settled in his eyes when he finished the story, so I asked him what was wrong.

He sounded angry. "It's a crime to kill animals for sport. We have no greater right to live on Mother Earth than the bison or the hawk or fish."

"But that was a long time ago," I told him.

The heat in his eyes melted and turned watery. "Yes, Little Bird, but man's selfishness leaves long ripples. How wonderful would it be if we could stand on the plains and see the great herds as our ancestors once did?"

"They're magnificent." Akari snaps me from my memory.

Sydney hoots. "They look like ugly beasts." She smirks at me, as if she's really talking about me instead of the bison. "Let's each pick one favorite animal to see. This way we'll make sure we get them all in. Juliet's already chosen the bison, so how about you Connor? What will it be?"

Connor turns and lifts his hand in the process. His fingers, coarse yet gentle, sweep against the length of my hand and send a tingling sensation up my arm.

"How about the gorillas? They're genetically close to humans. All of a sudden, I feel like we have a lot in common."

Blake smiles. It's the same genuine smile he had last night in the old building. It looks good on him. "Well, I thought you'd say the baboons. You share a few features with them also."

Connor scowls and raises himself up on his toes so he towers over Blake.

I can tell he's just joking, but from the anxious look on Blake's face, I don't think he realizes it.

"What are you trying to say?" Connor growls, doing his best not to laugh while he adds as much menace to his voice as he can muster.

I chuckle. "I think he's saying you look like a baboon. If I squint my eyes, I can totally see it."

"Do you think I have a baboon face?" Connor steps toward him.

"I-I wa-was just jo-joking." In full retreat mode now, Blake's gaze flashes off to the side, perhaps wondering if he could make a run for it.

A smile bursts on Connor's face. "Not bad." He slaps Blake hard on the back. "I didn't know you *could* joke."

"Now it's official. *Anything* can happen," Akari quips, and we all crack up.

Whether it's because of Akari's joke, the look on Blake's face, or the ridiculous situation we're in, it feels good to laugh.

I buy a pretzel on our way to the gorilla exhibit and stand close to Connor, but not too close. As we look through the glass, a mother swings her baby in one arm, which makes me feel guilty.

My mom is back home in Arizona. My dad knows we're okay and must have told her so, but she's probably sick with worry. I don't want to put her through this, but she'd be in real danger if I told her the truth. I almost lost her a week ago because of a Seeker, and I can't face that again. She'll have to deal with the situation. At least she has my dad.

Connor glances at me. "I wonder what they're thinking. Their eyes look so much like humans. I've known some blokes at the pub back home who look a lot dumber."

"Gorillas and humans share 96% of the same DNA." The figure pops to mind from my early morning date with the encyclopedias, and I feel silly as I spout random facts.

Connor's lips turn down, his face etched with real sadness. "I wonder what percentage of *our* DNA we share with humans." He turns and walks away.

He feels it too, this separation we have with everyone else, this isolation.

We have lunch in the African section of the zoo at the Flamingo Cafe. We eat nothing fancy—hot dogs and burgers for all of us except Sydney, who buys a salad.

"So what's next?" she asks.

"I'd love to visit with a polar bear." Akari is focused on folding a napkin, but she looks up and grins at us. "We don't have any in Japan. They seem magical."

"And deadly," adds Blake. "They're the fiercest type of bear, which is why you probably like them."

"What about you, Blake?" asks Connor. "What type of posh animal is your favorite?" Connor raises his voice an octave and talks in an upper crust accent. "One that's hygienic, I imagine. Maybe one that uses a knife and fork while out on the range eating antelope and drinking only sparkling well water."

"Giraffes. They're beautiful, strong and fast, and not carnivorous."

"They also have skinny legs like you," I joke, and we share a small laugh at his expense.

Akari hands me a carefully folded origami creature and bows her head slightly.

"Thanks," I say. "It's a bison. Awesome." I twirl the little figure in my hand and admire each fold, neat and exact. "I love it."

Akari beams. "I thought you would."

A gaggle of preschoolers race past us; they all clutch ice cream cones in their hands and wear shirts from someplace called

Treetops. The three adults who hustle behind try hard to herd the cats. One cute kid with a mop of black curly locks stumbles and drops her ice cream cone.

I catch it with my mind and let it hover in the air for a second until the girl reclaims it.

When she does, she looks around and finds me with her eyes. An uncertain smile sneaks onto her face before she races forward to catch-up with her schoolmates.

Blake watches the kids, cringes, pulls a pill bottle from his pocket and lifts it toward me. "Do you want one?"

"What is it?"

"Antibiotics. You can't be too careful with kids running around."

I shake my head.

He shrugs, swallows two pills and looks at Sydney. "How about you? What's your favorite animal?"

Sydney sports a mischievous grin. "We'll save that for last."

We finish lunch, check out the giraffes, which are beautiful, and amble toward the polar bears. We stop at different animal enclosures along the way: strange deer, wild horses, elephants and even the Monkey House, which Blake refused to go into because of a long list of diseases he was sure they would have. Still, he didn't deter the rest of us from exploring them.

When we stop to look at the polar bears, Akari stares at them wide-eyed and frozen in place, so Connor and I step back.

He gulps from his water bottle and catches my expression, which must be sour, because he stops mid-drink and asks, "*What?*"

"You don't need to drink."

Connor lifts the water bottle and smirks. "I'm thirsty. You want some?"

"You know what I'm talking about. That bottle has more than water in it. You had one at dinner last night filled with vodka."

His face reddens. "I didn't know you were in charge of monitoring my alcohol intake." He pushes the bottle toward me and scowls. "You'll be happy to know there's nothing but water in this one."

I can tell he's serious and that I've hurt his feelings, which was not my intention. "I'm sorry. I just thought that—"

"That I'm a drunk. I know that's what Troy thinks, but I thought you were different."

"I didn't mean that you're a drunk." He's so close to me now, his breath warms my lips. "I just want to...."

"You want what?" He leans closer to me.

"I don't know... to make sure you're okay."

"You don't need to worry about me." His face turns hard and he turns away.

My chest tightens. *I'm such an idiot.* Now he thinks I pity him, which is not at all how I feel. Of course, I don't know *how* I feel, or why I care about hurting his feelings so much when I didn't do anything wrong.

The sun has already started to sink.

"Last stop," announces Sydney. She leads us to the lions, and we stop and stare at a full-grown male. "The king of the beasts— so powerful and majestic—by far my favorite animal."

An enraptured look shines from her eyes as her mouth drops open. She's caught up in the power and strength of the animal. Perhaps that's why she's involved with us. She senses our strength, our differentness from normal humans. If that's her motivation, we have real issues. The Deltites are strong also, stronger than we are, and if what Stuart said is true about Elites, the Prime Elector will be much stronger than any of us. She might switch sides the first chance she gets.

I glance at Connor, but he refuses to look at me. Bloods races through my body like white water rapids and I clench my hands into fists. *This is so stupid. How did I get myself into this situation?*

Sydney leans against the fence, her voice breathless. "I wonder what it would be like to see the world through his eyes."

I need to take my mind off of Connor, and Sydney's words ring in my ear. *How does a lion see the world?* This is as good a time as any to find out. I turn my body, so my back faces Connor, and reach out to the animal with my mind. I sense his energy and push into his thoughts. For a moment I am the lion. Well, not really—I still have my own identity, but I can see what he sees. The world is washed in blues and oranges. I feel the sensation of strength and savagery. I arch my back, push my head back and shake the ground with a fierce roar. My vision focuses on Connor and then swings to Sydney and I roar again. A sink-my-teeth-into-flesh rage rips through me. It scares me, so I pull my mind away from the lion.

"Wow," says Sydney. "I've never heard him do that before." Just then her phone rings. "Yes, Stuart, we're just about finished at the zoo. Okay, I'll be right back." She turns toward us. "We have to go. Our excursion is over. Stuart needs me."

Her eyes crinkle at the edges and her jaw clenches.

I wonder what's wrong, and immediately worry about Troy.

What would Stuart do if he found him snooping around his apartment?

CHAPTER 24

Sydney pulls the car to a stop in front of the Inn, and we pour out of the cramped vehicle. A second later she motors off with a squeal of the tires.

Connor stomps inside without so much as a glance toward me. He hasn't said a word to anyone since we talked by the polar bears.

"What's up with him?" Akari holds the door open for me.

"Beats me," I lie, knowing he's angry with me even though he shouldn't be. If he had given me a chance to explain, I would have said *something*. I don't know exactly what, but it would have been reasonably good. I'm sure of it.

I take a deep breath and follow the others inside. They fade behind their doors, but I hesitate in front of mine and trace the twisted arrows symbol with the tip of my pointer finger.

Is this all that's left of me?

Is Juliet Wildfire Stone gone, only to be replaced by a silly symbol?

At least Troy remembers who I used to be and.... Thinking about him sends a shiver of anxiety roiling through me. I unlock the door, scan the rooms, and call out his name, but he's not here.

My heart thunders in my chest and my imagination races. What if Stuart caught him sneaking around his apartment? Would he hurt Troy? *We're still on the same side, aren't we?*

The dining room was bugged last night, but that doesn't mean all that much. There are numerous reasons to snoop on a formal dining room, many of which don't involve us. That bug could have been old. Stuart might not even know it's there.

Still, my gut tells me he knew all about the listening device. After all, he knew how Blake found the Inn, which must mean that he had listened in on our conversation.

There's only one way to find out if he's spying on us, so I search the two rooms that make up my suite. Three smoke detectors are stuck on the ceiling for just two rooms—at least one too many. Stuart has bugged my rooms, just like the dining room.

I can't escape the obvious: he's spying on us. But why?

I start to pace as my thoughts hopscotch between Stuart, Troy, and Connor. My insides twist when I think about Troy. I can picture him snooping in Stuart's bedroom when the diminutive Host waddled inside.

Though not physically imposing, Stuart probably has a gun or some other type of weapon. He poisoned us, so he won't hesitate to hurt Troy if he wants to.

But why would he want to?

Just when I picture the worst for Troy, I remember the hurt on Connor's face at the zoo. *What's his story?*

He hinted at something important last night. Did he kill someone, and now have a hard time living with it? Does he drown the memory with booze?

I would've thought that ridiculous a month ago, but I killed a Seeker. Sure, I wasn't left with any choice, but if I could kill a Seeker, why is it so hard to believe he might have had to kill someone too? Maybe in self-defense? Still, he shouldn't have gotten so mad at me.

Troy should have gone to the zoo. If he had been with us, none of this would have happened! Troy would be safe and Connor wouldn't be angry with me. They're both so – pigheaded!

I work myself up into such a satisfying righteous anger, it takes me a moment to notice the door open and Troy standing in the doorway. "Jules, are you all right?"

"Argh!" I practically growl at him and storm into the bathroom—childish, perhaps, but I need a moment before talking to him. I distract myself by searching the bathroom for listening devices, sweeping my hands along the edge of the mirror, opening the draws in the medicine cabinet, and inspecting the ceiling and walls. When I find none, my body relaxes and I can breathe.

Troy knocks on the door. "Jules, what's going on?"

I glance at my reflection in the mirror. My black hair rains down well beyond my shoulders. My eyes are not quite wide enough to be beautiful, and my nose is longer than I wish and pointy at the end like the tip of a dagger.

I sigh. I'm lost in a world I've never been before—a stranger in a foreign land where I don't know the language. I've never had a boyfriend. Maybe there's a reason why Troy and I have only had a platonic relationship. Perhaps he's only meant to be my friend, my best friend.

Connor could be different, or maybe I'm nuts. What would he see in me anyway? I look at my reflection in the mirror again, straighten my back and twirl my hair. I'm not special; I never have been. I'm fooling myself. Connor accidentally touched my hand on the fence by the bison, and I've spun some silly childish story. I've got to be stronger than this, so I push these thoughts aside and open the door.

Troy stands on the other side, worry clouding his eyes.

I lift my finger to my lips, wave him into the bathroom, shut the door behind him, and twist the faucet in the shower. The sound of rushing water should mask our conversation, but I whisper anyway. "I think the rooms are bugged. I'll bet there's a microphone in one of the smoke detectors."

He frowns. "Great. Are you okay? What happened at the zoo? You look angry."

I twirl my hair and look off to the side toward the towel rack. *What do I tell him about Connor?* I've never had a problem talking to him before, but the words stick in my throat, so I focus on the zoo instead of Connor. "The zoo was fine. No problems, although Sydney got a call from Stuart and had to rush back." I glance back at him. "What happened with you? Did you sneak into Stuart's apartment?"

He smirks. "For an alien, he hasn't invested much in security. I had no problem with the lock. He's a weird dude. First, he likes comic books."

"Seriously?"

Troy grins and nods. "The apartment is full of them, all stacked in cardboard boxes—Batman, Spiderman, Iron Man, Aqua Man. *All of the Mans.* Not the most inspiring stuff for our Host, but I found something else that's really weird. Guess what?"

"What, like on his computer?"

"No. You know I'm no hacker, Jules. He password-protected his computer. I tried a few of the superheroes, but that was a dead-end. Still, I checked out his closet." He hesitates. "You've got to guess."

I roll my eyes. "I'm not going to guess and don't tell me anything really gross unless it's important. I don't want to know about rubber superheroes or anything like that."

He whispers, "I'll skip that part then, but in the back of his closet, I found three white tunics. They were softer than anything I'd ever touched before. They're not made from any fabric we have on Earth. If that's not odd enough, they were way longer than old Stuart could wear. They'd look like dresses on him."

"So *who* are they for?"

He shakes his head. "That's the question."

Someone raps on the exterior door.

We leave the bathroom and find an envelope had been slipped underneath the doorway. I open it and find fine linen paper folded neatly inside.

The note is short:

Meet me in the dining room at midnight. Your training continues.
— the Host.

"Midnight," I whisper to Troy. "Why so late?"

As soon as we enter the dining room, I suspect we're in for a surprise—and not a good one. A screen hangs from the ceiling with the Inn's symbol projected on it. Troy and I settle into our seats across from Akari and Blake.

Connor saunters in last, a few minutes after us. I try to catch his eye, but he doesn't look at me. He hasn't brought a water bottle, so maybe some good has come from our argument. Maybe he realizes I only wanted to help... or maybe he hates me.

Lots of different maybes cross my mind in a heartbeat, and my face flushes with heat.

When Connor sits, the image on the screen flickers and Stuart's face replaces the circular symbol. "Good evening, Twisteds. I trust you had a most excellent day, but it is time to continue your training. Yes, yes, your training must advance. I suspect we are almost out of time, so I've had to accelerate matters."

My heart flutters. *Why isn't he here? This can't be good.*

His left eye twitches and little rivers of sweat trickle down his cheeks.

Connor says, "Why don't you tell us who this leader is, so we can get on with the important job at hand? We don't need to fiddle around with these bloody training sessions."

Stuart tugs on his beard. "Yes, yes, I understand your impatience. I feel the same way, but we must progress in the correct order. Your abilities must be tested. You will never survive unless you embrace and use the special abilities the Alphian DNA has given you.

"Each one of you has a special ability that I'm sure you know about by now. Yes, yes, certain that you know. The Alphian DNA helps you channel the energy around you, so you can perform certain feats like create wind or fire, or liquefy solids, and in Juliet's case, possess animals' minds for a short period. These traits are common among Alphians. Usually an Alphian will have two or more, but in your case, each of you has but one. We must make sure you can use these abilities when you face the Prime Elector, so this test is necessary. Yes, yes, this is your final test before we move on to more... practical items."

"Test?" Blake sounds worried. "You didn't poison us again, did you?"

Stuart arches his thin blond eyebrows and looks at us like we're the crazy ones. "Poison, no, no. Gratefully, you all passed that test. This test is a... scavenger hunt. Yes, yes, a scavenger hunt. To pass you will need to find four round crystals, one for each Chosen. Each crystal will have a different clue etched onto the surface. Once you have all four, you simply lock them together. The crystals will read your special electrical signatures and emit a beacon of sorts that I will register, so I will know when you have found all four and the test will be over."

"A bloody scavenger hunt. There's more to it than that," grumbles Connor. He glances at me for the first time, and I can tell we share the same thought.

This is no ordinary test. Stuart and Sydney aren't here for a reason. They're worried about our reaction to whatever he hasn't told us yet.

"So what's the first clue?" asks Akari.

Stuart smiles.

"Seek the grandest place:
A monumental holy space;
Never finished, it's a symbol of human struggles;
Choose unwisely and you'll never solve the puzzles;
Fire and light have both burned within its walls;
Find the statue that shows it all;
Moon versus Sun, good versus bad;
Peer into evil and you'll be glad."

Blake rakes his hand through his hair and sighs. "I hate riddles."

"Oh, there's one more item. Yes, yes, I should mention this." Stuart's eyes gleam. "You have one hour to recover all four crystals."

My heart plummets. "Or what?"

He shrugs. "The stakes have to be high. Yes, yes, without pressure you will never unlock your gifts and learn to control them. Better to know this before we confront the Deltites."

"So, what mental thing have you done now?" Connor barks.

"You can buy additional time, but it is costly. Costly indeed. Every additional half an hour will cost you one life."

"You're going to kill one of us for thirty minutes?" Akari's face twists into an angry scowl.

Stuart grins. "Oh no, not one of you Chosen. That test has been finished. Yes, yes, you passed that test. I will kill a person close to one of you. Your loved ones will be in danger. You will not know whom. This way you will feel the responsibility you share—to save your kind." He scratches his beard and his eyes turn to scalpels. "You all have people you love. Yes, yes, parents, a grandmother... and even you, Connor."

Connor's face twists with explosive rage.

"Maybe not family for you, but a certain pub owner's daughter? The test has begun." Stuart's face fades from the screen and is replaced with the time.

12:18.

CHAPTER 25

I've been run over by a truck. Black tire tracks are probably burned onto my face.

I came to New York to protect my family and friends so they wouldn't be thrown in the middle of this mess, and now a new wildfire threatens to burn them. The reality of my situation sinks in like a lead ball. They'll never be safe until this we finish this thing, until I find a way to defeat the Prime Elector.

How could they be?

My family isn't even safe from the people who are supposed to help me.

My stomach tightens for another totally selfish reason. I glance at Connor and find the truth on his face. He loves the pub owner's daughter, which only proves that I'm being silly. He loves a girl back home, probably someone with blonde curly hair and freckles and wide eyes and....

Just as my mind threatens to slip down that slide, Blake

thankfully interrupts my toxic thoughts. "Do you think he's serious? How could he know who we care about?"

"He looked serious to me." Akari throws a glass against the blank screen.

"He knows a lot about us." My voice turns grim. "He knows about your family, Blake, and how they use the twisted muskets, and he knows how Akari and I just barely escaped Seekers. He knows about Connor's parents and how they died, and he knows this *pub owner's daughter.*"

Did my voice really just go up an octave? I didn't mean to bring her up, but once my mouth starts to run, sometimes my foot gets lodged in it.

"That nutter is really winding me up," Connor grumbles. "But we don't have time to debate whether he's serious. We need to pass this bloody test so he won't do something stupid."

"Well, what was the riddle again?" Blake glances at us.

Troy has an amazing memory, so he repeats it for us.

Blake speaks first. "We have to focus on the beginning for now. The rest we can figure out later. According to the riddle, we need a grand holy place. It has to be St. Patrick's. That's the most elaborate church in the City. I went there once and it's amazing."

Blake stands. He's ready to go, but St. Patrick's doesn't feel right to me. It seems too obvious.

"Hold on," I say. "We need a place that's never been finished, and he mentioned that fire and light are both involved somehow."

Blake shrugs. "Are cathedrals ever really finished? And fire and light might represent heaven and hell. Who knows, but Saint Patrick's has to be our place."

I'm unconvinced, and a wisp of an idea floats into my mind. "Troy, what did Landon say about that church on the Upper West Side?"

He smiles. "He said St. John the Divine was the largest cathedral in the world and it's not yet finished because of a—"

"Fire! A fire damaged the cathedral so it's still being worked on! That's our place." I'm certain of it.

Blake crosses his arms over his chest. "I've never heard of St. John the Divine before. St. Patrick's is the most famous church in the City."

Connor stands. "He said grandest space, which could mean largest not fanciest. No offense, Blake. I'm sure St. Patrick's is a posh place, but I'm with Juliet. The clues fit her choice better."

He looks at me and his eyes pierce mine. An unspoken moment passes between us—he trusts me.

An inferno scorches my face. Lives are at stake and I'm acting like a silly girl with a crush over a guy who loves a mysterious, and probably I-can't-take-my-eyes-off-her beautiful, pub owner's daughter. *How stupid is that?*

"Let's go," urges Akari.

We bolt into action, racing for the church and leaving Troy behind to fetch a cab. We sprint north and practically fly to 112th Street and Amsterdam. We've become shadows in the darkness, blurs on the pavement, almost invisible until we stop at the church.

A massive stone gothic cathedral stretches for an entire city block. The front has two vast wooden doors in the center, a huge round stained glass window above those doors, and a turret off to the right that looks like it belongs to a medieval castle. No lights are visible from inside. A series of smaller doors flank the two large ones in the center.

"It's certainly giant-sized." Blake hesitates at the stairs that lead to the cathedral. "What next?"

"We need a statue with a moon and sun that depicts the struggle between good and evil. It could be anywhere." I spin in a tight circle, but no statues are out front.

"Could be," says a tired, gravely voice. A vague form appears on the steps in front of the cathedral. An old man who wears a dirty sweatshirt and jeans stirs to his feet, his face all bones, his eyes hollow in deep sockets.

Connor approaches him. "Do you know the statue we're looking for? The one with the moon and sun?"

The man shoots him a half smile and reveals a jagged, toothy mountain range with more than a few teeth missing. "Yes, I do. I'm the mayor of this city, but it'll cost you."

Connor digs into his pockets, pulls out a bill, and hands it to the homeless man. "How about a tenner? But you had better not be yanking my chain."

The old man takes the bill with shaky fingers, shoots us another craggy grin, and points to the courtyard just south of the church. "It's behind the fence. Can't miss it. Big black metal thing."

"Thanks," Connor says, and we jog to the ten-foot tall wrought-iron fence.

It's dark, but a streetlight from the corner sheds enough light onto a statue inside the courtyard that I can spot its outline.

It's hard to see clearly, but it looks like a giant winged angel.

"What's that angel standing on top of?" Blake points at it. "It looks like a ball."

"It looks like a moon or sun, which would make good the riddle." Akari puts her hands on her hips.

"We'd better get a closer look." Connor tugs on one bar of the fence and I pull on the other. We use our enhanced strength, so they bend easily, and we create a gap wide enough for us to fit through.

A second later, a taxi pulls to the curb and Troy hops out. When the cab rolls away, we race forward, leap over a short fence and approach the winged angel.

"That's the weirdest statue I've ever seen. What's it doing by a church?" Blake's eyebrows furrow together and his mouth hangs open.

The massive iron statue is totally bizarre. A giant winged angel holds a sword in one hand and a deer's head in the other. Another oddly-shaped deer climbs on his back. Underneath the angel's feet is a twisted human body that's hard to make out in the darkness, an odd moon face, some type of crown, and what looks like lobster claws.

Connor points to the base of the sculpture. "This has to be the right bloody statue. That's a moon face. The angel must be good and that twisted body underneath him has to represent bad. So now we need to look inside evil, whatever that means."

Troy glances at his phone. "We've spent fifteen minutes so far."

"*Great,*" mutters Blake.

We circle the statue and look for something, anything that might help. Time feels heavy, and I move as if weights circle my legs. The artwork is beautiful, the lines and dimensions stunning, the imagery startling. I could study it for a month and not catch all the details.

I pause at the moon face; Stuart mentioned the moon specifically, so maybe it's more important than just a weird part of the design.

Then I see it. "There. Underneath the moon is the devil's head, hanging from a lobster claw."

"Freaky, but that has to be what we need," says Blake.

Akari grunts and squeezes the head, but nothing happens. "How do we open it?"

"We can't crack it open like an egg." I catch Connor's eyes. "Stuart said we needed to use our abilities to pass this test. You'll have to liquefy the iron without melting the crystal inside."

Connor squints, touches the head by the horns, and looks at me. "I don't know if I can do it. What if I wreck the crystal? We'll be gutted."

I touch him on the shoulder. "You can do this. I believe in you." I've only just met him, but the crazy thing is that I really do believe in him. He radiates strength.

"Seventeen minutes," says Troy.

I glare at him, and he shrugs.

Connor closes his eyes. At first the skull bends and becomes pliable like putty, and Connor starts to shake as if he fights an urge to melt the entire head at once. A few heartbeats later, the iron drips away—not in a gush, but slowly, layer by layer. Sweat beads on Connor's forehead as the effort takes all his strength. He stares at the mess that drips from his hands, eyes blazing hot, until a crystal in the center catches the dim light.

I bend closer to the head. "I see the crystal. You have to stop."

He pulls his hands from what's left of the head and a crystal chip falls to the ground.

"Wow, that's gross." Blake steps back.

"You're a real samurai," snorts Akari as she lifts the crystal. It looks like a poker chip with grooves and writing on the surface. She shrugs and hands it to Blake, and I realize that she can't read English.

"Here's the next clue," he says.

"Into the church you must tread;
Find a magical beast filled with dread;
From ashes it's reborn;
Unlock the name its light will adorn;
A holy man will be revealed;
To be saved, he must be unsealed."

"Twenty minutes," says Troy.

CHAPTER

We race back to the front of the church. In the slippery moonlight it looks like a fortress. I've never understood why some churches look like castles. Who do they want to keep out? More to the point, how do we break in?

The homeless man watches us, dusts himself off, and meanders over. "Did you find the statue? I told you it was just over there." He points at the courtyard. "I'm the mayor of these parts. Nothing happens here that I don't know."

"You wouldn't happen to have a key to the bloody church, would you?" asks Connor. "We need to get inside."

The homeless man grins. "I might know a way in, but it'll cost you. Twice as much as before." He holds his hand out.

Connor hands him a twenty.

The old man pockets the bill and hobbles toward the front doors.

Connor and I share a look.

"They don't leave the front door open, do they?" I ask.

He reaches the massive wooden door on the left. "Not usually, but I saw this little guy come through it a few hours ago. I've never seen him before. He forgot to lock the door when he left."

"Did he have curly red hair and a beard and look a little like a troll?" asks Akari.

"That's him. He had blond eyebrows though. I can't imagine why. Weird, but I guess you see all types in the City."

"You'd be surprised how weird he really is," says Blake.

The door creaks when Connor pulls it open, and we move inside. At first it's so dark my footsteps are tentative, but Troy flips a switch and a few lights flutter on.

One time, when I was eleven, Sicheii took me rock climbing. We had just finished scaling a particularly steep stretch and reached a ledge high above Slippery River. A red rock collection called Devil's Peak soared across the canyon, reaching another fifty feet above us. Air froze in my throat when I first looked upon it, just like it does now.

When Sicheii noticed my reaction, he grinned and patted me on the leg. "Some places are spiritual in nature. You never know where you'll find them, but if you open your heart, they appear in the most unusual of places. This is one of them. The separation between the spirit world and the living world is thin here. It's easier to communicate with those that inhabit the shadow world when in a place such as this. Breathe deeply and you can almost smell the difference. One time, I had this same sensation in a donut shop in Old Town. Of course I was hungry."

We both chuckled, but he was serious. He saw what others could not. I've never communicated with spirits or dead ancestors, but I understood what he meant: some places are

188

special. I felt that connection one other time when I went to the Pacific Ocean on vacation with my mom. The vastness of the water, the motion of the waves, the sun as it glinted off the horizon—it sent butterflies fluttering inside my stomach. I felt connected to something permanent, something bigger and more substantial than I could ever hope to be.

I've always thought those special places had to be natural, like the ocean or on the edge of a cliff. I've never experienced this sensation inside a building before... until now. The cathedral speaks to me. Maybe it's the scale, which is huge, or the arched ceilings, which soar upward, or the way the pews lead to the altar and the massive organ. Probably it's all these features together that take my breath away. No matter the reason, this is a spiritual place.

"Well, at least we don't have to guess what the riddle is about." Blake points to two giant phoenixes that hang from the arched ceiling in the center of the church. They face us, and even though they're the size of small airplanes, the vast interior of the church swallows them whole. Made of hammered tin, they have red, gold, and green feathers, with long wingspans and heads that look more like dragons than anything birdlike.

"Now that we've found the phoenixes, what's next?" Akari walks toward one of them, her head tilted upward, her eyes fixed on the colorful figures.

The largest one of the magical birds faces a great round stained glass window, and I know what we have to do. This test is not *only* about our special abilities, but it's also about *controlling* them. "We need to know which saint that phoenix points to on the stained glass window."

Troy reads from one of the informational boards. "That window is called the Great Rose Window. It's over forty feet wide in diameter, made from over ten thousand pieces of glass, and is the largest rose window in the world. Jesus is in the center, but different saints surround him."

Connor turns toward Akari. "Phoenixes are supposed to breathe fire. You have to create a line of flames from the mouth of that phoenix toward the window. It should fall upon one of the saints. Then we'll know what to look for."

He's right. She'll have to control her ability for us to discover the right holy man.

"Once we know which saint is our guy," I add, "we'll have to unseal him somehow."

Akari balls her hands into fists and her face flushes with anger. "I *will* kill Stuart when this is over."

Blake shoots her a wry grin. "Just don't burn down the entire cathedral. It's been through one fire already."

She glares at him and turns her attention to the phoenix. The air sparks and crackles.

I hold my breath when a thin fireball erupts from the phoenix and shoots the hundred feet toward the window.

"Brilliant," says Connor. "It lit up Saint Cuthbert."

Troy looks at him suspiciously. "How do you know which saint it touched?"

Connor shrugged. "I spent too much time with the local vicar when growing up. St. Cuthbert is an English saint famous for uniting people. You can tell it's him because of that shield he's carrying with lions on it. That's the sign of Wessex, and he's their patron saint."

"Great," says Blake. "They're all dead old guys to me. We'll need to unseal him somehow."

There has to be an easy way to find this Cuthbert. We don't have much time and Stuart wouldn't make this part of the test too difficult. The scavenger hunt is designed for us to use our abilities, not to see how quickly we can search the church for a name.

I glance down at my feet and realize I'm standing on a round piece of marble with the name St. Patrick on it. "Look on the floor. These circular marble slabs have saint names on them. One has to be Cuthbert."

"Over here!" yells Akari a few seconds later. She points to a round black marble slab with the name Saint Cuthbert inscribed around the edges, and a shield in the center divided in fourths with a lion in each section.

Blake bends low to inspect the marble. "Well, how do we unseal this? It must weigh a ton, and there are no handholds."

"Okay, if Cuthbert is the saint of unity, then we have to pitch in and do this together," I say.

"Right, but how?" Akari grabs a heavy metal stand and bashes it against the marble. *Clang!* "Maybe it will." *Clang!* "Break." She doesn't even scratch the marble.

"That's not it." Then the answer hits me. "Stuart wants us to use our abilities. We can't bash it to bits or pry it open by hand. What did the leprechaun say in The Underground?"

"Why use your hands when you can use your minds." Connor grins. "That's it. We need to use telekinesis. If we concentrate on lifting it, it'll budge."

We circle the marble tile.

I concentrate hard on the edge. Energy pulses around me as I use my mind, wrap the edge of the marble with a mental band of pure power, and tug. The marble sways and then it shifts from the opposite end where Connor stands. *He's moving it also.* I bear down and the marble circle starts to rise. My head begins to pound and my entire body coils together.

The disc lifts, and I shout, "Slide it toward Connor!"

We push it two feet toward him and let it drop. Troy reaches into the newly created hole and removes another crystal chip. "We have to move faster. We've already spent forty-two minutes."

He reads it.

"Music soothes the soul;
You'll need to hear it toll;
Find number 671 in the book;
You don't have much time to look;
One verse is all you'll need;
Play the proper notes to succeed."

Troy hands the disc to Akari, who twists the two crystal chips together. They make a snapping sound when they lock in place.

This test has to be about either Blake or me. I spot pipes out of the corner of my eye. Toward the other end of the church, a massive organ stretches toward the ceiling on both sides of the altar. Thousands of pipes peek out from the carved mahogany.

"The pipe organ." I point at the metal tubes. "We need to play a song on it."

We jog toward the altar and the organ.

"What's this book he's talking about? Is it the Bible?" Blake glances at Connor, who's become our religious expert, or at least our Christian expert, by default.

"No, the Bible doesn't work that way. This is an Episcopalian Church, which is basically the same as the Church of England where I grew up. They should have a hymnal around here that'll list songs by number."

"Got it!" Troy grabs a blue book from a table and flips it open to hymn 671: Amazing Grace.

At least I know that song, and it fits. All the clues are connected to us somehow. 'Peer into evil' could mean we need to match wits with the Deltites. Cuthbert is the saint of unity and

Amazing Grace could describe us when we learned we were Chosen—*I was blind and now I see.*

I nod. "Blake, you've got to blow wind through those pipes and play the first verse of that song."

The color drains from his face as he looks up at the plethora of pipes. "How?"

"The longer pipes will make the deeper notes and the shorter pipes the higher ones. Just pick a few and play the tune." Troy thrusts the book at him. "You *can* read music, right?"

Blake grabs the hymnal. "Of course I can read music. I took piano lessons for eight years. I'm actually pretty good."

Some color returns to his face as he studies the notes. He puts the book down and stares at the pipes. Wind rustles and a low rumble blares from one of the longer ones, then another note from a different one. After a minute he seems to have the hang of it.

"We don't have much time." Troy looks at his phone. "Only thirteen minutes left."

"Okay, okay, here goes." Blake narrows his eyes and the beginning of Amazing Grace fills the church. When he finishes, nothing happens. "I don't know what I did wrong. It should have worked."

"You played it too fast," says Connor. "I'll sing it, so you have the right tempo."

Blake starts and Connor sings, "Amazing...."

My mouth drops. He can sing.

Full of emotion, his voice has a slightly raspy quality that only makes it more authentic. The cathedral echoes with the song. It's not perfect, but when they finish the first verse, a hydraulic hissing sound escapes from a marble crypt off to our left.

The lid lifts.

One more crystal chip left, which means it's my turn.

CHAPTER

We don't have much time left, but I can't run to the creepy coffin, so I'm the last to arrive. It looks just like what I would have guessed—totally gross. A skeleton lies on his back, dressed in a white robe, long bony fingers crossed over his chest, wisps of gray hair stuck on his skull. The smell is also exactly what you'd expect—musty, full of decay and death.

I wrinkle my nose. At least there aren't any spiders.

Connor hands me the crystal chip, which I read for everyone.

"The test is almost finished:
Your achievements should not be diminished;
Find the angel in copper;
He'll be holding a horn proper;
You'll need wings to take flight;
To save your friend from his plight."

When I finish reading the riddle, I hand the chip to Akari, who adds it to our collection. This test is for me, but what does it mean? *A copper angel?* I scan the church and don't see any copper statues at all, but....

Troy wanders off to the left muttering to himself.

"Troy, where are you headed?"

He calls back over his shoulder as he picks up speed. "I could swear I saw the twisted arrows sparkle in this baptistery."

How will that help us?

He crosses into the small prayer area, where a red light blinks by the open gate that protects the space. Something's wrong. The last riddle is for me. What did it say exactly? "Save your friend...." *My friend?*

"Stop!" I yell, but it's too late.

He has already entered the baptistery, triggering a motion sensor and causing red laser beams to crisscross the opening. He reaches for the twisted arrows symbol, which is just a projection against a wall, and pulls off a plain post-it note.

The color drains from his face as he reads the message.

"Troy will be the first to die;
There's no time to be sly;
Do what you must to save your friend;
All four crystals are needed in the end;
The Chosen must work hand in hand;
Only together will they understand."

My eyes lock on the blinking light. It's attached to a timer and what looks like a brick of plastic explosives. A countdown has already started—four minutes and 35 seconds, which is the amount of time left before our hour is up.

The world spins and the air whooshes from my lungs. For a heartbeat I'm about to fall, but Connor props me up.

A chuckle drifts from the far end of the church, and I catch the vague outline of the homeless man before the door slams shut. Stuart must have paid him. That's why he knew which statue we needed and how to get into the cathedral. He must have triggered the projection to lure Troy to the baptistery.

I see red and resist the urge to chase him down. We don't need him; we need the fourth crystal.

I shrug Connor off and race to the gate and the laser beams.

Troy holds his hands out. "Don't break any of the lights, Jules. I'm sure that'll trigger the bomb."

"Don't worry, we'll figure this out." I can't utter any other words because I'm sure my voice will break, and that would be bad.

He smiles with his lips but it doesn't reach his eyes. "Me worry? Never. I've got the easy job." He sits with his legs crossed. "You've got the harder one. Just don't come back without the crystal." He closes his eyes and hums, just like I've seen Sicheii do hundreds of times. He's reaching out to the spirit lands to find guides for strength and wisdom.

My heart aches.

He's always sacrificed for me. In the third grade, he took the blame when I unscrewed the bolts that held the teacher's chair together. In fourth grade, he stood up for me when I got into a fight with a middle schooler, even though it was totally my fault. He joined the Order of the Twisted Arrows to protect me. He left home and traveled across the country just to help me, even though he probably can't, and now he's only put himself at risk.

I'd trade places with him if I could.

I swallow my fear. "We'd better get started then. All these tests require us to control our special abilities. This one has to be the same. He mentions wings, so I probably have to possess a bird."

Connor nods. "An angel with a horn is a common Christian symbol. Usually you'd find one outside. The angel is supposed to trumpet the arrival of the savior, so everyone knows he's coming."

"Well, we use copper weathervanes in New England on top of roofs," Blake adds.

"That's got to be it. We need to get on top of the roof!" I take a last look at Troy, who opens his eyes long enough to smile at me, and then I bolt for the door before I lose it.

Three minutes 45 seconds left.

We plunge into the cold night and stare up toward the roof of the Cathedral. "I can try to climb it," says Connor, "but the stone face looks smooth."

I grab his arm; he only wants to help, but that's not how we're going to pass this test. "Let me try." I reach out with my mind. I need it to switch into super-concentration mode, like it did when Blake needed the cure, so I can see the auras from the other life forms around me. That's the only way I can find a bird to possess.

Time starts to slip away. My head aches. "It's not working." My heart feels as if someone has pulled it from my chest, stomped on it and jammed it back into my body. "Why isn't it working?"

Connor grabs my hands, and for a second I focus on his face. His eyes radiate into mine. "You can do this. Just let it come to you. Troy will be fine."

He sounds so confident and relaxed, it puts me at ease. I close my eyes and absorb his strength. When I open them again, his aura flickers on and so do the auras of the others. Light also emanates from animals: a cat stalks across the street, two rats race in the other direction, a squirrel climbs a nearby tree.

I study the trees around us and find a hawk perched on an oak along Central Park West. The hawk is Sicheii's animal spirit guide, and I can't help but think he's here with me somehow.

I project my mental energy toward the bird. He's beautiful with a strong beak and intelligent eyes. I push into his mind, and suddenly the world looks sharper. His vision is extraordinary. I will him to look at the cathedral's roof. A copper statue stands on top of the slanted tiles with an angel who holds a horn.

The hawk has to fly toward the statue, find the crystal, and retrieve it for me, but how do I command him to do it? Time fades, along with Troy's chances. My connection with the bird weakens.

Then Connor grabs my hands again. His strength and energy flow through his fingers and into mine.

My connection with the hawk strengthens and now I'm inside his head. *Fly*, I mentally tell him, but he doesn't budge. *Get the chip.* Still he just stares at the statue, both claws clutching the branch.

How do I get him to do my bidding? Obviously, words won't work. That's stupid. He doesn't know what they mean. I picture him flying toward the roof and sense him stir.

That's it. I have to use images.

Concentrating with all my ability, I picture the hawk unfurl his wings and beat the air. A second later he launches himself from the tree.

It's working!

Two beats of his wings and he circles the statute. He sees the crystal at the base of the angel even though it's pitch black out.

I imagine him swooping low and grabbing the disc, and a heartbeat later he's done it. He circles directly overhead and lets the crystal fall from his talons. It seems to float toward me in slow motion. I grab it and give it to Akari.

She locks it in place.

My mental clock tells me we still have thirty seconds left. Troy should be safe. I can breathe again.

Connor's fingers are still laced in mine. Heat scorches my body, but I pull my hand free.

When I race into the church, my heart lumps in my throat. Troy sits cross-legged in the center of the baptistery, the lasers still in place while the clock continues to count down.

Twenty seconds left.

No! This can't be!

Nineteen seconds left.

CHAPTER

"We have all the crystals! The bomb should stop ticking down!" My heart hammers against my ribs.

Troy opens his eyes, shrugs and waves at me. "Run, Jules! I knew what I signed up for when I joined the Order. This is my choice."

He's sacrificing himself for me again, but I won't let him.

Akari holds the interlocked crystals in her hand. "The last clue! All the other riddles helped us in some way. We have to solve that last one."

She's right. What are we missing?

"There's no time!" says Blake. "That bomb will level this place."

I need to concentrate, so I close my eyes and time stops. My mind spins at supercollider speeds. The words to all the riddles float around me in a slow motion twister. The last two lines were always the most important. They tell us what to do.

What are the last two lines from the post-it?

"The Chosen must work hand in hand; Only together will they understand."

What does that mean?

Sicheii's face appears in my mind's eye. Maybe the cathedral *is* a spiritual place and the separation to the spirit lands is thin, or maybe I'm so desperate I'll imagine anything. Either way he's relaxed with a confident smile and a twinkle in his slate-colored eyes.

"What do I have to do?" I ask him. "There's no time left."

"What else do you know about Stuart? Use everything you've learned."

I groan. Even in the spirit lands he refuses to answer my questions. My mind torques—all I know about Stuart whirls around me at the speed of light.

One item burns brighter than the rest: *he loves romance novels.* He always has one with him. Troy said he crammed his apartment full of them.

That has to be it. Air comes in gulps now. "We have to hold the crystals together. It won't work unless we're physically linked."

Blake's face has turned to ash. "There's only five-seconds left. If—"

"Better grab the bloody crystal then." Connor yanks Blake's hand and pulls it on top of Akari's. I cover them with both of mine, and energy flows through us. I feel Akari's anger and Blake's insecurities, and from Connor, a mix of strength and vulnerability, as if the two characteristics weave around each other to form one new stronger one.

My hands start to burn and the crystals turn from opaque to blood-colored. The lasers disappear and the clock stops at two seconds.

Sweat rolls down my face, and Blake sinks to the floor.

Connor laughs. "Wow! That was *absobloodylootely* brilliant!"

201

Blake rises unsteadily to his feet. "I have to find a bathroom," he says as he meanders off.

"I'm still going to kill Stuart." Akari's hands are clenched into fists, her eyes smoldering red-hot coals.

I turn to face Troy. He's cross. I've seen that expression before, but this is the first time it's meant for me. He's angry and disappointed at the same time.

"*What?* Should I have let you get blown up?"

He strolls toward me. "*Two seconds, Jules!* You should have left. What if that didn't work?"

I narrow my eyes. "Then we all would have been blown up! I did what I had to. I'm not going to apologize for it. I can't let you die. I'm not the one who got stuck in the baptistery with a bomb! You did that on your own!"

When the last words burst from my lips, I wish I could take them back. It wasn't Troy's fault he got trapped; Stuart did that to him.

"*Really?*" Troy simmers, stomps past me, and dives on one of the pews with his head in his hands.

"I think we could all use a drink," says Connor.

"We're in the middle of a church." Akari waves her arms in a circle as if he hadn't noticed.

Connor smiles. "Yes, that's true. And they always keep some red wine around here someplace. I'll find it." He saunters toward the altar.

I bounce my gaze between Connor and Troy and feel like I'm stuck in a ping-pong match. Does one of them always have to be mad at me?

Connor returns with an open bottle of red wine that swings from his hand. He hands the bottle to Blake, who takes a small drink and passes it to Akari, who also takes a sip.

"Sake's much better," she says before pushing the bottle toward me.

I shake my head. I'm not a drinker and I have no desire to start now.

Connor shrugs, reclaims the bottle, takes a swig, and hands it to Blake.

"Well, you have to give Stuart credit. He's certainly gotten us to do a lot with our enhanced abilities in a short time." Blake takes another drink from the bottle.

"*Aho ka, omae*? There had to be a better way." Akari's face is still flushed pink, although the heat in her eyes has cooled to a low simmer.

"I'm not *aho ka*... whatever that is. I'm just saying, he gets results." Blake shrugs his thin shoulders. "His methods aren't that different from our families. They injected us with the DNA not knowing what it would really do to us. Then they send us out to face the enemy without being prepared. At least—"

"They believed that...."

I have a hard time keeping track of the conversation between Blake and Akari because my eyes keep turning to Troy, who hasn't budged since he sat in the pews.

What's he thinking? Is he all right?

Connor takes a gulp from the bottle; a small red trickle leaks from his lips and down his chin. He uses the back of his sleeve to wipe it clean. "At least now he has to tell us the name of this bloody Prime Elector, so we can get on with the important job."

Blake tosses out guesses as to who the Deltite leader might be.

My thoughts keep returning to Troy. *How angry is he? Should I apologize?*

Connor must have noticed my attention fixed on Troy because he hands me the bottle. "Let me have a go at him, Juliet. I think he and I need to talk for a bit."

He strolls over to Troy and sits next to him.

Great.

CHAPTER

The waves ripple against the dock while Gagarin sits comfortably in a teak chair, a glass of bourbon held lightly in his hand, and a pleasant smile plastered on his face. The moonlight glistening off the rolling water has a hypnotic effect on him. He removes his prize possession from a velvet pouch, a crystal ball no larger than the palm of his hand, and uses his mind to hover it before him.

The small round crystal is a miniature world, created by the Memory Librarians centuries earlier. When his ancestors were banished from Alpha, the Memory Librarians pulled memories of the planet from the Deltites and locked them into a dozen miniature worlds, none larger than the palm of his hand. They used the memories to re-create Alpha as it was, right before they were sent away—every detail exact and polished.

Only this planet has no Alphians or animals on it. They could only capture the bones of the world as it once existed, and because they were limited by the amount of collected memories, not all twelve of the miniature worlds have the same level of detail. Gagarin's is eleventh out of twelve, so some of the more remote portions of Alpha are blank. Still, many would kill for his treasure.

He certainly would.

He stares at the beauty of the crystal for a moment and projects himself into it. Having no physical form in this world, he can only drift along the planet's surface as if he were a ghost. The most powerful among them can take solid form on the imaginary planet, even touch the structures and smell the air, but that power lies beyond his abilities. Still, he can float and see his home world, and that satisfies him for now.

He travels to his favorite landmarks, the Crystal Caverns, a vast underground space with an endless supply of crystals that enhance natural Alphian power, and the Elder Canyon, which by comparison makes the Grand Canyon seem puny and dull in size and beauty. He also travels to the Alphian Gardens, the true Eden of the universe, filled with a plethora of wildflowers and the intoxicating wide-leafed Linutai Plant with its mind-bending powers.

He lingers at all these places and imagines possibilities, probing beauties he's been banished from, but eventually he drifts toward the crowded stadium in the capital. He always visits the crystal structure last—a soaring demonstration of Alphian advanced architecture. Used for the most important Gatherings, it holds over two hundred thousand Alphians and has a beauty without equal in the known universe—even the Memory Librarians had a hard time recreating its majesty and allure. He feels a deep sense of melancholy as he looks upon it now, empty and lifeless, its true greatness diminished.

He imagines it packed with Alphians—two hundred thousand of them. They crowd the stadium bringing their own spirit energy, their own light, which transforms the lifeless structure into a truly remarkable, dazzling kaleidoscope of color. The Deltite flag billows in the sweet-smelling breeze.

He pictures himself dressed in an Elder's shimmering tunic as he sits on the dais in one of the crystal throne chairs. A Heart, a simple red crystal, hangs from his neck on a golden chain. The Heart acts as a turbo boost for Alphian power, much stronger than normal crystals. Only a few exist, and only Elders are permitted to wear them. He sits in one of the six chairs on the dais, but not the tallest one—not yet anyway. One day he might be elevated to Leader, but for now, just sitting on the dais would be enough.

The former Elders, chains linked around their necks, squirm on their hands and knees before them. Defeated, they have been stripped naked in shame for how they betrayed their kind. When he decides their fate, the Heart pulses with energy and fills him with power and greatness he could only dream about.

As he reaches the climax of his short daydream, Bailey and Caleb, his two subordinates, arrive and interrupt his musings, which spoil their purity and intensity. The spell broken, he opens his eyes, pulls away from the miniature world, and replaces the crystal into the velvet pouch.

"Yes? Since you've come without an invite, I presume you two have important news to share with me, critical data that could not wait."

A sly smile graces Bailey's thin lips. "Our computer experts have found an interesting symbol that's connected to the hybrids and the Elders back on Alpha."

"Really? Let me see it." Gagarin's interest is piqued. He knows the Elders cannot help but feed their own warped sense of poetry. The twisted arrows and the samurai swords are ironies created to amuse them.

He takes the sheet of paper from Caleb and laughs. The bit of mirth escapes from his lips involuntarily. "How remarkable, and how arrogant of them. Did they think we would not notice? Four twisted weapons together all in one circle. They might as well have stamped the words *Alphian Elders* on it. What fools."

"We thought you'd find it amusing." Caleb smiles.

"I do not understand why the Elders persist in this ridiculous version of the universe where we live in harmony with the inferior species. We are meant to dominate them. A child could see it. They exist for our control. It is the only natural order that makes any sense."

Gagarin glances at his two fellow Deltites as they nod along. Even they understand natural selection. It's so simple really, a pattern repeated everywhere in the universe. Even humans understand that the most powerful among them are meant to rule, their democracies nothing more than failed attempts to disburse power. In the end, the wealthy and powerful govern, and deep down they know that's how it should be.

He sighs. "I imagine you found this symbol in the City?"

Bailey beams such a bright smile that her violet eyes glow in the moonlight. "Yes, and there's more."

He leans forward in his chair.

"We found the symbol in an old article about walking tours in Greenwich Village. It's the sign used by a small hotel on Perry Street, but that's not the best part. Check out this photograph we took from outside the hotel earlier tonight. The individual in the photograph is the owner and manager of the hotel."

She hands him a color photo that he brings close to his face. "It can't be.... They brought an *Ugly*, but surely there is an Alphian master nearby. He must work for one or maybe two Alphians sent by the Elders."

Bailey shakes her head. "Our guys interviewed the neighbors

208

who live near the hotel. No one has seen anyone who could be mistaken for an Alphian. The Ugly is the owner and manager. We even had the computer experts check the ownership and there is no sign of any Alphian involvement—just an Ugly."

"Why do they insult us so?" Gagarin starts to pace. "Sending an Ugly to help these hybrids? Do they think so little of us that they believe this creature can defeat our efforts to take the planet?"

He had hoped to kill Alphians from the home planet, perhaps even an Elite sent by the Elders. Only by defeating a worthy opponent can he advance and prove himself, but now there's only an Ugly to face. They should have sent someone powerful, unless they have other plans.

But what?

He glances at the photo again. "Who's this woman with the Ugly. They appear close."

"Her name is Sydney. She works at the hotel for him," says Bailey.

"We could go tonight and kill the lot of them." Caleb reaches for the handle of his sword at his waist. "How hard could four hybrids and one Ugly be to kill? I'm sure I could do it on my own."

"I am confident you could, but it would be messy to kill them in such a public place, and we do not need the attention when we're so close to our goals. Besides, we must be missing something. Why would they give so much authority to an Ugly? Some caution is called for. We should not forget the lesson Damien taught us. Have our people watch this hotel for the next day and report back to me. Let's see if an Alphian shows up. Otherwise, I have a more delicious plan in store for them, a glorious plan that will truly make them pay for their arrogance."

He crumples the picture in his hand. "The woman in the photo... what do we know about her?"

209

CHAPTER

I toss the last encyclopedia onto the bed from my perch by the window, and gaze outside. The first rays of dawn start to lighten the morning sky as I try to make sense of what's happening.

Back at the cathedral, Troy and Connor chatted for what seemed like forever, but in real time lasted probably no more than ten minutes. I kept waiting for fireworks, but their conversation stayed cordial. In the end, they meandered over to where the rest of us sat, and Troy even took a swig of wine. Still, he refused to look at me and subjected me to the silent treatment for the rest of the night, which I totally hate. He knows how much it bothers me, so I refused to apologize to him.

He *did* almost get himself blown up, so technically I *was* right.

After we finished the bottle, we lingered in the church for an hour or so. Connor regaled us with stories of his altar boy adventures. Not surprisingly, many involved him stealing the sacramental wine. One time he added food coloring to it. Hours later, parishioners complained that their mouths had turned purple. Some even thought God had sent them a sign, until the vicar realized what he had done.

As the stories waned, no one wanted to head back to the Inn, but where else could we go? We strolled back downtown at a leisurely place.

With no sign of Stuart or Sydney in the lobby, we disappeared into our rooms.

Troy fell asleep instantly on the couch, but I tossed fretfully for a few hours in the bed before I gave up.

Troy grumbles, rolls over and plants his face firmly into the cushions on the couch. He's probably having a bad dream, which is totally understandable since Stuart almost vaporized him with a bomb only a few hours earlier.

I can't watch him sleep any longer. Besides, too many thoughts bump into each other looking for space in my head, and the hotel feels like a prison, so I sneak past him, go down stairs, and stroll out the front door onto Perry Street.

The soft morning light takes the edge off the City's rough corners. On the street I can finally breathe. With no destination in mind, I head west toward the river and grab my burner cell phone from my pocket. I need to talk to someone—someone not named Troy or Connor for that matter—so I dial my father's cell.

He answers on the second ring, his voice rough with sleep. It's three hours earlier in Arizona, which means it's not yet four in the morning. "Juliet, are you okay?"

"I'm fine. I'm sorry it's so early. I forgot about the time difference."

"Don't worry about that. Are you safe? Have you found the others?"

"I'm safe for the moment." I don't want to worry him anymore than he is already, so I won't tell him about the poison or the bomb. "I've connected with the three other Chosen. We're working together."

"So things are going according to plan?"

I chuckle, unable to help myself. Nothing seems like it's going as planned. "You could say that — "

"What's bothering you? I may not have known you for long, but I am your father. I can tell by your voice that you're upset. What's up?"

I try to avoid the question. "How's Mom?"

"She's... doing as well as you'd expect under the circumstances. I won't lie to you. Once she found out that I helped you leave she wanted to kill me, but so far she hasn't snuck up on me with a knife in the middle of the night. She'll be fine when you come home."

If I come home....

I squeeze the phone. "You're watching over her, right? They might have figured out my identity, and then you'll be in danger." Nothing I can do short of killing the Prime Elector can keep them truly safe.

"Don't worry about us, Juliet. I drive your mother to work and back and keep an eye on her. I will keep her safe. Now tell me what's bothering you. You don't have to continue on the path your grandfather set for you. You can come home. We'll disappear someplace. We can go to Ireland. I still have some family left there."

"No, it's not that. I have to see this through. It's the only way to keep everyone safe. They'll find me no matter where we go, and I'd rather *hunt them* than the other way around. I just... there's one Chosen here named Connor and he's driving me crazy." As the words blow from my mouth in an emotional gust, I instantly feel better and completely stupid at the same time. *Weird.*

"Crazy how?"

"That's the problem. I don't know. He's stubborn and funny and strong and vulnerable and smart and can be really stupid. He's a pain in the ass sometimes, but he has... a lot to offer." I don't mention his rugged good looks or his eyes that seem to have no end or his drinking or his girlfriend back home. *I'm hopeless.*

"Oh... he sounds like an interesting person. What does Troy think of him?"

I've only spent a few days with my father. We first met two weeks ago, a short time before I had to kill the Seeker to save Mom and escape from town with Troy. When he was sixteen, he took over his brother's drug dealing gang, so he knows that teenagers are capable of doing a lot more than adults usually give them credit for. He believes in me, and that belief is why he let me leave without putting up a stronger fight. That and maybe he knew I was going anyway and didn't want to snuff out the kindling that represented our newly formed father-daughter relationship.

Still, he doesn't know me that well yet—not like my best friends or Mom—but he's perceptive enough to bring the conversation back to Troy, which he must have figured out is at the heart of the problem. I can't like them both. Troy's always been my best friend and I love him, but do I *love* him? What does he want?

I've just met Connor, but I feel a spark and can't seem to get him out of my mind. Since I barely sleep, that's twenty-two hours a day with a boy in my head, which is way too much.

I sigh. "Troy's not a big fan of his. He thinks he's *unreliable.*"

"Reliability is important when you're part of a team. But if you see qualities in him that'll be helpful, give him a chance to prove himself. Some people appear unreliable on the outside but are rock solid on the inside."

He's talking about himself. Mom trusted him even though no one else did, especially Sicheii. "Thanks, Dad. I've got to go. I just wanted to hear your voice."

"Say the word and I'll come help, wherever you are."

I smile because he's serious. It's nice to have a father after not knowing one for the first sixteen years of my life. Just talking to him has made me feel better. "Thanks, and I'll call if I need help. Just watch after Mom and tell her I love her."

"You got it, Love. Don't worry about us and don't forget to toss the phone. I'll do the same. You remember the next phone number, right?"

We agreed to use each burner phone only once. After that we switch to the next one. "Yep, and thank you."

"For what?"

"For listening and not asking too many questions." I disconnect the call, remove the battery from the phone, and toss it in the trash.

I've wandered to the banks of the Hudson River. For a long moment its tranquil beauty transfixes me, makes me feel small in comparison, and that makes me smile. I know the sensation won't last, but it allows me to relax and rest, which is what I need. I'm not sure how much time passes, but the sun starts to beat down on me and the temperature gets warmer.

I return to the Inn with the same questions I had before I left. My only resolution is to stuff my feelings for Troy and Connor into a mental closet and keep them locked away until after we've dealt with the Prime Elector.

Troy waits for me when I open the door.

"Where'd you go?" He looks worried.

"Out." My tone is colder than I intend so I soften it and add, "just for a walk by the river."

"They're waiting for you downstairs in the dining room. Stuart is ready to tell us the name of this leader dude."

CHAPTER

We're the last to arrive at the dining room. A strangling early-morning frost hovers in the air that's cold and biting.

Troy grins at Connor before he plops down next to him.

Great. All of a sudden they're best friends.

Connor points at Stuart but looks at me. "We decided against killing him until you showed up. I thought it would only be fair if we all voted on it."

"I vote we kill him," growls Akari.

"That's good enough for me." Connor bolts from his seat and grabs Stuart's neck before his chair hits the ground. He moves so fast Stuart can't create a force field in time to protect himself.

Connor squeezes and Stuart's face turns pink. "Listen, *Host*, how do you like having your life on the line?"

Stuart paws at Connor's hands, but can't weaken his grip. It doesn't look like Connor is letting him breathe.

I shift forward, ready to jump in because, as pissed as I am with Stuart, I can't let Connor kill him.

Troy grabs my hand under the table and whispers "Wait!" in my ear.

"You threaten the people we love again, and I'll pop your head clear off. Got that, *Stuart*?" Connor's face blazes white-hot.

He's probably thinking about the pub owner's daughter back home. He must love her a lot, which only makes sense. He's the type of guy who would love someone completely.

At least that's what I imagine. I'm such an idiot to believe he could have fallen for me.

He releases Stuart, who gasps for air and slumps forward on the table, but remains standing over him.

"That was the final test, right?" Akari spits the words out with a hard edge.

Stuart straightens his shirt collar and his face turns back to its normal pasty white. "Yes, yes, the final test from me indeed. Of course you will have to face the Deltites, and they will be harder to defeat than my tests. Yes, much harder, but I promise that all my tests have been finished. You all passed, so we can now move on to the real challenge."

Connor saunters back to his chair, unable to hide a smirk as he winks at Troy.

They must have planned this together while I was out. I'm jealous for some reason I can't quite name, but I shove those emotions back into the mental closet where my confusion over the two is locked away — *supposed to be*, anyway.

When Connor sits, Stuart tugs at his beard and stares at him with slanted eyes. "Now that the threats are over...." He waves his hand at a plate of pastries and a carafe of coffee in the middle of the table. "Please help yourselves. I assure you the pastries are

217

perfectly fine to eat. Actually, they are delightful, and from the looks of you, the coffee will come in handy to create a little spark. Yes, yes, a spark would be good."

I can't disagree with him. It looks like no one has showered, and everyone's eyelids hang heavy. I grab the coffee first and it makes the rounds, as does the plate of pastries.

Troy grabs three.

Stuart taps on a laptop and the screen from last night jumps to life.

Two men appear in sharp color, both standing. One towers over the other, and I know instinctively he's Alphian. Both wear dark blue suits, but the taller one wears his loose, almost as if it's a size too large. He's bald, light-skinned with electric blue eyes and a handsome face with fine, perfectly symmetrical features.

Stuart clears his throat. "The taller man is named Alex Gagarin. Don't be fooled by the dark blue eyes—a simple trick made by contact lenses. He is the Prime Elector on Earth."

He pauses to let us soak in the image of our enemy, and I feel like a cold slushy fluid has replaced my blood and chills my bones. I'm staring at the face of the person we're supposed to murder.

He's not some abstract idea or concept. He is real. He's flesh and blood with his own spirit and soul.

Can I seek him out and murder him in cold blood?

Stuart continues, "He's the principal of Stellar Capital."

"Stellar means star," says Connor. "So he's playing bloody games right in front of our noses."

"There's more." Stuart works the laptop and Stellar Capital's logo appears on the screen below the photograph. The logo depicts three different interlocking circles. "That, my twisted friends, is the outline of Alpha's three moons."

"What else do we know about this guy?" I lean forward.

Stuart scratches his beard. "Not much. That photograph is the only one I have been able to find. His company is located in Manhattan, so I think he lives nearby, but he is a reclusive individual and not much is known about him. He publishes a highly regarded investment report at the beginning of each year, and his private equity company is extremely successful. They manage just short of ten billion dollars worth of assets, which is sizable."

"If he's such a big shot, there's got to be more about him on the Internet. Let me get my computer. Yours is a slug. Mine's custom-made and has to be three times faster." Blake jogs out of the room.

"So you've never met him?" Akari shoots Stuart a questioning look.

"Me?" Stuart points to his chest with a surprised expression on his face, as if he's just won the lottery. "No, I don't think that would be very prudent. You see, some of my kind were exiled with the Deltites all those many centuries ago. I am afraid, yes, I am certain he would spot me as an Ugly right away, and that would simply be no good. No good at all. He'd be curious and then...."

"Right." Connor rolls his eyes. "You'd be at risk."

Blake rejoins us with his laptop in hand. "Well, okay, let's see. I'm sure Stellar Capital would have to file reports with the SEC if they manage that much money."

Akari stands and leans over his shoulder.

"Yep, they have a number of filings that go back ten years. The most recent one says they use Swiss Bank to hold their accounts."

Blake continues to work his laptop. "Stellar is the world's largest owner of cell towers. That's interesting."

"I've never heard of them. Are they like T-Mobile or Virgin?" asks Connor.

"Well, no," says Blake. "They own the physical towers, not

the networks. Those providers pay them rent." Blake continues for a few minutes spouting random facts, none of which pique my interest or seems helpful.

"What about that bloke who's shaking his hand? Who's he?" Connor points to the original photo on the screen. "He looks chummy with our guy."

Stuart sighs. "Yes, I can see where that information might be helpful. Sadly, I have no idea who he is."

"Not to worry," says Blake. "I'll run it through a facial recognition program."

Just then Troy's phone buzzes. He checks the message, grumbles, and shows me the screen. Landon's outside and wants to talk. Either we see him now or he'll come inside and cause a ruckus.

"He tried to reach us twice this morning already," he whispers to me.

The last thing we need is Landon barging into the Inn, so I stand. "We've got to go for a few minutes. We'll be back as soon as we can."

Connor smirks. "Don't worry. You know where to find us. We'll be here watching Blake fiddle around on his laptop."

Blake grins. "Everyone leaves a digital footprint these days. It's impossible not to, even if you are some super evil alien villain. We'll find out all there is to know about our mysterious Alex Gagarin by the time you get back."

I get the feeling it's not going to be so easy.

Landon leans against a Con Edison truck with a sour expression on his face.

The truck looks familiar. I saw it out front this morning and glance around. No workers are in sight.

Troy walks a step in front of me and greets Landon. "Hey, Cuz, I'm sorry I didn't call you back."

"Right," says Landon. "We've got to talk about the other night. How did you really find out about Lilly, and who helped you take out those thugs?"

Troy smiles. "I thought we settled that. Some guys on the street—"

Landon raises his hand. "Don't start with that crap. It stinks all the way to the spirit world. I'm worried about you two. I know we have a deal and your week isn't up yet, but you're still family." He looks at me. "That includes you, Juliet. I'm worried you're dealing with some dangerous characters. You have to be careful in this city. Situations can escalate in a heartbeat and turn lethal."

"We're not involved with any criminals," says Troy.

I add, "We should be finished by the end of the week and we'll tell you all about it."

Landon rubs his hands over his face in the same way Troy does when he's frustrated. The similarity between the two makes me grin.

"You'll come to me next time *before* you attack an entire gang?"

Troy raises his arm. "Scout's honor."

"They wouldn't have you in the Boy Scouts if I remember correctly." Landon's phone rings and he digs it out of one of the pockets in his cargo pants. "What's up, Amare?"

I can't hear what Amare says, but Landon's back stiffens and his eyes sharpen. "You're sure it's the same tall bald guy who you saw around Marble Hill the other night?... Okay... stay right there. Don't do anything stupid."

221

My instinct perks up like it's been jolted with a triple shot of espresso. Tall, bald, and creepy sounds like a fair description of a Deltite. I shoot Troy a knowing look and he shrugs in response.

Landon disconnects the call. "I've got to hustle and check this out. Amare has found a guy who I think is trouble."

I step toward him. "We'll go with you."

Troy follows my lead. "Yeah, maybe we'll come in handy." He beams his most helpful smile.

Landon looks us over with a sharp intensity in his eyes.

"We promise to do whatever you say." I shoot him my most trustworthy face.

Troy nods enthusiastically next to me.

"I must be crazy." Landon rubs his hands over his face again. "If you don't do exactly what I say, then you'll tell me what you're up to. The whole story?"

"Deal," I say, not having any choice. We need a lead, and my intuition tells me this guy is a Deltite. I have to trust my intuition. It's all I have.

Landon hails a cab, and we scramble in back as he directs the driver to the Upper East Side.

"So what's the deal with this bald guy?" I ask him.

"He's been surfing the projects for six months. At first we heard rumors about him and really didn't believe them—some tall, bald, rich dude hanging around—but the stories kept popping up. And the kids that go with him never return. At least six have disappeared, and I'll bet there's a bunch more."

"Did you tell the police?" asks Troy.

Landon shakes his head. "Come on, cousin. These are project kids. They disappear all the time. Most of them run away. Even my NYPD friends won't take us seriously without some hard evidence."

The cab pulls to the curb on 82nd Street and 2nd Avenue. Amare is just up the street, smoking a freshly lit cigarette, crouched behind a beaten-up bike, pretending to secure it to a tree with a chain that doesn't exist.

He straightens up and smiles when he sees us. "That was quick, Bear. And I see you've brought Little Cub and his friend, Juliet." He shares a fist bump with us.

Five-story townhouses line both sides of the block. Most are made from stone with a few brick ones thrown in. They all have garages and look expensive.

"So which house is he in?" Landon scans the buildings across the street.

Amare nods toward a stone townhouse with a green door. "The one with the flag."

"How'd you find him?" I ask.

Amare takes a puff from his cigarette and shifts on his feet. "I work as a bike messenger. I saw him stroll down Second Avenue. He went into that building twenty minutes ago, and then he left in a black Mercedes just before you guys showed up."

"What's the deal with the flag?" asks Troy.

"This neighborhood is full of consulates where diplomats live," Landon says. "That's probably one of them.'

There's a small brass plaque next to the door. "It belongs to the Island of Guernsey," I say.

"You've got some sharp eyes. Where the heck is Guernsey?" asks Amare.

"It's a small island near the UK."

They shoot me a weird look.

Guernsey was in the encyclopedia I had just finished reading, but they'd *really* think I'm strange if I told them that I read encyclopedias to waste time, so I roll my eyes and say, "A friend

of mine came from there. She used to have a flag in her room."
Even with all the changes taking place in me, I'm still a horrible
liar, but no one calls me on it.

"I don't think anybody's home." Amare flicks a long line of
ash from the tip of his cigarette that looks like a pencil eraser on
steroids. "We could break inside and do some exploring."

Landon checks both sides of the street. No one's around.
"Normally I'd say no way, but if this guy's taking kids, we need
some evidence implicating him, and we don't have time to wait."
He looks at Troy and me and says, "You guys stay here."

I grab his arm. "Why don't I come with you? Troy can stay
here as a lookout. We'll be able to search the place faster with
three of us."

"You could get into serious trouble." Landon frowns at me.

Amare grins. "I like her, Bear. She's got spunk. You're
always saying how New Beginnings is a family. Families go all
in. Either she comes along or I'm out, and you need me to get
inside."

Troy's about to object, but I blast him with a dangerous look
that stops him before he complains.

"You're both a pain in the butt." Landon grabs us and digs his
fingers into our shoulders. "Okay, we're a team, but listen to me.
If I say run, we take off." He looks at Troy. "Call us at the first
sign of trouble."

He leads us across the street at a leisurely pace and pauses at
the stoop, where he points at a video camera above the door.
"Heads down and don't look at that camera. Amare, there's a
security keypad on the left side of the door."

Amare lifts his hood over his head, tosses his cigarette to the
ground, and smiles. "Got it. It's very expensive, but I'll have no
problem with it. I'll fix the security system, and you pick the lock.

Juliet can stand behind and block us from any nosy people who happen to walk by."

We march to the stoop with our heads down.

Landon rings the doorbell. "Let's hope no one's home." After a few seconds, and when no sounds come from within, he nods at Amare.

They young man pries off the cover to the security panel and starts to rewire the system. "When I connect the power source directly to the keypad's blue wire, the entire system freezes. It doesn't know what to do with the power, but it won't short out because of a safety feature." A few seconds later, the light on the keypad turns from red to green. "You're up, Bear."

Landon uses two small tools that look like needles and messes with the lock.

"How come I get the feeling you guys have done this before?" I whisper from behind them.

"Only when we've had to, and always for a good cause."

The lock clicks.

Landon smiles, turns the doorknob, and we enter the fancy townhouse. The entire break-in takes no more than a minute.

When he shuts the door, an arctic blast whistles through me. An Alphian lives here. I can sense a residual trace of his energy like a bad aftertaste.

I reach for my sword and realize it's back at the Inn.

I'm an idiot, charging ahead as usual without thinking things through.

CHAPTER

A few pieces of modern furniture decorate the inside of the townhouse. Painted white, the walls contrast with natural maple floors, and metal tables with glass tops. The place feels like a trendy hotel, as if the people who live here expect it to be temporary.

Amare holds his nose. "What's that smell? Is it some *white person's* thing?"

"It smells like incense to me. It's a little sweet," I say. The Seeker from back home burned incense in his villa and said how he hated the smell on the planet. Another sign that I'm right—at least one Deltite lives here.

Landon turns toward me. "Here's the plan. Amare and I will start on the top floor and work our way down. You search here and go up. Let's be quick before someone comes home. We're searching for anything that indicates what he's doing with the kids."

They race up the stairs, taking two at a time, leaving me alone to search the main floor.

A living room appears off to my left with a pass-through kitchen that stretches beyond it. The house is surprisingly narrow, like the deck of a small boat.

I wander through the living room, not sure what to look for. The limited pieces of furniture have crisp edges and are made from a shiny white material that looks hard and uncomfortable. An out of place, soft, white shaggy rug lies in the middle of the room. Except for a glass cocktail table by the leather couch and a huge flat-screen TV mounted on the wall, it looks like a snowstorm had just blown through the place.

It reminds me of my room at the Inn.

The few paintings on the walls feature various geometric shapes, all in different shades of white and cream. There are no earth tones, beiges, or browns. I spin in a circle. Nothing looks *natural*. The living room is oddly disconnected from the planet.

I open a drawer to a thin desk in the foyer and find nothing. There's really nowhere else for me to search in the living room—no hiding places or drawers to rifle through—so I head into the kitchen, which favors the same color scheme and contemporary design.

At least the major appliances are stainless steel, which breaks up the otherwise plain whiteness of the room. The cabinets have the stuff you'd expect to find: plates, glasses, spices, pots, and pans. The huge double refrigerator is mostly barren except for a wide variety of meat that's crammed onto three of the shelves. I'm not a vegetarian, but this diet strikes me as extreme. Then again, who knows what Alphians like to eat?

I find nothing interesting in any of the cabinets or drawers, so I leave the kitchen and continue my search farther toward the back of the house and find a door that leads toward a courtyard out back. I ignore it and turn left into the last room—an office with a desk, a chair, and a computer. There are no filing cabinets to open and the desk doesn't have a drawer, but before I turn to leave, the massive painting on the wall catches my interest. It looks oddly out of place as it takes up the entire wall.

It's a simple painting of a lavender circle with a golden triangle inside of it, but it steals my breath away. My legs go weak and I fall back onto the desk chair. I've seen that symbol in my dreams. That's the Deltite symbol, the one they rally behind. One more bit of evidence that the Deltites exist and that we'll have to kill the Prime Elector. I guess there's always been a small part of me that hoped this situation wasn't real, that Deltites weren't threatening our world. That hope is totally gone now.

A moment later, Landon calls from the staircase, "Juliet, have you found anything?"

I join him and Amare in the foyer. "Nothing." My face burns a little because I wasn't fully truthful with him. Still, I'm not stupid enough to tell him about the painting. He doesn't need to know about it. It has nothing to do with runaway kids. He'll ask too many questions that I'll never be able to answer without giving away my true purpose in the City.

"At least two people live here," says Amare. "A man and a woman. They have clothes in different bedrooms and personal items in the bathroom, but other than that, they don't have any of the things normal people collect, like pictures and stuff. There's barely any furniture."

Landon nods. "The top two floors are completely empty. Have you found the stairs down to the basement yet?"

I shake my head.

"All these townhouses have basements." Landon spins. "They usually run below the road out front." He opens what looks like a coat closet, but it's empty. "That's weird. I've never seen an empty coat closet before."

"Bear, this whole place gives me the creeps. What's with all this white?" Amare shudders. "It's not natural."

Landon taps on the walls inside the closet. On the third knock we hear a hollow thud. "This isn't a solid wall. This is a door." He sweeps his hands along the edges, presses a button concealed in the corner, a latch pops, and the door swings open. "Bingo."

"If there's some type of chainsaw-wielding, blood-soaked, zombie maniac down there, I'm gone so fast you ain't gonna even see my shadow," says Amare, his breath fast, sweat sprinkling his forehead.

Landon flips a light switch. "Stay here if you like." He disappears down the stairs.

I nudge Amare in the side and tease him. "Come on. Do you want me to hold your hand?"

"Very funny." He follows Landon down into the basement with me a step behind.

A laboratory runs the length of the townhouse, complete with expensive looking instruments, examining rooms with glass doors, florescent lights, desks with computers on top of them, and a full-sized fridge that contains glass vials.

Landon whistles. "This is quite a setup. I've got a really bad feeling. Check this out." He points to a massive map of the area around New York City pinned on a wall above a desk.

"What are those small blue patches circled in yellow?" I ask.

Landon leans closer to it. "They're aqueducts that supply water into the City."

Amare lifts a translucent crystal the shape of a small tablet. "What the heck is this?"

He's found an Alphian crystal. It looks like it's made from the same material as my sword.

"Let me see that," I say.

He hands me the crystal, and when I touch it, an electric current burns through my fingers, as if I've stuck my hand in a wall outlet. I shriek and toss the tablet on the desk. For a heartbeat, the world turns gray and I feel unsteady, as if I'm on a raft in the middle of a storm. After a few moments, color returns around the edges.

The crystal is some type of Alphian computer. My touch activated it, and images raced through my head in a stampede of data.

"Are you okay, Juliet?" Landon grabs my waist.

"I-I-I'm... fine." My tongue feels twice its normal size and tastes metallic.

Amare swings a chair toward me and gravity pulls me down. "What happened?" he asks.

"It must have been static electricity." Another lame lie, but my mind still recoils with the Deltite data so that's the best I can do.

Landon pats my shoulder. "Take it easy while we search the rest of the lab."

I try to make sense of the images that whipped through me. I saw a graph with a curved line, which sloped downward like a ramp where it crossed a horizontal line. The graph had unfamiliar symbols on it, yet I understood what they meant.

It must be knowledge from the Fusions. The vertical side is a mortality rate and the horizontal line represents twenty-five percent.

A twenty-five percent mortality rate is the goal and they've reached it. It must be connected with the lab and those vials, and I check out the map on the wall.

Water basins? Are the Deltites about to poison the City's water supply? Why?

I try to wrap my mind around the idea, when Sicheii's voice rings in my head. "He's returning."

I feel as if someone has stabbed my eyeballs with needles, and an image flashes in my mind.

A black Mercedes is only a few blocks away. If he gets here before we leave, we'll all die.

Only Troy can help us.

I reach for my phone to call him, but it's gone. I haven't replaced the burner phone I tossed this morning.

CHAPTER

Landon has stuck his head in the fridge to check out the glass vials, while Amare searches the other side of the lab.

There's no time to tell Landon to call Troy, and besides, what would I say—that I have a psychic connection to an extraordinarily powerful alien that wants to enslave the entire planet and possibly poison all of New York City killing millions of people in the process? Oh, and if he catches us in his evil lab he's sure to torture us and devise a truly horrible way to murder us?

I close my eyes and kick my mind into hyper-drive, projecting my thoughts outward to search for Troy.

His spirit is across the street.

I speed toward him like he's a magnet and my thoughts have turned into a metallic cloud. In a heartbeat, I'm inside his head.

His mind is troubled as he searches both sides of the street for Deltites.

How do I communicate with him? I remember my experience last night with the hawk. I have to project images into his mind and hope he understands what they mean.

I recall the picture of the Mercedes and concentrate with everything I have, trying hard to add urgency to my thoughts. Hopefully, he'll get the idea and figure out a way to slow down the Deltite. Either way there's no more I can do with him, so I pull back and return to the lab.

"We've got to go! The guy's on his way back. He'll be here in a few seconds."

Landon slams the fridge closed and races over to me, with Amare by his side. "Come on!" He grabs my arm and we fly up the stairs. When we reach the first floor hallway he pauses. "How close did Troy say he was?"

"Close." I can't correct him about Troy.

"We can't go out the door or he'll see us. Are there any windows around here that don't lead out front?" Landon twists, but there's only the two in front of the house.

The garage door opens with a screechy whine.

Amare removes a small club from inside his sweatshirt. "He'll be here in a second. We'll have to take him out."

He doesn't know what he's about to face. If we try to fight the Deltite, it will only get us killed.

I remember the door I saw earlier. "There's a door to the backyard!" I sprint past the office and fling open the back door, hoping they'll follow me.

The backyard is a simple courtyard with neatly cut grass, a few metal chairs, a table, and a stone fountain off to the right. It's hemmed in by ten-foot brick walls on three sides, and the back of the townhouse on the fourth, completing the square.

Amare's voice sounds two octaves higher than usual. "When

233

he comes in the house, he'll know someone's screwed around with the alarm. In this neighborhood the cops will be here in a minute. They don't like me. We're not on speaking terms."

The last worry I have is the police—we'll never live long enough to see them.

"Over the wall, then." Landon makes a basket by interlocking his fingers and a second later he boosts Amare, who just manages to grab the top of the wall with both hands.

He swings for a second, appearing as though he might fall back down, but he manages to pulls himself up with a grunt.

The garage door closes with a thump.

"Your turn, Juliet."

I don't need the lift, but I play along, step into his hands and leap. My enhanced strength makes the ten-foot jump feel like a short hop, and I easily reach the top of the wall, grab the ledge and swing myself on top in one smooth motion.

Amare reaches down with his arms. "Come on, Bear! Just make believe you're on a hoops court."

Landon backs up two steps.

The front door opens.

He takes three steps and leaps, but he doesn't make it to the top. He falls a good foot short of the ledge, but he manages to catch onto Amare's hand.

Amare tries to wrench him to the top of the wall, but he's not strong enough.

Stomping noises and an explosion of energy burst from inside the house. The Deltite knows something's wrong. He's coming for us.

I reach down, grab Landon's shoulder, and whip him over the wall.

The back door opens.

Amare and I jump.

Landon is already on his feet.

I bounce to mine and grab Amare.

This courtyard looks the same as the one we just left. "Should we jump the next wall and keep going?" I ask Landon.

He shakes his head. "That way is a dead end. The last house on the block won't have a wall for us to jump. We have to go through this house and out the front door. Let's hustle. Be quiet, but don't stop for any reason. Once we hit the street, turn right."

Landon reaches the door first.

I glance back at the wall and questions twist inside my mind. Did the Deltite see us? Is he about to leap over it? How can I keep Landon and Amare safe without my sword?

Amare tugs on my shirt.

Landon opens the door and leads us through the hallway at a quick pace. Noises cascade from upstairs. A woman talks on the phone. A miniature poodle yaps at us.

"Keep moving," whispers Landon.

A second later we open the front door, plunge into the City, turn right when we reach the curb, hit 3rd Avenue and blend into the chaos and the busy street around us. After we've gone two blocks, we stop and lean against the side of a deli.

Landon breathes heavily, sweat soaking his shirt.

Amare smiles. "Man, that was wild."

A few seconds later, Troy wheels Amare's bike over. He limps as he walks toward us, his shirt sleeve torn, blood smeared across his arm.

"What happened to you?" Landon asks.

"When I saw the car, I knew I had to slow him down, so I hopped on the bike and cut in front of him. He didn't stop in time."

Amare grabs the bike. "You didn't mess it up, did you?" He spins the wheel, which wobbles. "The rim's bent."

Troy speaks in a mocking voice, higher pitched than usual. "Thank you Troy for throwing yourself in front of a car to save my sorry ass. I hope you didn't break anything important."

"Are you okay?" My eyes stick on the blood splashed on his sleeve and my heart twists. He's always getting hurt when he tries to protect me, and we haven't even started the truly dangerous part yet.

"No major damage. I have two arms. The other one works fine. Did you guys get what you need?"

Landon grins and removes a glass tube from his front pocket. "I pinched this vial. I'll have a friend at the hospital do an analysis. Whatever it is, it's got to be bad, and then I'll have some concrete evidence to tell my police friends. That should be enough for them to conduct a search."

The sun sparkles off the glass in Landon's fingers. The clear liquid sloshes to one side.

I don't know what's in the vial, but it's way worse than he suspects, and based upon that graph, we're out of time.

CHAPTER

Amare and Landon bend the bike wheel back into shape, and after a few swear words, Amare peddles away with the bike shaking only a little bit.

Landon claps Troy on the shoulder. "Thanks for jumping in front of that car. That extra time really saved our bacon. I owe you one."

"Consider it payback for helping us find the Inn and not telling our parents where we are," Troy says.

"About that... time's ticking. I'm still holding you to our original deal. One week."

We fist bump, and he takes off to see his friend who works at the hospital.

When he's gone, Troy turns to me. "How'd you do that? One second I'm keeping watch on the street and the next you're inside my head and I see the Mercedes."

I want to downplay the whole telepathic thing, but I've already added it to my list of aberrant behaviors, which makes the number too high and means I'm already lost. "I projected my thoughts at you. It worked for the hawk last night, so I thought you'd have no problem picking them up. After all, that hawk is way smarter than you." I punch him on the arm.

"It was weird. I felt this electric shock in my head. Not pleasant."

"Must be all that empty space in there. Did you get a good look at the guy? Is he the one we need?"

Troy shakes his head. "He's in the same tribe, but he's not our man. His face is too narrow and his nose too long. He was pissed when I ran into his car. I tried to ham it up a bit and lie in front of the car to stall for more time, but he wasn't buying it. He threatened to run me over if I didn't get out of the way, and he looked serious. When he got back in the car he started forward and I had to jump back to the sidewalk or he would have nailed me."

"Great, a Deltite with an attitude."

When we return to the Inn we pass the same Con Edison van that was parked out front when we left. "Check out that truck, Troy. It hasn't moved the entire day."

"It's probably a different truck. They all look the same to me. You're just paranoid."

"Maybe." We circle the van and find no one in sight, and I shake off the uneasy feeling. "You're probably right."

"Don't act so surprised. I've been right before." He smiles, so I shove him inside the Inn and straight upstairs to our room where we find a first-aid kit under the sink in the bathroom. After he pulls off his ripped shirt, we run cold water over his forearm.

I gently guide the water over his copper skin and wash away the blood. The cut doesn't look too deep. It's already scabbed over, so I remove a bandage and some antibiotic cream from the first-aid kit and patch him up.

He shoots me a weird look.

"*What?*"

"I've never thought of you as the nurturing type. You'd make a good doctor when this is all finished."

I ball my hands up into fists. "Stop doing that!"

"Doing what?"

"Making believe we're going back to normal when we finish this."

His eyes widen and glisten. He's hurt, but he has to hear this.

I can't pretend any longer. "Whatever happens, I will never have a normal life. I'm not normal anymore. I'm not...." I want to say human, but I can't. That's too much for me to utter out loud. It's absurd, but if I speak those words, I'm afraid there's no return, so I use other words instead. "I'm not... the same person I was before."

Troy grabs my hands and wraps his warm fingers around mine.

For a moment I close my eyes and we're back home on top of the cliff that overlooks Slippery River, or maybe in line at Tito's Tacos, but when I open them again we're in the bathroom with the Deltites hovering over us and this destiny that presses in on me that I can't dodge.

"You're the bravest person I know." His face is inches from mine. "This is scary, but we'll find our way. We aren't alone. Sicheii's spirit is with us, and he's one tough old bird. He'll guide you when you need him."

239

I throw my arms around his shoulders and pull him into me. He doesn't understand. *How could he?* I don't even understand myself. Yes, I'm afraid the Deltites will kill me, but I'm more afraid that I'll live and cease being human—that I'll be alone—so I cling to him like a life preserver in a vast ocean with no land in sight. He's my last connection to my old world, my only connection to a normal life.

Tears roll down my cheeks. I know I'm being selfish. *What if he gets hurt or killed?* I hold him tighter still and feel his heartbeat through my clothes. Mine slows to match his.

I'm not sure how long we stay like that in the bathroom, but when I've soaked up enough of his strength, I release him. "We had better go downstairs and find out what they've discovered." I wipe the tear tracks from my face.

"You know there's a good chance someone's dead."

"Dead?"

"Either Connor's killed Stuart or Akari's killed Blake or—"

"Or Akari's killed all of them."

We both chuckle, but it's out of nervousness more than anything else. He leaves and I wash my face. When I reach for a towel, something in my pocket pokes me. The vial—I had almost forgotten about it. It's supposed to open when I'm ready, whatever that means.

I lift the crystal and mutter, "I've passed Stuart's stupid tests. I've got to be ready now." I shake the tiny container and the liquid sloshes around. I hold it tight and concentrate on it. I try to make the top disappear like I have with the prior crystals, but it stays in place. My hand starts to hurt because of my death grip on the vial, but nothing happens.

I must not be ready yet.

I slip it back into my pocket and check to make sure all the traces of my tears are gone, and march with Troy to the dining room.

To my relief, we find the entire gang still alive and clustered out around the table.

It's obvious Blake hasn't made much progress. The strain on his face is palpable as he bites his lip and runs his hands through his disheveled hair.

Akari still hovers over his shoulder, frozen in the same spot since we left, which I'm sure only intensifies the stress Blake's under.

Connor uses telekinesis, crumpling a piece of paper with his mind and sending it flying toward Blake.

Akari growls and the paper erupts into flames and turns to ash that falls to the table on top of a growing pile of charred paper.

Connor is about to send another one at Blake when he notices us in the doorway and greets us with a broad grin, but it doesn't mask the anger that burns behind his eyes. And the water bottle has returned. "Welcome back, mates. I'd like to report a few breakthroughs, but our computer genius hasn't found any useful bits of information yet."

Blake peers up from his fancy custom-made laptop. "The facial recognition software is running a little slow, that's all. It hasn't been a total waste. We've found out a few other things."

Akari speaks through a clenched jaw. "Nothing helpful. Stellar has an office in some little island place called Guernsey. Who cares?"

"That's interesting." I recount our adventures at the Guernsey consulate: the painting with the Deltite symbol, our narrow escape, and what I know of their plan to poison Manhattan's drinking water. I leave out my telepathic communication to Troy. They don't know I can read thoughts, and I don't want to share that with them. It's bad enough that I'm the Alpha, whatever that

241

means. I don't want them to believe that I can read their minds, which I can't do anyway.

"That really throws a wrench in the works." Connor swigs from his bottle. "Any idea when they plan to start?"

I shrug. "I'm not sure, but I feel it could be soon."

Stuart tugs on his beard. "You saw images when you touched the crystal tablet?"

"Yeah, so?"

"That's just a bit odd. Those computers are geared to receive only Alphian brainwaves. If I touched one, nothing would happen. I'm surprised, yes, yes, more than a little surprised that it responded to your touch."

"The swords work when we touch *them*," says Akari.

"True, true, but they were specially calibrated for your... your uniquely twisted DNA."

Heat flushes my face. I don't like the look on everyone's face, as if I'm some type of traitor. "It didn't work. Not really. I felt a shock and saw a few images. It probably would have happened to any of you guys."

"It doesn't matter," says Connor. "At least we have a lead now. We know where there's a Deltite. He could lead us to this Gagarin we need to find."

Stuart leans forward on his elbows. "No, no, that would be highly unadvisable. We need to surprise the Prime Elector. This Deltite will know you are nearby because of your unusual signature. Our element of surprise will be ruined and without that...." He frowns and places his hands on the table palm down, his unspoken meaning clear.

We'll all die.

"Signature?" asks Troy.

"Yes, yes, all living animals have a unique electrical signature, like a fingerprint, but each species gives off a distinct signal. For example, an Alphian can tell all horses just by the signature, and an adept one could identify a specific horse if he is acquainted with that animal."

"So we won't be able to sneak up on the bugger. This cock-up just gets better and better." Connor smolders.

"You'll be able to surprise them for a few moments. That's our window. It takes time for the Alphian mind to sort though all the life forms around them. If they don't expect you, they won't look for you—and that, my twisted friends, is our best chance." He shoves the last pastry into his mouth. His fluffy cheeks jiggle as he munches the dessert like a squirrel eating a handful of acorns.

A trumpet blares from Blake's computer, and I jump.

"What's that?" asks Sydney.

Blake beams. We've got a hit for Gagarin's friend. "His name is Peter Smyth. He's a Senior Vice President at Swiss Bank."

"How does that help us?" asks Troy.

"Well, I have a plan." Blake takes his time and stares at everyone before speaking. "But it isn't an easy one."

Gagarin sits alone at a long oak table in a dark windowless room. Light from two tall candles dances across the porcelain plate and crystal wine glass in front of him. He lifts the glass, swirls the Malbec inside, and stares intensely at the heavy liquid coating the crystal sides. After he takes a sip, he lifts a silver knife and fork.

Before Caleb has a chance to knock on the door, Alex opens it with his mind. He studies the young Deltite as he marches toward him, and knows instinctively that his charge has bad news to report. The young man's hesitant strides and downcast eyes give him away.

He stops a few feet from Gagarin and refuses to look at him.

"Another unexpected visit? My, we are making a habit of these interruptions. What difficulties have you run into this time?"

Caleb reluctantly lifts his eyes to meet Gagarin's. "There's been a break-in at the townhouse on the Upper East Side."

Gagarin gently places his utensils on the plate and leans back in his chair. He speaks through gritted teeth, each word slow and rich with tension. "Did they discover the laboratory in the basement?"

Caleb nods, looks down at his feet and talks into his chest. "One of the vials of our brainwashing drug was taken. But there's no way they could possibly know what the drug is or what it does."

Gagarin steadies his breathing with effort. Steam threatens to escape through his ears, but he wants to stay in control, at least for a little while longer. "And you know who broke in, right? I can tell by your expression."

He recognizes the fear in Caleb's eyes, which could mean only one thing, so he guesses. "One of the hybrids discovered the townhouse, broke in and stole a vial—all because of your carelessness!"

"I-I don't understand how she could have found the townhouse. But the video camera caught her on tape and she wasn't alone."

Spit flies from Gagarin's mouth. "She? Is this the one from Arizona? This Juliet Wildfire Stone who killed Damien! The hybrid he believed to be the Alpha!"

"That's the one, but she wasn't alone." Caleb stiffens his back. "She brought two other guys, one Native American and one African American. They avoided the video camera by the door, but failed to realize we had another one hidden in the front hallway."

Gagarin rubs his smooth head. "We need to find out who these friends are. Put our best people on it. I want them both dead. We can't afford any loose ends. We will have to kill them and all their acquaintances."

"That won't be a problem, but what about the hybrids? I can take care of them now. Maybe it would be best to eliminate them."

"No!" Gagarin pounds the table; his plate jumps and wine sloshes inside his glass. He takes a deep breath and hesitates for a few moments, and does his best not to explode. Eventually, when he feels his temper subside, he lifts his knife and fork and studies his plate. His voice sounds calm and measured. "Where's Bailey? Are we ready to proceed with our plan for the drug?"

"Yes, she estimates the mortality rate for the latest version to be twenty-five percent. She's at the lab in Westchester now and tells me it's proven to be highly effective. We should have enough made by tomorrow to dump into the water supply."

"I'm happy *she's* performing to expectations. The cell towers are properly programmed. Once the water's been contaminated we can send out the pilot signals and test the drug on the entire city. When our little experiment succeeds, we will have a compelling case to take to our leader. He will have no choice but to pick Earth for our next conquest. The other targets will be forgotten, and I will have my victory. I will succeed. We will be one step closer to Alpha, and my glory will have no bounds."

"Yes, but how shall we handle the hybrids?"

Gagarin slices into the meat on his plate. "Have you ever eaten alligator?" He glances at the four-foot alligator pacing in the cage on the floor behind him. The cage isn't made from steel. It is infinitely stronger—made from pure energy from his mind.

When Caleb shakes his head, Gagarin says, "You must try it. The animal is a natural born killer. You can taste its power through the blood." He nods to the table. "Lay your left hand flat on the table by my plate."

"My hand?"

"Yes, just place it flat on the table." Gagarin could force Caleb's hand to the table if he used telekinesis, but he'd rather have Caleb lay it down voluntarily.

Caleb shuffles forward and places his palm on the table, fingers spread wide. Fear flickers behind his eyes and the thin line made by his lips.

Gagarin swallows a large chunk of meat. "You don't have to worry about the hybrids. I have a plan—a poetic plan that will give me great pleasure to carry out. It's already in motion. When your services are needed I will let you know."

Caleb nods.

Without warning, he jabs the knife into Caleb's hand.

Thunk!

The blade pierces the flesh.

Caleb screeches, but Gagarin jammed the blade so hard it punctured the table, so Caleb can't move his hand away.

"Fail me again and I'll cut it off!"

CHAPTER

"Here's what I'm thinking." Blake pushes his laptop away from him, looking relieved his computer investigation panned out and that he didn't finish last in another race. "Antiterrorist laws require every bank to know who owns and runs the companies they do business with. They need to have information about the key people — who they are, where they live, etc."

"So bloody Swiss Bank knows where Gagarin lives." Connor takes another healthy gulp from his vodka-filled water bottle. His impatience level climbs with each drink, as he grips the plastic bottle harder and takes bigger gulps than he had before. "How do we extract the bloody information out of these buggers?"

"Peter Smyth is the key. According to their website, he's an investment banker who handles private equity companies like Stellar. He became a Senior Vice President ten years ago just when Stellar first showed up. I bet that's not a coincidence. He has to be the connection between Swiss Bank and Stellar. He'll have info about Alex Gagarin, including where he lives. No one messes with these laws. They could get serious jail time."

Akari finally gives up her vigil over Blake's shoulder and settles into the seat next to him. "So we grab him and make him tell us where Gagarin lives. Bankers are wimps. I'll crack him in no time." She cracks her knuckles, grins, and leans forward with an eager gleam in her eyes.

"That *could* work," smiles Blake. "It's a little Neanderthal, and Smyth's apparently in Europe meeting with clients, so that would take some time."

"Too long," I say. "We don't have that kind of time. Traveling to Europe and finding Smyth would take a week. They'll have poisoned the City's water by then, and millions of people would die." I have an idea that could work though. "I bet Swiss Bank has a branch in the City. They probably keep that information on their computers here somewhere."

The switch goes on and Blake's face lights up as he speaks loud and rushed. "Smyth has an office on Madison and 23rd in their main US building. He'll keep all his most sensitive stuff on the computer in his office. All we need to do is access his desktop and clone it on a flash drive. Once we have the drive we'll find some email or other document that'll tell us where Gagarin lives."

"How do we clone his desktop?" asks Troy.

Blake turns a light shade of pink and fiddles with his computer. "Well, I had a slight problem last year in honors Chem. My teacher kept all her tests on her laptop and she had a sloppy habit of leaving her laptop in the classroom during lunch. I kind of—"

"You bought a cloning program and stole the final from her computer. Wicked move, Blake. I'm impressed." Connor grins.

Blake shrugs, obviously embarrassed, providing a glimpse of the pressure he must feel as the son of two perfect parents. He *couldn't* afford a bad grade in honors chemistry for fear he would disappoint them. That's a heavy burden to lug around—the weight of unrealistically high expectations. He's probably had to carry it his whole life.

Stuart pulls up images of Swiss Bank from the Internet and flashes them on the screen. The bank looks impregnable with a vast stone facade, giant steel gates, and heavy glass doors. Inside, armed guards man the entrance and there's a metal detector for visitors.

"Is there a back door?" jokes Troy. "We're never sneaking past *that* security."

"Well, we don't have to sneak our way in. We could just ask for a tour." A sly grin sweeps across Blake's face.

Akari scowls at him. "What aren't you saying to us? Don't make me hurt you."

"My parents have an account at Swiss Bank. I've actually been *inside* the offices once with my dad."

"If you call the banker, he might give you and your friends a quick tour of the place. *Right?*" I say.

Blake nods.

"Bloody brilliant," says Connor.

"Well, that's the good news. The bad news is the bank's setup. The private bankers have a floor all to themselves. That's where my dad's banker has an office. The investment guys are on a different floor. We won't be able to march onto Smyth's floor or office without an escort. They take their privacy extremely seriously."

"How does the security work?" Troy asks.

"They give you a pass when you go through reception and the metal detectors. You take the elevators behind the desks and a person meets you at the floor you're headed to."

"We can't *all* go see your dad's banker. We'll never be able to sneak away long enough to find Smyth's office." Connor furrows his eyebrows. "There has to be another way."

All four of us can't sneak around an investment bank without raising suspicion. We'd stand out like a Rolls Royce on an Indian reservation. "We need to split up. That way some of us can snoop around without an escort. Blake can take one of us to see his dad's banker and the rest will take the elevator to the right floor. We'll bluff our way to Smyth's office, sneak in, and clone his computer."

"That's doable." Blake purses his lips. "If the banker asks what happened to my other friends, I'll just tell them you couldn't make it. He won't call down to security to check, but sneaking into his office will be tricky. All the offices are made of glass. There's no way you'll get into his office with everyone hanging around."

"What about the fire alarms?" says Sydney. "If you pull one, everyone has to leave the building, right? You'll have a few minutes to find his computer and clone it."

I hate to admit it, but that's a good suggestion.

Stuart jumps in. "Sounds like a workable plan. Blake and Akari should see the private banker while Juliet and Connor bluff their way onto the right floor. When they find Smyth's office, they will pull the fire alarm, hide until the floor clears out, and then clone his computer."

"Why do I have to go with Blake?" Akari's eyes turn into slender angry knives.

Stuart strokes his beard pensively. "The cover story is better if Blake brings a young lady to impress. That will give him a reason for coming to the bank. Yes, yes, that works well. You two can pose as a couple and that leaves Juliet and Connor to snoop."

251

"If you try anything, I'll break every bone in your body," Akari warns Blake, but her voice sounds light and her face hints at a smile.

"We'll have to make it seem realistic," quips Blake, and she swats him on the arm.

"What about me? What do I do?" asks Troy.

"There is no need for you to go with the Twisteds. No, your presence will only make the sortie more difficult. Juliet and Connor will be fine without you. Besides, you do not have any special... qualities to add."

Blake says, "It will be harder to sneak five people in and have only two that show up at the banker's office. Three people wandering around will definitely be more suspicious than two."

They're right. I don't want Troy to feel left out, but he'd only make it more difficult.

Akari and Connor both nod along with Stuart and Blake.

"Sorry, mate, three's a crowd." Connor waves his water bottle, and the liquid inside splashes over the top.

Sydney leans forward. "While they snoop around Swiss Bank, we can keep a watch at the consulate. Our DNA isn't twisted with Alphian DNA, so the Deltites won't suspect us. We can blend in with everyone else."

"Yes, yes, that's a good idea. There's nothing special about you two." Stuart's eyes twinkle more than I like.

"We have to move fast," I say. "Blake, do you think you can get us in tomorrow?"

"I'll find out." He leaves the room to make the call.

Sydney tosses a cotton candy smile at Troy. "I've never been on a stakeout before. We'll get a car and find a spot to park near the house. That way we can stay comfortable while we keep a watch on the place."

Troy nods, but deep, angry ridges etch into his face and he shifts his body away from mine, as if I've betrayed him somehow.

Blake comes back a minute later. "It's all set. We'll see the banker at noon tomorrow. That'll give us time to get ready. We have other things to do before then."

"Like what?" asks Akari.

"Well, we'll need to get the right clothes. Everyone has to be dressed like they belong. That means suits and ties for us, Connor, and business wear for you two." He points at Akari and me.

Connor groans. "I don't have any posh clothes. I don't even own a suit and tie. Never have."

"No problem. We'll go to Brooks Brothers. You'll look like a banker in no time." Blake grins.

I glance at Akari. "We can go to Bloomingdales. We'll find something there. My mom's a lawyer, so I know how to dress adult-boring."

"One other thing." Blake stares at Connor. "You have to cut your hair. It's too shaggy for a bank—you'll stand out too much."

Connor's face turns red. "Never!"

"I have some scissors and a bowl in my room." Blake cracks a smile.

"Come near me and I'll show you what you can do with those scissors."

We all start to laugh—everyone but Troy. He's never been left off a team before. He's always been picked first or second, so this is new to him, and he's steamed. He'll get over it, but what bothers me is how quickly everyone else agreed that he shouldn't go with us to the bank. It's almost as if they discussed it beforehand and decided he would be a liability.

The worst part is that I agree with them.

CHAPTER

Most adults look at teenagers and never see beyond the obvious stuff: clothes, hairstyles, tattoos, make-up, or the music they listen to. They get stuck on age, as if that's a fair measure of maturity, but that's stupid. Chronological age doesn't have much to do with maturity; experience does. A twenty-something who has never struggled or faced adversity hasn't matured much, yet a sixteen-year-old who has fought through life is, in all the important ways, older.

I feel ancient, as if my back has been bent from a lifetime of troubles, my skin turned to leather, and my face wrinkled like a raisin. This weariness that has seeped into my bones shouldn't be there. Perhaps I just need a breath, a moment to rest and think, but I have a sinking suspicion no such break will come.

Troy stayed back at the Inn after we argued for half an hour. He wanted to go to Swiss Bank with us, and was angry we didn't have a role for him.

I could see it clearly in his eyes and the strain on his usually carefree face. I tried to make him feel better about it, and explained that, of all the tasks we have to perform, this one is the least dangerous.

He didn't buy it, and when we started round three of the exact same argument, I had to walk away. Still, a certain undercurrent flowed below the surface of our conversation.

Troy *isn't* a Chosen. No matter how special he is, he can never truly be one of us. We've avoided *that* discussion so far but those issues lurk just below our words. So I hugged him and left him by himself, and our most important conversation remains unspoken... for now.

I've never been much of a shopper. Most of my clothes are casual—shorts, T-shirts, jeans, and an occasion sweatshirt or sweater—typical Arizona wear. Still, I look forward to shopping with Akari. It feels *normal*—even if it's a mirage, even if it's only a few hours at a store.

I forget about my role as a Chosen, the disappointment on Troy's face, and all the struggles we still have to face as Akari and I take a cab to Bloomingdales on the Upper East Side.

Her eyes widen as we get out of the car—Bloomingdales takes up an entire city block and towers six stories high. She speaks with a breathless I-can't-believe-my-eyes quality in her voice. "Is that one store? It's a *bakemono*."

"*Bakemono?*"

She shrugs. "Oh... I think the word is... monster."

I grin. "Yes, it certainly is. It's an American monster called Bloomies." I point to a black art deco sign with white letters on top of the main entrance. "There's one back home in Arizona, but this one is way bigger."

We cross the street and she hesitates at the entrance. "We only have one general store in my village. People have to mail order everything except the basics."

I open the door and smile. "Welcome to America."

We move from the main entrance and down three steps, into a vast open space filled with circular stalls, sales people, and customers who race around at a frantic pace. Akari gasps beside me, and I can't imagine what she's thinking.

A certain pattern emerges before us, as if the sales area is transformed into a dance floor and all the dancers circle the floor in one direction. The stalls on the main floor are filled with jewelry and cosmetics.

This is the wrong floor for us, so I grab her hand and pull her into the dance. "We need to find a directory."

We let the momentum of the other people pull us toward the shiny gold elevator doors. A directory can't be too far off from them.

We find one in front of the elevator bank. "We have to go to the third floor."

When the elevator doors open, we cram in with the eclectic mix of people: two older women with gray hair, fancy dresses, gold necklaces, and a cloud of perfume that hovers over them; one guy in his twenties with a mohawk, a sleeveless T-shirt that show off arms covered with tattoos; two young men with suits and ties; and one mom with a double stroller, rocking twins who are either on the verge of sleeping or crying.

Akari looks uneasy as she shrinks against the back of the elevator. Her eyes flash from side to side and her breaths comes in short bursts. Luckily, the guys step off at the second floor and no one new jumps on. When we get to the third floor, she's frozen, so I yank her around the stroller and through the cloud of perfume.

We stand off to the side of the elevator bank. "Are you okay?" I ask.

She's still gasping for air and her body trembles. It takes a few minutes before her breath steadies and color returns to her face. "I'm sorry... I get these... panic attacks."

"Have you always had them?"

"Not always. The first time was when one of the fishermen in the village told us that my father went missing. The walls closed in on me and I couldn't move or breathe. I thought I was about to suffocate, but air finally came. The attacks were bad for a few years after that. My grandmother helped me deal with them."

"What did she do?"

Akari looks away. "It's stupid."

I grab her hand. "You can tell me."

"She'd say I was stronger than the fear. She'd repeat it over and over again. I'd listen to her voice and start to think positively. After a few minutes, I'd start to breathe in the same rhythm as her voice and eventually I'd break through." Her voices jumps and her eyes turn electric. "Don't tell the others! I don't want them to think I have a problem."

I smile. "There's something wrong with all of us, but this'll be our secret. I promise."

"Thanks, but I haven't noticed anything wrong with you." She shoots me a half grin. "Connor drinks and Blake needs some confidence, but you don't have any obvious problems."

I laugh. "Oh, there's plenty wrong with me. You'll see."

We drink water from a water fountain and turn our attention toward shopping. The third floor isn't as crowded as the main one. It's separated by designers as if they each have their own island with their own flag. The names don't mean much to me: Burberry, Canada Goose, Dylan Gray, Eileen Fisher.

"Where do we start?" Akari looks lost.

"We have time. Let's float around."

We wander among the islands like castaways adrift on a raft. Akari pulls out dresses at random—nothing we should buy or can wear to Swiss Bank, but it's fun to watch her face light up. She smirks at a particularly horrible electric blue piece littered with silver sequins, a plunging neckline, and virtually no back.

"I bet that would make quite a stir if you wore it back home," I joke with her.

She laughs. "My own grandmother wouldn't recognize me. Heck, no one would." Some of the hard edges in her face soften when she laughs.

"It's good to see you joke. Most of the time you seem *angry*."

She waves her hand at me. "I've always had a quick temper. Besides, in my country women are still supposed to be submissive to men." She lowers her voice. "Sometimes I'm not quite as angry as I seem. It helps me get my point across. Otherwise they won't take me seriously."

"So, it's an act."

She lifts her finger to her lips. "Not always, but every now and then. Don't tell Blake."

I chuckle. "He's certainly scared to death of you."

"He's not so bad." Her eyes sparkle. "But if I'm stuck as some kick-ass Chosen, I'm not taking crap from anyone. There has to be perks for this crazy situation we're in."

We continue to wander among the designer islands, and Akari's enthusiasm becomes infectious. We both pull off the racks dresses we love or hate or really can't decide how we feel about. Finally, we spot a designer that has blouses and slacks that Mom would wear to work. We sail in that direction and find some items, which are mostly boring but serviceable and workable. All the clothes are locked to the racks, and every time I try to catch the eye of a salesperson they conveniently look the other way.

Akari catches on right away. "I guess we don't look like customers. We'll have to corner one." She points at a saleswoman firmly planted in a neighboring island. "I'll scoot around to her other side and flush her toward you. We'll meet in the middle and grab her."

Akari's plan works, and when trapped, the saleswoman has no choice but to help us. She's all bubbly and says, "How can I help you?" and "Let me carry those for you."

We find clothes that fit and look *almost* pretty on us. I pay for them with cash. Now that we carry Bloomingdales bags, we've passed a seriousness threshold, so the people at the shoe department can't wait to help us. Their friendliness is fake, but it feels good to have them fawn over us.

On our way out of the store, we pass the perfume stalls and an overeager saleswoman sprays Akari in the eyes.

Her face turns red. She swipes the bottle from the saleswoman, sprays her in the face, and growls, "How do *you* like it?" with each spray.

After a half dozen spritzes, I grab the bottle from her before security comes over. I hand it back to the ash-white woman, who probably wishes she had never come to work that day, and pull Akari outside.

I chuckle. "So, were you really angry or just putting on a show?"

She laughs. "The first three times I sprayed her, I was angry, but the look on her face made me keep going. Did you see how her mouth dropped? I bet she swallowed half the bottle."

We hail a cab and my head splits open like someone has taken a nutcracker to it. The auras switch on and my mind races into hyper-drive. I try hard to shut it down, but I can't control it. My arms and legs tingle and energy flows through me. My body has been set on fire and flames lick my skin. Pitchers full of sweat pours out of me, and then....

The auras and weird sensations switch off as suddenly as they started.

Akari asks if I'm fine, so I complain about carsickness.

CHAPTER

Blake paces the dining room with his hands stuffed inside his suit pants pockets, while Akari folds small pieces of paper into perfectly shaped horses.

She's already created a full-sized herd.

"It's after eleven o'clock. Where can he be? We only have one chance at this. We can't be late." Blake huffs for the third time in the last ten minutes.

No one has seen Connor since we returned from dinner last night in China Town. Generally sullen during the meal, he didn't say much. He disappeared into his room when we went back to the Inn, mumbling about a football match on television, which made no sense because of the time difference between New York and England. Any match would already have been over.

Connor is not the only person missing.

Sydney didn't show up this morning either. She left a note for Troy that she'd meet him by the Consulate. I'm not sure what she's up to, but she was supposed to go with him in a Zip Car.

Instead, Troy trudged off on his own to start the stakeout without her. I'm not happy with him spending the day with the super-beautiful, flirty, perfume-wearing Sydney, but that's a whole lot better than having him around sulking with an "I told you not to trust the drunk" look on his face.

"He's going to mess this up if he doesn't show soon." Blake stops pacing and fiddles with his gold tie, flipping it against his white shirt.

"Yes, yes, he certainly will." Stuart frowns. "Imbibing spirits is a nasty habit. It makes one so unreliable."

I glare at Stuart. "He's fine. I'm sure there's an easy explanation. I'll find him."

"Yes, certainly," says Stuart. "If you can't locate him, I suggest you go on without him and we hope for the best."

I shoot Blake and Akari a half-hearted smile. "We'll meet you at Swiss Bank by twelve. Don't worry so much." I clasp Blake on the shoulder and try to sound confident, doing a poor job of hiding my worry about Connor, who could be anywhere.

I leave the Inn and mumble, "Now what?"

I picture Connor's face in my mind's eye and start walking the streets. Moving swiftly, I make turns without thinking, the pull stronger and more confident than that first time I searched for him. Still, my eyes are drawn to the window of every bar along the way, and I wonder whether he's inside watching a soccer match, drinking himself into a stupor, and getting into a fight. I thought we were beyond that, but he's still a mystery and anything can happen in mysteries.

Oddly, I stop outside of a huge Barnes & Noble bookstore on 17th Street. There's no bar nearby or other place he might have settled into, so my gaze returns to the bookstore. He has to be inside.

The first floor has more toys than books, so I ignore them and follow my instincts up the escalator to the third floor. This area holds stacks of the less popular books: literature, poetry, and college textbooks. Three people stroll about, taking hesitant steps as if they're lost.

Connor sits on the floor in one of the isles, his back against a bookshelf, holding a paperback in his hand. He wears a navy suit and white shirt, but no tie. The clothes transform his good looks and make him appear older and more refined. His shaggy hair still drops below his eyes, but he could pass for someone in his twenties, a college student on an interview maybe.

I stroll over, press my back against the bookshelf, and slide down until I'm sitting next to him.

He doesn't look up, and a full water bottle is perched between us like a neon warning sign.

I smile and bat my eyes at him. "So, do you come here often?"

He grins and closes the book. "That's the best line you have? Complete rubbish. How'd you find me?"

"You don't think I came here to look for *you*, do you?" I point at my chest in an exaggerated show of indignation. "No way. I was in the neighborhood and thought I'd do some reading, maybe buy one of the latest bestsellers. I'm a big Ruby Standing Deer fan."

"Right." His eyes flicker between the full water bottle and me.

I breathe a little easier knowing he hasn't drunk any alcohol yet. "So, what's up? Just thought you'd do some reading?"

He smirks. "I only have three hobbies." He ticks them off with his fingers. "Football, and there are no bloody matches on, drinking, and reading. It was a close call between those last two, but I found this place and thought I'd try reading."

"How's that working out?" I glance at the water bottle.

"I know what you're thinking. It's not that I'm a drunk or anything. It's just that...." He shrugs. "I don't know. I always end up drinking when I'm pissed, and this whole situation really turns my head inside out. I mean, what were my parents thinking when they injected me with that DNA? I was only a baby. How stupid were they? Then they go ahead and get themselves killed running from a Seeker and leave me with the cold-hearted vicar so.... What? So I can grow up as an orphan and work for the bloody pub owner, spend all my time carting around kegs and cleaning up after the drunks."

His face heats up and turns a light shade of pink when he stops himself. His left hand shakes when he places it on the bottle. His eyes stick to it.

I place my hand on his.

After a few moments he locks his eyes with mine. They're ringed with red and burn through me. "I'm a bit of a mess. I want to be angry with my parents, but I'd forgive them in a heartbeat if they were still here."

"I'm sure they did what they thought was right."

He snorts. "Bloody good choice. They've placed the weight of the world on our shoulders. What's this world ever done for us? It dumped me at a pub. Left me with no one. I'll tell you the truth. I almost didn't come to New York. I had my mind made up to take the gold coins they gave me and find an island to spend my time. Drink myself from sunrise to sunset."

"Why didn't you?"

"Curiosity at first. I wanted to see the others. You know, others like me. But once I met... once I met you, I couldn't leave you holding the bag with Akari and Blake while I took off to build sand castles. That'd make me a right big wanker."

I chuckle. "You're still a wanker, but I'm happy you stayed. I'm sure I couldn't do this without you. Besides, my grandfather used to tell me that the heaviest burdens were given to the strongest people. I know you're strong. You don't *have* to drink."

He curls his hand around mine and lifts if from the bottle. "You sure you don't want to run to Fiji with me?"

I laugh—a nervous type of giggle that I'm not fond of. "No way. I hate sand. It gets between your toes and in your hair. Do you know how long it takes me to wash sand out of this much hair?" I flip my long black strands at his face. "*Forever*. That's how long. I still have some sand in there from my trip to the beach three years ago."

He smiles and we stare silently at the books around us for a few moments.

He's not the only one who uses a crutch. We all do. Blake hides behind his family's wealth and Akari uses anger to mask her true feelings. My crutch is the worst of all. I use Troy. I know I have to send him away before he gets himself killed, but just the thought makes my chest tighten and my stomach churn.

If Connor can find the strength to stop drinking, can I find the willpower to turn Troy away?

"What about you?" he says. "Why did you let me win in The Underground when we were training with the swords?" He tightens his lips and shakes his head. "Don't deny it."

I sigh. "I don't know."

"Did you think I'm too fragile to lose to you?"

"No, it's not that. It's silly, really. I just don't want to stand out from everyone else. I'm tired of being different."

"You're the strongest among us. Everyone knows it."

"So you don't mind if I crush you like a tin can?" I smirk at him.

He snorts. "It's only temporary. Next time I'll best you fair and square. So long as you promise not to go easy on me."

He holds out his hand and I shake it. "Deal."

"We had better get a move on. Blake's probably wet himself by now."

"Not so fast." I release his hand and swipe the book he had put down. "What were you reading, anyway?"

"Give me that!"

I hold the book away from him, and the pages flutter open. A passport-sized photograph floats to the floor.

"Who's that?" I reach for the photo.

"Michelle, the pub owner's daughter."

My fingers clasp the edge of the picture. It's facing downward so I can't see her. The world seems to stop in the same way I imagine it does for a terminally ill person who faces the reality of her situation for the first time, staring at a grim-faced doctor with bony features and sad eyes that hide behind metal frames. Just the sullen expression from the doctor should tell her all she needs to know, but she holds out for the slightest whisper of hope, fleeting and temporary as smoke. Once the doctor explains the dreary situation to her, the hope dissipates in swirls as if never really there, because, of course, it wasn't. It was an illusion the entire time. Just like this connection I've manufactured between us.

"Go ahead," he says. "You can turn it over."

I don't want to flip over the photograph and see the perfectly beautiful Michelle with her curly blonde hair, small button-nose, and moon-shaped blue eyes. Still, that whisper of hope floats above me, so I turn the photo over. It takes me a full minute to focus on the face that smiles back at me.

"When was this taken? She looks so young." Michelle is indeed beautiful, with freckles, red hair tied in pigtails, and a bright smile.

Connor takes the photo from me. "This snap was taken the

day I left. She's only twelve. She's also an orphan, really like a little sister to me."

Emotions whoosh through me like a sudden blast of heat. He's not in love with a girl back home, at least not in the way I had feared. A smile starts in my toes and travels all the way to my face. "She looks special." I try to hide the giddy feeling that threatens to overcome me from my voice.

"She is. She's too good to be stuck in that pub. When this is all done, I'll rescue her." He shifts his weight to get up, and reaches for the book to reclaim it.

I swing it away from him. "Hold on a second." I grab his shoulder and push him down. "Let's see what you were reading." The book opens to a bent page. "*Yeats?* Who's that?"

Connor's eyebrows arch upward. "You don't know Yeats? What do they teach you in these shoddy American schools? He's only the best English poet that's ever lived. I'm buying you this book." He stands and helps me up.

"I know all about Yeats."

As we head to the escalators, he says, "Okay, what poems have you read?"

"Well... none, but that doesn't mean that I don't like poetry."

"Sure." He smiles and starts to recite lines from Yeats' poems in a booming voice as we drop down the escalator. "Think where man's glory most begins and ends; And say my glory was I had such friends...."

I give him a shove, but he won't stop.

Other shoppers stare at us, but he still won't stop.

He pays for the book and continues his orations all the way out of the store.

CHAPTER 39

Connor and I arrive at the entrance to Swiss Bank two minutes after twelve.

Akari greets us with a smile, but Blake's lips turn down and one of his eyebrows arches upward, which gives off the impression that he's annoyed and confused at the same time. "Where's the tie? We bought a perfectly good tie yesterday. What did you do with it?"

Connor yanks a new, yet wrinkled, navy tie from his suit pocket. "I have no idea how to fasten the bloody thing."

"It's silk. You're not supposed to stuff it in your pocket like a used handkerchief." Blake waves him over. "Give it to me."

When Blake finishes, Connor straightens it and grins. "So, do I look like James Bond, or what?"

"Or what!" Akari and I say at the same time.

"Come on! Not one of the early geezers but the last guy, Daniel Craig." He lifts his chin and sports a sly smile in his best Hollywood pose.

Akari bursts out laughing.

I shake my head. "Not even close." If I squint my eyes, the comparison actually isn't horrible, but he'll never hear me tell him so.

"You guys are cruel!" He frowns playfully.

"Let's go." Blake hands me the flash drive, yanks Connor's arm, and pulls him through the glass doors into the building.

I hesitate just inside the doors. I've never seen a more elaborate building. Even the casino back home would not compete with this one. Huge arched ceilings with carvings etched into stone overhang the main floor, expensive old-looking portraits hang on the walls, and marble floors squeak under our shoes.

We follow Blake as he strolls toward a black marble reception counter with golden block letters that spell Swiss Bank in the center. He moves easily, as if comfortable among all this excess.

Three women and one man sit behind the counter, waiting to greet clients. A beefy security guard stands on each side of the reception desk, with a metal detector and operator behind them. All this security looks like overkill, but I guess if you're rich you want to know your money's protected.

Blake leans against the counter and talks to a tastefully dressed middle-aged woman on the far left. "Blake Richards to see Darryl Formato. I have three other guests with me. He's expecting us."

The woman offers a totally phony smile, checks her computer and prints four passes. "Place these stickers on your chest and take the elevator to the fifth floor. Mr. Formato will meet you there."

We stroll past the security guards, through the metal detectors and over to the elevators. When a bell rings, the brass doors open and a dozen harried people file out. When the crowd clears, we move inside and press the buttons for the fifth and sixth floors.

"We're lucky it's lunch time," says Blake. "Most people will be leaving and the floors won't be too full."

The bell rings for the fifth floor and Connor grins. "Shouldn't you two hold hands or something? I mean you've got to act like a couple."

Blake actually looks at Akari with a hopeful shine in his eyes.

She swats Connor in the stomach. "We'll be fine. Don't worry about us." She steps off the elevator and they're gone.

We pull the passes from our clothes and leave the elevator when it stops at the next floor. A glass door with a card reader blocks our way onto the floor.

"What now?" whispers Connor.

A group of three youngish men ambles toward us. They must have just shared a joke because all three are laughing. The slight bounce in their step likely means they're headed to lunch.

"Follow me." I saunter toward the glass door and time my arrival for a second *after* they reach it. Since they arrive at the door first, they unlock it from their side and hold it open for us. I smile and, just like that, we're in the clear and on the investment-banking floor.

"Wow." Connor whistles.

The floor is a vast cubicle farm, every inch crammed with people and computers. Flat screens drop down from the ceiling every twenty feet and blare the latest financial news. A long flat table centers the space where two-dozen people sit with headsets plugged into their ears. Each person has at least four computer screens streaming data at them. One guy has six.

How can anyone pay attention to six screens at the same time?

The floor reminds me of the casino back home, with the same electricity and buzz from all the different conversations that blend together. A siren blares from the far end of the floor with swirling lights. A banker raises both hands in triumph, shouts something I can't make out, and hits a button that makes the lights stop.

"We have to find Smyth's office before we trigger the fire alarm." I nod toward the exterior offices that ring the floor. "Blake said he's a hotshot, which probably means a corner office."

We can't just stand by the elevators and gawk, so we start out toward the right.

A pleasant looking young guy with a fleshy face, wire rimmed glasses, and eager brown eyes walks toward us. He's definitely spotted us and slows to a halt as we approach.

"Hi, I don't think we've been introduced. My name's Michael Weber. I'm in Structured Products." When he mentions the name of the group he works for, he lifts his chin and smirks in a self-important way.

I nod my head seriously, as if I'm impressed. "I'm Juliet Stone and this is--"

Connor thickens his accent. "Daniel Craig. We're interns from the London office, just flew over the pond today. Be a good chap and point out Peter Smyth's office, will you?"

I fight hard not to roll my eyes.

Michael smirks. I'm not sure he has fully bought Connor's act, but he seems like a nice guy who doesn't want to stir up any trouble. "Smyth works in Investment Banking. They're on the other side of the wall." He points toward the far end of the floor and a glass wall that separates those cubicles from everyone else. "You'll need an ID to get through. Compliance worries we might overhear *secret* client information."

He uses air quotes when he says secret, which totally annoys me.

"No problem," says Connor. "You wouldn't happen to know the whereabouts of a pub around here that might play the football matches? Chelsea has a big match—"

I stomp down on his foot, but it's too late.

"Who do you work for in London, again?" he asks, but before we need to make up a name, his phone buzzes and his eyes squint. "Sorry, got to go. Polen's looking for me. I'm sure you've heard about his temper." He hustles away, taking short brisk steps, glancing at his phone as he walks while muttering to himself.

"Laying it on a little think, don't you think, Connor?"

He beams a bright smile. "I told you I could pass for Daniel Craig."

"Right." This time I roll my eyes.

We head toward the investment banking area. Storage rooms, vending machines, and bathrooms are on our left, and a fire alarm hangs near the glass wall. No one pays any attention to us. We won't get a better chance, so....

I pull the red lever down. Sirens go off immediately and the lights flicker. A collective moan erupts from those around us, and a voice from a loudspeaker tells everyone to evacuate the floor.

I drag Connor inside an empty women's restroom not more than ten feet away, and we sneak inside a stall, the two of us pressed close together. His face inches from mine, his breath tickles my cheeks, and his eyes are so close they seem to reach inside me.

"If you wanted to be alone with me you just had to ask," he jokes.

The trance is broken, so I punch him in the stomach. "Be serious."

"Why is everyone hitting me?"

I count off thirty seconds in my head and crack the door open. The floor is deserted, so we hustle to the glass door that leads into the investment banking offices. It's locked. We don't have an ID, so I shove with my enhanced strength and the metal latch snaps.

We race toward the larger of the two corner offices. The brass plate identifies it as Peter Smyth's office.

Connor is first through the door. A computer screen sits on top of a clean oak desk with the tower on the floor underneath. He takes the flash drive from me and starts the computer. When he plugs it in, the words "Cloning in Process" appear and start to blink in red.

"How long do you think we have before someone shows up?" He turns his head to glance out of the office.

I see two guards strolling toward the door I just broke, and pull Connor down to the floor behind the desk. "Not long. Two guards are coming our way."

"So much for having a few minutes." He peeks over the edge of the desk. "The cloning is almost complete, but those two goons are closing in on us."

"We need to get out of here fast," I say, still crouched on the floor. "They have radios on them. If they report us, the floor will be flooded with cops and security."

My heart rate picks up, and when the computer pings I almost jump up. With the cloning finished, Connor disconnects the flash drive, and I shut off the computer.

We don't want them to know we were here. If we run for it, we'll probably get out before they grab us, but they'll know we snuck onto the floor and word would get back to Gagarin. That would be a disaster. We'll be back where we started and lose the element of surprise altogether.

"Follow me. We'll crawl out."

Connor grabs my blouse. "One wrong turn and we'll be face to boot with one of the security guys. I don't fancy that. Believe me, we don't want to be on hands and knees if we run into one of those beefy blokes."

"Just follow me." I crawl from the office and use my mind to scan the floor for others.

They appear like beacons. Three security guards patrol the floor now — one on the other side of the building and two with us in the glass-enclosed restricted area.

I navigate us among the cubicles, zig-zagging down aisles and turning into different rows, always a step ahead of the guards. We stop with our backs pressed against a cubicle wall, stuck one row away from the door while a guard stands only twenty feet away.

He smells like cigarettes and pepperoni. He's standing in place, and we're running out of time.

He barks into the radio, "Better send up the police. There's no fire and I don't like how the door's broken. Something smells fishy."

We're bound to get caught. My hands turn clammy and my stomach feels like I'm plummeting down a roller coaster.

Connor whispers, "Don't worry, I've got this." He sneaks a look over the desk. A second later, files flop from a filling cabinet on the other side of the floor.

"What the heck?" says the security guard as he jogs in that direction.

Connor smiles. "After you, my lady."

We race through the door and down the staircase.

By the time we reach the main floor, the "All Clear" signal has been given, and we have to swim through a stream of bankers who are trying to get back to work.

Akari and Blake wait for us outside.

"Did you clone the computer?" asks Blake.

"Of course we did," says Connor. "Piece of cake for James Bond."

I groan and shove him in the back. "Let's hope there's some useful information on the flash drive, because we need a break."

Blake pockets the drive. "We'll find something."

Akari smirks. "I know... everyone leaves a digital footprint."

"Right." Blake smiles.

I'm not so sure.

CHAPTER

Technology isn't always good. Yes, it's often great. Almost every conceivable piece of information is literally one or two clicks away—the latest in movies, music, trends, books. Oppressed people around the world use social media to stage revolutions and gain freedom. Yet like everything else, technology has a dark side.

Blake is right about digital footprints.

Everything posted online, every transaction, every search and link and photograph and stupid site we visit is recorded somewhere and can be traced back to us. Buy a book at two in the morning and someone, somewhere knows about it. Search for the latest diets and magically *Google* will flood your other search requests with all things diet. Privacy doesn't exist anymore because we rely too much on technology. We don't even think about it. We just assume there are no secrets, that there's no place to hide, no way to stay anonymous.

I doubt the Prime Elector will have the same relationship with technology as we do. He's probably accustomed to technology way more advanced than ours, and not interested in the stuff we have to offer. He'll only be concerned about his plan to take over the planet and enslave us for his own purposes. He'll be smart and careful.

Still, it's easy to mess up, and Smyth could be his weak link.

"The good news is our Peter Smyth is a very organized person." Blake taps on his laptop and the screen in the dining room jumps to life. "He has folders for everything."

Connor points to the top of the screen. "Check out that one. It's labeled Stellar, which seems like as good a place as any to start."

"Sure," says Blake as he rummages through the folder.

It doesn't take long. We only find a few memos about accounts, and wiring instructions, but no address.

"Try emails. Yes, yes, people write the dandiest things in emails." Stuart tugs his beard and flickers his eyes around the room.

When he greeted us at the Inn upon our return, he looked disheveled, his shirt wrinkled and his gaze haunted.

We all deal with stress differently, but it's weird that he looks as if he's about to unravel.

Different file folders appear in Smyth's email account. One is marked Gagarin.

Blake clicks on the most recent email, which came only two hours ago. "Bingo."

The message is short:

Meet me at the Boathouse in Central Park midnight tonight. We need to discuss phase two of the Launch Project. Come alone. G.

"The meeting must be planned for tonight," says Blake.

"I thought Smyth was traveling in Europe," I say.

"He must be on his way back," says Stuart. "This is good news. Time is not on our side. Yes, extremely good news."

Silence covers us, thick and syrupy. It sticks to my skin and seeps beyond, toward my lungs. It replaces the air and steals away my breath. I taste acid in my throat and feel like I've been on a long trip to someplace unpleasant, turned the corner, and found my destination suddenly in front of me.

Can I complete the journey?

If we go to the Boathouse we'll have to murder Gagarin. We can't have any doubts. Doubts will only get us killed.

"What's the Launch Project?" asks Akari.

Blake shrugs. "Could be a new investment strategy."

"Or it could be connected to that drug they want to put into the City's water supply," I say.

Connor says, "It doesn't matter, either way. To finish this thing, we'll have to surprise him at the Boathouse." He sounds confident and sure of himself. "We should go early and stake the place out. That way we can be sure he's alone."

"No, no, that's not a good idea. We can't give him the opportunity to sense our presence. We will lose the chance of surprise. Surprise is essential. No, a better plan is to arrive a few minutes after midnight and then rush him. It's the only way." Stuart glances at us. "It is the only way we can defeat him."

"*We?* You're coming with us?" I thought for sure he'd make up some excuse why he couldn't be part of the mission— something weird about being an Ugly or how he detests violence or how he needs to catch-up on his reading. He doesn't strike me as a brave person.

Maybe this explains why he's so agitated. Now, his life is at risk.

His eyebrows arch upward. "Yes, yes, certainly I will be with you. This is the final test. Just me and you four, I should think."

"What about Sydney and Troy?" asks Akari.

Everyone looks at me. This is my decision, the moment I've dreaded for so long. I can't be weak.

I lock eyes with Connor. "They can't come with us. We are the Chosen. This isn't for them."

He nods.

Troy returns to the Inn two hours later.

I've run through countless versions of our conversation in my head. None end well. The last thing I want in this world is to hurt him. He's my best friend and has always been there for me, but I can't let him face the Prime Elector with us. Maybe that's selfish or maybe it's not. I don't care anymore. It just is.

Finally, the key enters the lock and Troy stands at the doorway. He shuts the door behind him and strides into the suite. His shoulders sway confidently the way they usually do. "So, how did it go at Swiss Bank?"

"Good. We've got a lead on the Prime Elector." I don't like to call the Prime Elector by his name, Gagarin. Prime Elector makes him sound more like a robot and less like a real person. "When did Sydney show up?" Even now I can't keep the frost from my voice when I say her name, and I start to twist the end of my hair.

Troy shrugs. "She was a couple of hours late. It was no big deal."

"I don't trust her, Troy. She's manipulative and acting weird." We have more important things to talk about than

Sydney, but my mouth flaps open and words spew out as if they were a flock of birds heading south for the winter. I can't stop them.

Troy touches my arm, his hands warm and strong. "Listen, Jules, there's no reason for you to be jealous of Sydney. You and I are just...." He hesitates.

I want him to say it. On some level I need him to tell me. "Just what, Troy?"

"You know. We're best friends. I love you like a sister. Always have."

The word "sister" magically solidifies in the air, turns into a sledgehammer, and hits me in the stomach.

He's never led me on. He's always had girlfriends. We've never kissed, or even come close to kissing.

I guess I've always known that we weren't meant to be together in a romantic way, yet *knowing* something and having proof smack you in the face are two different things altogether, and this feels like I've flunked out of school. All those fairytales I used to spin about us will need a different ending.

I pull my arm away from him. "Of course, I know *that.*" My face burns. "I just figured you were too fragile for me to say anything. Besides, you're completely not my type."

Troy crosses his arms and grins. "What's wrong with me?"

"Just about everything. For starters, you eat too much and you have a horrible sense of humor."

He lifts his hand. "Okay, we don't need a laundry list."

"Oh, there's more. You snore like a truck driver."

"Hey, that's going too far. I don't snore!"

I do my best imitation of Troy snoring, and we both crack up. Just like that, the pain breaks and we're good again. This is part of growing up. Fairytales with "happily ever after" endings aren't real. Reality is messy, muddled, filled with gray and red and sometimes brilliant yellows.

"What's this lead on the Prime Elector?"

His question reminds me what I need to tell him. My stomach twists and my voice sounds detached. "We have something else to talk about."

He looks right through me. "What's wrong? What aren't you telling me?"

"Why do you think something's wrong?" I turn my back on him and drop on the couch.

"You've never been good at hiding your feelings. Not from me. Remember when you failed the math mid-term in sixth grade?" He sits next to me.

I shake my head. "That was a long time ago. My mom got me a tutor the next day."

"Right, and now you've got the same expression on your face, only worse."

I sigh and tension-filled air blows out of me. "We have a way to get to the Prime Elector. It'll go down tonight. We have to kill him. I'm not sure if I'm ready for that."

He takes my hand. "That's *good* news. I knew the Wind Spirit would help guide us. The Prime Elector is a dark spirit who must be dispatched back to the spirit worlds—the sooner the better. It's the right thing to do. You wouldn't be asked to complete this journey if you couldn't handle it. You have the strength. I know it."

I half smile at him. He reminds me so much of Sicheii, sharing the same belief system. He's a rock—strong and true to his nature—and so much stronger than me. "I wish I was as sure."

He squeezes my hand. "Let me do it then. I'll kill him."

My chest tightens as if a clamp squeezes my heart. I'd rather jump from the window, land on the concrete, and break every bone in my body than have this conversation. I should never have let him come with me. I should have been stronger. It would have been easier back then. I should....

All these alternatives whip through me in a guilt-ridden tsunami.

"That won't work. You...." My voice cracks and my eyes flutter to his duffel on the table. I've already packed for him.

He follows my gaze and sees the bag. "You don't want me to come with you? You want me to leave?"

I fight back tears. I can't cry now. I have to do this one thing right. He can't fight the Prime Elector with us and be in harm's way. "You have to go home. I'll see you when this is over. You've done everything you can—more than you should have. I wouldn't have made it this far without you, but now you have to go."

"This is my choice." He squeezes my hand a little tighter and his eyes pinch together. "Don't send me away. I can help."

I summon all my strength and reach deep inside, deeper than I've ever had to reach before. "No, you can't help." I steel my eyes and turn my heart to stone.

Troy rubs his hands across his face.

Part of me breaks, but I don't—I can't—let those emotions seep into my eyes. I stand because sitting on the couch next to him is no longer an option. He's too close and I need to put distance between us.

He moves next to me. "It's just the same as when you went to that private school. You left me and your other friends behind. We barely got to see you, and now you're doing it again!"

"I hate Bartens! You know that!"

His face reddens. "Part of you hates it, and the other part wants to be accepted by... *them*. You want to be just like *them*!" He spits out the word "them" with such venom. A lifetime of unfair treatment has scratched his voice and made it sound harsh, rubbed raw.

"That's not true." I can't look at him and see the pain and confusion, so I turn and face the window.

The back of my throat burns. I wish he was completely wrong, but a kernel of truth hides in his words.

I *did* separate from my old friends. I told myself the heavy workload at my new school kept me busy, and that we had different stuff going on in our lives, but the materialistic pull from Bartens tugged at me. Even though I never belonged with them, they had everything I was *supposed* to want. I found myself stuck between two worlds, frozen in place, standing on a lake while the ice cracked around me.

"Now you're leaving me for the other Chosen—Connor, Blake, Akari, and Stuart. You think you don't need me, but you're wrong. This is a big mistake." His voice has a pleading quality to it. "We've come this far *together*, and we need to finish this *together*."

When I turn back to face him, all I want is to hold him, but I grit my teeth instead. I have to be stronger. I have to become the Alpha and think of him first, so my voice comes out hard and loud. "That was never your role. You'll make it more dangerous for me—for all of us." I start to tick off the instances and a little of my soul dies each time. "The burglar at the hotel. The fire at the warehouse. The bomb in the church. The car that ran you over by the consulate."

"I was trying to protect you those times, and you can't hold the car against me. I did that one on purpose."

I wrap myself around his shoulders and bury my head into his chest. I won't look into his eyes and I don't want him to see the tears rolling down my cheeks, so I talk into his chest. "I don't hold any of them against you. You get credit for each one, but if you're with us, I'll worry about you and that will —"

"Only make it more dangerous. *I get it.* I'm really just a liability. I can't be trusted. You're better off with Connor and the rest. Except that he can't be trusted. None of them can be!" He pushes me away, his voice toxic.

I wipe the tears from my eyes before he can see them, and grab the leather straps to his duffel.

"So this is it then? You don't need me anymore? You're tossing me out? I've risked everything for you and now you're trading me in?" Fire burns from behind his eyes.

"It's not like that. I'll always need you, but with you, I'll be weaker."

He spins from me and looks out the window.

Part of me wants him to stay more than ever, but this one time his safety has to come first.

I touch his back. "This is the only way."

He turns back toward me. "Give me a chance to prove myself. Just one more chance to protect you."

I can't speak. I can only shake my head.

He pushes past me, takes the duffel from the table, opens it, pulls out our folder of cash, and flips it on the couch. "Sicheii saved that for you, not me. I don't want *your* money."

"How will you get back home without it? I don't need it. The others have plenty."

"I'll make do. It's not mine."

Just when I expect him to storm from the room, he brushes the back of his hand against my cheek. It's such a loving gesture; I almost lose all my resolve. My legs go weak and my knees wobble.

He sighs. "Are you sure?"

"I'm sure."

He turns and stomps from the room, taking with him my last connection to humanity.

I am the Alpha.

CHAPTER

Gagarin studies the self-assured smile on Bailey's face. She is capable, talented even. Perhaps he should invest more time in her, train her, and see how much potential she might possess. Maybe she could evolve into a worthy mate. She's young still, and could advance beyond a Level Two to a Level One Alphian.

There are so few Level Ones among the Deltities. "You've dumped the brainwashing drug in all the aquifers that hold New York City's drinking water?"

"As you wished."

"Good, and you project the mortality rate to be 25%."

She nods. "With a 1% margin of error."

"Excellent." He starts pacing. "The drug is harmless until we broadcast the cellular signal, correct?"

"That's right. The cellular signal activates the drug in the human brain. It will make them compliant with our commands without them knowing it. Twenty-five percent of the time it will create a brain aneurism that causes immediate death."

"Perfect." He smiles as he stops in front of her. "They will be at our mercy. How long until the contaminated water seeps into their drinking supply?"

"Areas in the Bronx will be impacted tonight. It will take a full week for the entire drinking supply to be poisoned."

"That's ideal. We don't want everyone dying in one day. That would look suspicious. They need to believe that a plague has fallen on them. Yes, a plague brought down by their God. Panic will grip them and we will hold the key. We will start the Launch Project tonight."

"They will panic."

"Yes, at first, but our strength will save them. We will free them from their oppression. They don't know it, but they need us."

Her eyebrows arch upward. "They need us?"

He strokes her moist lips with his fingertip. "Of course they do. They need a strong master. All this freedom oppresses them. They don't know what to do with it. They squander it on base pleasures and ruin their own planet. Without us, they will make Earth uninhabitable. It's only a matter of time. We will give them a purpose and set them on a path for the higher good. They will be fulfilled and be more content because of it. The Elders will say we are enslaving them, but they don't understand the natural order of the universe. We free them by dominating them."

His grip tightens on her lip and he breaks her skin with his fingernail. A trickle of blood winds down her chin, and he smiles.

CHAPTER

As I head down the stairs to the lobby, one question blocks my thoughts like a boulder in the middle of a narrow road that can't be avoided. Circling it, I examine it from all angles.

Is killing the Prime Elector our only option?

I think it is, and Stuart says it is. Reasoning with the Prime Elector seems futile and way too risky—he'll be too powerful and we'll lose any chance at surprise.

If there's some other way to defeat him, we had better think of it soon, because the objective of this mission is simple and direct—murder. In truth I couldn't have killed the burglar we faced at Roy's Red Roof Inn, or the greasy-haired guy at the warehouse. A part of me wanted to, but the rest, the part raised by Sicheii, would not have let me. So the current plan fills me with dread and doubt, but I can't think of another way around the boulder.

The others wait for me by the door.

Blake wears a Polo shirt, khakis, and fancy loafers, as if he's headed to a country club for a round of golf.

Akari wears a loose-fitting T-shirt and jeans, and the handle of her fishing knife shows where it's tucked into the back of her pants.

Stuart looks like a shadow in all black.

Connor has the Chelsea jersey he wore when I first met him.

We all wear what makes us comfortable, what fits us.

I touch the wind catcher pendant tucked under my shirt, the only personal item I have to bring with me. Sicheii said it would protect me when I need it, and I'll certainly need it tonight.

"It looks like the gang's all here," says Connor, his voice serious for once.

In an effort to lighten the somber mood a little, I say, "What stinks?" and wrinkle my nose. "It's the jersey. It smells like beer. You could've washed it."

Connor grins. "It's my lucky shirt. I never clean it. All the luck would wash away with the suds."

"Oh, that explains it." I force a grin.

"We should leave. Yes, yes, I think it's time." Stuart solemnly holds the door open for us and glances toward the floor. I try to catch his eye, but his gaze stays downcast. He must know the long odds we face, and doesn't want me to see his lack of confidence.

I walk past him, into the cool night and toward my destiny. My sword pulses from inside the string bag that's once again slung over my shoulder. The pulses match my heart rate—fast. The odds are against us, but I don't care about the odds—not now, anyway.

We get into a car out front.

Stuart drives us to 72nd and 5th Avenue, where he parks in a tow zone. I glance at the sign, and he just shrugs. He's right: that's the least of our worries.

When we enter the park, Blake asks, "Do you think he'll be alone?"

"I doubt he's got mates with him to play poker," says Connor

"No," I say, "but we can't assume he doesn't have another Deltite with him either. We know two live in that consulate."

"Yes, yes," Stuart says, "but it seems like he wants to meet Smyth alone. That's what the email said. Either way we must concentrate on Gagarin. He's the key. The other Deltites are not important." He leads us toward the lake and the Boathouse.

"Not important so long as they're not trying to kill us," Blake mumbles.

I grab his arm and pull him to a stop. "Everyone we find in that Boathouse will try to kill us. It's them or us. Don't hesitate to act, because *they* won't." I don't mean to be harsh, but he's got to hear the truth and be prepared, or it will flatten him.

He nods.

We continue to walk, until the slippery moonlight dusts against the lake in the distance, revealing the outline of the Boathouse.

Stuart checks his watch. "12:15. We should hurry."

I survey the faces around me—good faces, trustworthy, brave. "When we go in, we use all our abilities—wind, fire, water, telekinetic, whatever. Feel the power surge and it'll be enough."

"Do you sense anyone in the Boathouse?" asks Connor.

I quiet my thoughts and switch my mind to hyper-mode. Auras burst and energy flows around me in waves. "At least one Deltite is inside. I can't get a specific read on how many. It's not clear, but the energy is intense."

When I grab the Seeker Slayer, the blade appears and sends a shudder through me. My body feels electric as the blade senses what's next, as if it has a mind of its own. I get the weird feeling it wants blood.

290

Connor stands next to me, so close, only a heartbeat away. His eyes pulse and his shaggy hair flips in front of his face in the breeze.

When I sweep his hair back, his eyes lock onto mine and time freezes. He leans into me and presses his lips against mine, soft and eager.

My world spins.

We separate for a second and I reach for him, pushing my lips against his, feeling a heat I've never known before. His lips part and we collide. My body is engulfed in flames and every nerve sparks. My insides turn volcanic, but then I push him back. Another second longer and I might not have been able to stop.

We're both out of breath.

He grins mischievously. "Now I have something worth fighting for." He winks at me, glances at the others and shouts, "For King and country!"

He bolts forward and we follow him.

I can't even feel my body. I'm floating on a wave of energy.

Connor hits the doors to the Boathouse first and dashes through them with me close on his heels.

We pause when we enter the high-end restaurant. Picture windows face the lake, and at the end of the main dining room, we find an open door with light flickering from inside. The smell of incense hangs in the air.

Connor surges forward, and in a second we burst into a large round banquet hall ringed by six-foot candles.

We stop a few steps inside, Blake and Akari breathing heavily at our sides.

The Prime Elector sits at a table facing toward us.

A man dressed in a suit has his back to the door — the stranger must be Smyth.

The Prime Elector smiles as we enter.

Connor and I step forward with our swords out front.

The man in the suit stands and turns—he's big, his jacket fitting tightly over well-muscled arms and a massive chest—and points a handgun at us.

He's not Smyth.

CHAPTER

Two other Deltites charge into the room from a back door, holding swords in their hands. A second later, two granite slabs of muscle burst through glass doors by the terrace, wielding pistols.

We're outnumbered and surrounded.

"Oh, bloody hell!" says Connor.

"You knew we were coming." My face burns and the muscles in my jaw ache.

"Of course I did," says Gagarin. An arrogant edge cuts his words as he lifts a sword in his hand. "*You were invited.*"

"How could you possibly know?" asks Blake. "We just intercepted that email today."

"Unless a snitch betrayed us." Connor spits out the words.

"It must have been Sydney." I clench my hilt in a death grip as I imagine chocking the life out of her. I knew we couldn't trust her. She's no better than the girls back at Bartens—only interested in herself.

We can still retreat. Maybe the others can escape, if I buy them time. I'm about to shout at them to run, when Stuart locks the door behind us and blocks the way out.

Light bends around him and the doors, but the distortion from his force field can't hide the guilt carved into his features.

Heat singes my face. "You're the traitor. It isn't Sydney, after all."

Stuart nods. His eyes look sad, and his voice lacks its usual bubbly character, as if regret weighs down his words. "Once Blake came up with the plan to clone the computer, the rest was easy. Yes, yes, easy."

"You mangy runt!" grumbles Akari.

Stuart betrayed us; Troy was right.

"If you put down those swords, I give you my word that I'll finish you off quickly," says Gagarin. "This way none of your families will be harmed. Otherwise, this will be a very long night, indeed. It will be morning by the time I finish torturing you, and then I will have to kill everyone you care about. You hybrids are no match for us. Don't be foolish and make this worse for you than you must. Now is not the time for mindless bravery."

He makes it sound as if killing our families is just a simple chore.

Worry ripples through me and keeps me grounded. I turn to face the other Chosen. Grim determination is chiseled into their faces and etched in their eyes. We might have lost the element of surprise, but we haven't lost our resolve.

I turn back to face him. "We'd like to thank you for gathering so neatly together. We really only wanted to kill the Prime Elector, but since you all came with him, we might as well clean out the entire rats' nest."

Gagarin cackles. "You know nothing. You are all silly pieces in a game you can't comprehend."

"Comprehend this!" Akari pushes her hands forward. The air sparks and a fireball flies toward Gagarin.

He flicks his wrist and a disc shape of reddish energy shields him and blocks the flames.

A wolf four times the normal size materializes before us, made of pure energy. It bounds toward Connor, mouth open, razor sharp paws about to carve into his chest, and jumps.

Connor slices through its neck with his sword and rolls to the side at the last second.

The energy creature bounds past him and turns. A gash appears in the creature's neck, but it closes almost instantly. The wolf howls and charges. Connor flips a table across the beast's path, but the apparition leaps and smashes through it.

It will land on him. Connor won't stand a chance.

I react on instinct and create the same energy bands I used at the abandoned warehouse. I whip them around the wolf's neck and it squeals as I yank it to a stop mid-leap.

Connor thrusts his sword into the animal's chest and the beast vanishes in an explosion of light.

Another energy creature appears in front of us, this time an eagle the size of a small car. It squawks and flies toward Akari. She blasts it with a fireball, yet it still comes.

Blake generates a wind gust that slows the bird, but it'll be upon her in seconds.

I imagine a spear, which appears in my hand — made from my energy. The bird is about to reach Akari when I heave the spear at it. It scores — the eagle screeches and disappears — but I drop to my knees, all my strength drained from me.

Gagarin chortles.

My head spins; I can't concentrate, and the room turns gray.

Gagarin can lop off my head with one easy stroke. I'm defenseless.

295

"You're nothing. What a pity." Gagarin clicks his tongue. "I was hoping for something *extraordinary*. Once again I'm disappointed. You're no better than the miracle child."

His sword swooshes in the air.

I struggle to lift my head, to at least see the end, but Connor jumps between Gagarin and me, and then Akari and Blake join him.

"You'll have to bloody well go through us." Connor challenges him.

"When I want her dead, she will be dead." Gagarin laces his voice with amusement. "There's nothing you can do to stop me."

I shake my head to clear it. Flashes of light appear in front of my eyes as energy from the other Chosen flows to me. Life sparks and returns to my body, and color seeps back into my vision. I stagger to my feet and notice red vines slithering around my legs. By the time I turn to face Gagarin, vines cover my whole body; they're too strong for me to break free.

Connor curses. Similar vines wrap around him, Blake, and Akari.

Gagarin has frozen us with his own energy bands. The animal creatures were a mere distraction.

Creating the spear stole all my energy, and I didn't have enough left to prevent the vines from binding us.

Fear grips me. I try to break his hold, but he's too powerful, too focused.

He lifts us off the ground and howls with pleasure. "Your powers are childish." He marches toward me and stops only two feet away. "You are Juliet Wildfire Stone, correct?"

When I don't say anything, he squeezes the vines and I gasp from the pain. "Yes!"

"I thought you were the Alpha. Interesting, but I do not see anything extraordinary in you. The Ugly warned me to be careful with you, but really, you are nothing more than a child."

I grit my teeth. "Your plan won't succeed."

"Oh *please*." Gagarin removes a small glass vial from his pocket. It's the same size and shape as those in the fridge at the townhouse. "I see from your expression that you recognize this. We've dumped enough of this drug in the City's aquifers to poison the entire drinking supply."

"Why kill everyone?" I snarl at him.

He laughs.

"He's gone mental," says Connor.

"No, not mental, you insignificant worm." He waves his hand at Connor and a gash appears across his forehead as if he's sliced into him with a knife.

I struggle but his energy does not slacken.

Gagarin turns back toward me. "We won't kill everyone. Once I broadcast a signal from our cellular towers, humans will be susceptible to my suggestions. Sure, millions will die, but the others will do my bidding without even realizing it. My superiors will be very pleased with me."

A flash of light from outside catches my attention. I sneak a glance and see Sydney, Troy, Frankie, Landon, and Amare— they're standing on the terrace that faces the lake.

It seems I have misjudged Sydney.

Troy signals for me to keep talking and buy them more time.

"How sad! I would have thought you'd be able to conquer a planet without drugging everyone." I snicker. "Some Prime Elector you are."

The bands tighten and it feels as if an elephant sat on my chest and crushed the air from my lungs.

297

"I'm not the Prime Elector, you fool. Do you really think the Prime Elector would be the face of a private equity fund? Someday I *will* be the Prime Elector on this stinkpot of a planet, and much more than that. Unfortunately, you won't be around to see it."

Frankie and Troy creep toward one of the doors that separate the banquet hall from the terrace, while Landon and Amare move toward the other. Sydney stays back.

Despair builds inside me as my eyes fix on Troy. I couldn't keep him away. I failed at the one task I couldn't afford to fail at, and Gagarin is too powerful for me. When Troy tries to save me, he'll die.

Connor curses from behind me, but I don't pay any attention. My angst turns to anger that erupts inside me and threatens to consume me. It feels like it did in the sweat lodge when I had to pass the first test to survive. I used the anger then to focus my energy. *Could it work again?*

Gagarin lifts a crystal tablet. "I guess you're wondering why I haven't killed you yet...."

Anger shoves aside my fear. It grows from a spark until it blazes into a wildfire. I mold it and power surges in response. His grasp is still too tight, but the bands loosen, so at least I can breathe and focus on what he's saying.

"By using this tablet, I can start broadcasting the signal. All it will take is one touch of my hand." Gagarin takes his time, a smug look on his face. He's enjoying himself.

He moves his hand inches from the crystal. He's about to start the broadcast and kill millions.

The doors crash open.

Troy, Landon, Frankie, and Amare charge into the room.

Surprised, Gagarin loses his focus on us and spins, and his grasp weakens even further.

I concentrate all my mental power on the vines that grip us, and snap them.

We fall to the floor and total havoc breaks out.

I'm in the eye of a tornado.

Time slows to a crawl.

Connor leaps forward and swipes his sword at the male Deltite off to the left, filling the room with the sounds of shattering glass.

Landon struggles with one of the security guards while Amare swings a club at another one.

A fireball erupts and is whisked aside by the female Deltite, but Blake uses the moment to slice into her side with his sword.

Akari bends her knees, ready to leap, but she freezes. Strain shows on her face, her eyes widen, and she lowers her sword.

The female Deltite whirls from Blake. Nothing separates her from Akari. She smiles and bends her legs to lunge forward.

Blake's too far away to block her, so I try to grab her with my mind, but my thoughts bounce off her.

Akari's still frozen, stuck in a panic attack.

Blake conjures a tornado and spins it around her, creating a wind funnel with her in the middle.

The Deltite thrusts her sword forward, but the wind is too strong and knocks her blade to the side.

Blake leaps forward and tackles the Deltite, and they go down in a jumble.

I can't see who has the advantage, but Blake stands, blood dripping from his blade.

From the corner of my eye, I notice one of the security guys leveling his gun at Troy. My heart stops.

He pulls the trigger and Troy dives to the side. The guard aims at him again.

This time I use telekinesis to yank his arm upward, and though the guns fires, the second shot misses.

Frankie bull-rushes him and tackles him in a full-on collision. I can hear the thud from across the room as they crash through a table.

"Troy!' My breath catches in my throat. I expect his aura to turn black but it stays white.

He grins at me, jumps to his feet, and runs to help Connor.

I can breath again.

I want to protect him and Connor and the others. My instinct tears at me to make sure they don't get hurt, but they'll never be safe unless we get Gagarin. I need to take him out to protect them.

I search the chaos and find him across the room.

His eyes find mine, and a flicker of doubt crosses his face. He turns and plunges out a side door.

I take one last look at the others and race after him.

Connor screams, "Juliet, don't!"

I ignore him and race toward the door. A heartbeat later I'm through it and in a courtyard.

The fear from Gagarin's eyes is gone.

The door slams shut behind me. Red energy seals it.

"Now you're mine. They can't help you, and once I kill you, I'll kill the rest."

CHAPTER

In my haste to protect the others, I've left myself vulnerable, on my own away from the herd.

The red energy he's projecting totally seals the door back into the Boathouse.

I won't make it through his blockade, but I don't want to go back. It's time to stand on my own. I want him. I'm the Alpha and this is my responsibility. "It looks like it's just you and me."

"Good. We can fight to the death. It has been too long since I last killed someone."

I point the edge of my sword at his chest. "You'll find out that I'm not so easy to kill."

He waves his arms over his head in a grand gesture and conjures a massive creature of pure energy. It resembles a lion with three heads, sharp talons instead of front paws, and two massive back legs. When it roars, all three heads bellow at once.

I shudder. This energy creature is worse than anything I've ever dreamed of, but I can't let fear overcome me.

I have to create my own creature to combat his monster. Like so many other bits of knowledge the Fusions have given me, it triggers at the right time, and I know how to do it. I generate the first animal that comes to mind — Sicheii's animal guide.

I imagine it — and a giant hawk soars above us.

The lion creature leaps.

The hawk swoops.

Sharp jagged teeth are about to rip off my head when the hawk snatches the lion in its claws and lifts the beast above me. Still, the lion's talons swipe at me. Hot wind blows against my face and heat fries my hair.

As the hawk soars upward, the lion creature turns on it. The middle head sinks its teeth into a leg and the hawk let's go of the beast. Wings instantly sprout from the lion's body and it flies toward the hawk. The two apparitions collide with a massive explosion, as if a bomb has detonated.

The ground shakes.

Gagarin claps his hands together. "You are more powerful than I thought. Good. I hoped you would present some challenge, even if it will be meager. At least you are not a coward. You will have to die the old fashioned way — my sword shall drink of your blood."

He flicks his sword in front of him and half bows his head. The muscles in his hand tense and his eyes narrow.

A wind rustles.

I need to be unpredictable, so I take the fight to him and leap forward.

We collide in a blur, the swords swirling at blinding speeds. The crashing and shattering sounds of our swords connecting explode around us, and we move so fast that sparks fly when the blades connect.

I swipe at his left side just as he spins away and rakes the edge of his sword across my left thigh. The blade cuts through my jeans, blood seeps from the wound, and my leg buckles.

He cackles.

I scramble to my feet and fly toward him with my blade thrusting at his chest. He parries my thrust, and I swipe at his neck.

He ducks under and nicks my other leg with his blade.

It feels like ice.

He slices at me from every conceivable angle: downward chops, then sideswipes followed by thrusts. He moves so fast, he's a blur.

I react instinctively more than by sight.

We lock swords for a second, his pushing against mine. He's not even sweating, whereas I'm drenched. I shove with all my strength and we separate.

He's too fast and his arms are too long for me; I need an advantage, some new weapon I can use. For the first time, the details of the courtyard come to view: a brick floor, low four-foot brick walls, a couple of black metal tables and chairs.

I flick a chair at him with a mental shove, but he blocks it with his own mind and sends it crashing into the Boathouse.

"The Elders are such cowards. Do they really think a few hybrids and one Alpha might defeat us? What arrogant fools." He jumps forward and plunges his sword at my chest.

I knock it away, a hair's breadth from my body, but he flicks the tip up and it nicks my ear and draws blood.

"They've summoned a Gathering." I try hard not to let my voice crack. "They'll come for you."

He smiles and a chill settles in my bones. "By the time the Alphians have enough courage to face us, it will be too late. Earth will be ours and that will be enough for us to defeat them. Not that it will matter to you—your time is finished."

I slide behind a table to keep some distance between us, but he glances at it and throws it off to the side with his mind.

Nothing separates us now.

As he's about to attack, the sound of footsteps draws our attention.

Connor appears—he's raced around the outside of the Boathouse.

Gagarin forms a new force field over the four-foot brick wall, which blocks Connor from joining us.

He throws himself against the reddish light, but it does no good. "Juliet!" he screams.

"I'll kill him soon enough, when you're finished. They won't stand a chance without you."

Akari and Blake appear at Connor's side. They all dive into the red force field, yet it holds.

Gagarin smiles and plunges forward in a wild attack. He moves so fast, I barely have time to leap out of the way as he swipes his blade at my legs.

I backflip away from him a second before another swipe would have cut me in half, and land with my back against the wall.

"There is nowhere else for you to hide, Juliet Wildfire Stone." My blood drips from his blade. "You and your friends are about to die. Where should I cut you first?"

"You can have me, but let them go. They're no threat to you."

He chuckles. "The time for deals is long past. I'm going to drain their blood, preserve their bodies, and throw them at the Elders' feet."

I can't let them *die because* I *failed.*

Sicheii's voice fills my head. "Little Bird, have you learned nothing?"

Help me.

"Remember the test in the Cathedral? When you joined hands you were connected with the others. That was the true purpose of the test. You are the Alpha — you can harness their power and use it to defeat your enemies."

I concentrate on the other Chosen and send them a vision of us joined together at the Cathedral. I hope it works like it did for Troy when we were at the consulate. It's all I can muster.

Gagarin sneers; a lethal twinkle sparkles in his eyes.

Connor's energy floods to me. The link comes easily, and a rush of power bolsters my own energy.

Then, Blake's and Akari's energies links to mine.

Our collective power channels through me and I feel like the sun, full of unspeakable strength.

He must sense that I'm different because his voice falters. "What's happened to your aura?" He squints his eyes. "It's so bight and full of... color?"

"I'm the Alpha."

He attacks, but he seems to move in slow motion. I easily knock his side cut away with my blade and slap him with the back of my left hand across his face.

He spins around, blood dripping from his lips. When he regroups, he jabs his blade at my chest.

I sidestep the thrust and plant a front-kick in his stomach.

He stumbles backward. "What's happening?"

"For an advanced race you're not too smart."

I flick my wrist and cut his arm with my sword before he can react. Another flick and I slice his chest. "You're losing."

He glances toward the other Chosen, but his strength is gone and the force field shatters. He swipes his sword at my head in desperation.

I duck and punch him in the face with the hilt of my sword.

Crack!

His nose breaks as he stumbles against the Boathouse. He drops his sword and it clatters to the ground. His hands shake and blood gushes from his nose.

I point my blade at his throat.

His eyes narrow to small pricks of light. "I can't believe they would stoop so low. You're an... an *abomination*. It's prohibited!"

"What are you mumbling about? I'm the Alpha."

The other Chosen crowd around me, with Connor right beside me.

Troy joins us and stands beside Connor.

Gagarin smiles a sickly grin. "You'll find out."

I press the tip of my sword against his flesh, and blood trickles down his neck in a small river. "Where can I find the Prime Elector."

"Never." His eyes are wild like those of an untamed horse. "Some fates are worse than death."

He won't tell us where to find the Prime Elector. He'll stay defiant until the end.

The moment I've dreaded for so long is here. *I have to kill him.* He deserves to die and we have no other choice. Still, I hesitate.

"Ha!" he laughs. "You are too weak to kill me. You can't do it!"

I've lost the connection with the other Chosen. The sword is frozen.

He starts to use his mind and the blade trembles. In a few more seconds, he'll turn it on me.

Connor wraps his hand around mine. "We're all in this together. You don't have to do this alone."

Akari and Blake add their hands. We are linked again and the power returns.

Troy layers his hands on top of ours. "It's time to send this devil back to the spirit lands."

My sword's blade blazes with an intense bright light that threatens to blind me as I glance into Gagarin's wild, defiant eyes.

He's too strong to keep as a prisoner. He'll either escape or find a way to kill us. He's chosen this fate for himself.

His sneer turns to panic at the last second.

I nod and we push the blade into his neck.

He gurgles as blood spills from his mouth. He opens his mouth as if to utter a last defiant word, but he can't. He collapses to the ground and reaches out for his sword. The hilt slides into his outstretched hand. As his aura fades, the hilt cracks and turns to dust.

An eerie quiet settles over us as we stare at his lifeless body. I expect to feel remorse for killing him, but I'm numb. Maybe it will hit me later, but I don't think so.

The blood has drained from Blake's face and his voice trembles. "We had to kill him, right? We had no choice."

Troy nods. "He was a dark spirit. We did the right thing."

I stare at his lifeless figure and can't help but wonder what he was going to say with his last words.

I have the sinking feeling they might have been important.

CHAPTER

Connor grumbles. "All this and he's not the bloody Prime Elector. We're back where we started."

"Well, what about Stuart? Maybe he knows how to find the real Prime Elector," Blake says.

Akari pushes through the door and we race back into the banquet hall.

Stuart has collapsed against a wall.

Landon stands over him, his expression grave. "He's been shot. It doesn't look good."

Stuart's aura flickers. He's still alive but just by the smallest margin.

I bend down and stare into his eyes. "Why?"

He looks at me, his eyes wide and moist. "Yes, yes, why indeed. They captured me and dragged me away in a Con Edison truck." He half coughs and half laughs. "A Con Edison truck. They wanted me to betray you. They always expect the worst from Uglies. I helped them plant the email, but I told Sydney and Troy about it. That was the only way we could truly surprise them."

Sydney nods at me.

I remember the tunics Troy found in his closet. "You weren't really sent here to guide us, were you?"

He tries to sit up, but he can't summon the strength and slides back down. "No, no, not me. There was an Alphian master who was supposed to be the Host. Yes, yes, he was to help, but he died after we arrived. I did my best."

"You did good."

He grabs my shirt. "I did this for you, not for them! To us Uglies there is little difference between the Deltites and the Alphians. We are nothing to either of them. The slave doesn't care who his master is. But you are better than they are. You don't deserve this fate."

"Who is the Prime Elector?"

"I don't know. I thought it was Gagarin, but he isn't strong enough. Yes, yes, he was not strong enough." He glances behind me. "If you could access the computer, you might find out. He uses it to communicate...." He coughs and spits out blood. "I'm sorry I wasn't stronger, that I wasn't special."

He closes his eyes and they won't open again. He's gone.

He was special, in his own way. He, a slave, ended up sacrificing himself for us, and we were so self-absorbed that we barely noticed. He could have hidden from us, lived on Earth with his freedom. Still he tried to help.

Would I have done as much in his place?

Connor touches my arm. Drying blood is smeared across his forehead and his shoulder, but neither wound looks too bad.

Blake limps a bit and has a nasty burn on his arm.

Akari appears untouched.

Troy smiles at me even though blood has crusted on his lips and cheeks and drenches his shirt.

"You got hit in the nose again?"

He shrugs. "It's my weak spot."

I wrap my arms around him. For a heartbeat, I'm the girl I was before, before I knew about the Chosen or the Deltites, but that moment quickly vanishes.

I'll never be that girl again. I'm the Alpha. I must stand apart, and for the first time, I think I'm strong enough to do it.

I whisper in his ear, "Thanks. You're amazing. I should never have sent you away."

"You can't get rid of me that easily."

I push him away and stomp on his foot.

"Hey!"

"Why didn't you tell me you were coming?"

"Sydney only told me an hour ago. We were the back-up plan. We didn't know the whole situation."

I survey the rest of the damage.

The banquet hall has been through a war. Both Deltites are dead. Blood pools on their chests. One security guard is knocked unconscious. The other two are missing. They must have run when things got weird.

Frankie limps over. He has a gash in his leg, and has tied his shirt around his thigh in a makeshift tourniquet. His bare chest looks like one of those ancient Greek statues. He shakes his head. "I thought I'd witnessed some intense stuff before, but that was the craziest shit I've ever seen. Good thing you're in our family, sister."

Amare stands right behind him. He looks unharmed, but his face is pure ash. He holds a lit cigarette in one hand that shakes, and lifts a crystal sword hilt in the other. "Where's the blade?"

I chuckle. I'll have to tell them the full story later, but first I need to try the crystal computer. If there's a chance that it will lead me to the Prime Elector, it can't wait. I lift the thin crystal and study it. It's a little larger than my hand—beautiful, thin—and bluish light reflects from inside its structure.

Gagarin was about to place his palm in the middle to start it.

I lift my hand and inch it toward the center of the crystal. It vibrates as I press against it. It feels cool to the touch.

I feel as if I'm standing on the edge of a platform and trains are whooshing past me at top speed—not one train, but an endless progression of trains, one after the other. Each zips past me from different directions and misses me by inches. I'm whipped in all directions at the same time as thoughts, images, and ideas ricochet through my mind with each whoosh. I concentrate on only one thought: the Prime Elector.

My hand starts to burn, sizzling from the heat emanating from the computer.

The crystal cracks.

The trains stop and I see a face. He looks young, his eyes an arctic blue—the color of pure ice, with electric lavender swirls that pulse inside them.

They blink.

I realize he's looking back at me, and I drop the tablet.

I fall, and the world spins from gray to black.

CHAPTER 46

A soft breeze warms my face as the sun brightens a cobalt sky. It's a spring sun, the kind that lightens the world with color and clarity. The air smells fresh—a mix of grass and earth and recently fallen rain.

Sicheii stands next to me, wearing a white linen shirt that billows in the breeze. His favorite pair of Lucky jeans fits loosely around his legs. Comfortable deerskin moccasins cover his feet, and a wide brim hat with a hawk's feather stuck in the band tilts on his head the way he always used to wear it.

We're standing on a small nob of a hill with a herd of buffalo grazing around us. They stretch out as far as I can see, an ocean of brown furry giants content to munch grass and soak up the sun.

He grins at me.

"Am I dead? Is this the spirit lands?" I'm not scared. I just want to understand.

"Yes and no. Maybe some of both." He shrugs. "Do you remember the conversation we had when you were little? How I wondered what it would be like to stand among the great herds as they existed when our ancestors roamed the plains?"

"Yes, but those herds have died away. This has to be my imagination."

He lifts his arms outward, the wind gusts, and his shirt flaps in the breeze. "The spirit of the herd lives. Such a strong spirit could never vanish completely. Time does not run in a straight line. It flows like an ocean with currents that move at different speeds. The surface travels much faster than the deep bottom."

I turn and watch the animals in silence for a long moment, transfixed by their beauty and power—not individually so much, but collectively, as if they are of one mind and body.

"I'm not like them. I have no herd. I'm alone."

Sicheii frowns. "You are not alone, never alone. You stand apart, yet you remain part of the herd. You are strong enough to face the wind without shelter from other trees. So you must face the wind even when it gusts."

I recall how I linked my energy with the other Chosen. We *were* joined, if only for a moment. Still I had to face Gagarin alone. It was my responsibility to defeat him. But I'm not finished. Not yet. I remember the young eyes in the crystal computer and shudder. My destiny is intertwined with those eyes, the electric orbs of the Prime Elector.

Sicheii touches my cheek with his fingertips. "I never told you this, but you have your grandmother's smile. There is much of her in you."

I grab his hands, the strongest hands I have ever known. "Will you stay with me?"

He pulls them from me. "I am always with you, but you know that already."

313

"I'm afraid this destiny will be too hard, that I'm not strong enough."

His stare reaches deep inside of me, to a place deeper than muscle and blood and bone. "We all have demons to contend with and fears to conquer. True strength is fighting back against them and still doing what is right."

I think of Landon and the demons he brought back with him from Afghanistan, and of Frankie, who regrets his early life in the projects. I think of the other Chosen and Stuart. They all have flaws. No one is perfect. Still, they wrestle with their faults and find a way to overcome them.

"But what if he's stronger than me? Those eyes from the crystal scare me."

"Those are Coyote's eyes, the trickster. They should frighten you. Only a fool or a child would not be afraid of him. You are neither." A hawk squawks above us. "There is more I must tell you."

He looks remorseful as he sweeps his long white hair from his face.

"Tell me now."

"Coyote is not all bad, just as the Wind Spirit is not all good. You will be faced with a choice. Follow your heart."

"What choice? What should I do? Tell me!"

"This I cannot help you with." He turns from me and strolls down the small hill. "You are the Chosen. Only you can decide our fate."

"Come back!"

He waves at me and blends in with the herd.

I try to follow him with my eyes, but he's gone.

He's left me with more riddles and questions, just as he always does.

314

A howl from a pack of wolves pierces the air, and the ground shakes. The herd has been spooked, and they stampede in an explosion of energy.

I open my eyes and see Troy hovering above me.

CHAPTER

47

It takes a moment before my eyes bring Troy's face into focus. I sit up, but it takes a few seconds for me to realize where I am, my mind still a little foggy. "We're in The Underground?"

He nods.

Connor, Blake, and Akari join us.

Blake speaks softly, as if worried a loud noise might hurt me. "Well, we couldn't go back to the Inn. It isn't safe. This was the only place we could think of."

A drill bores a hole into my head and my brains want to gush out. I wince.

"Are you okay?" Connor's face twists with worry as his hand strokes my hair.

The hole closes and the pain in my head subsides, leaving behind a dull ache that I shake off. "I'm fine. I feel as if one of those paving trucks rolled over my head and flattened it. How long was I out?"

"A day and a half," says Akari. "We were going to take you to a hospital if you didn't wake soon."

I scan the abandoned pub and find no one with us. "Where's Landon?"

"We told him and Frankie everything," says Connor. "They wouldn't have believed us except they saw too much with their own eyes, and we all know how bloody convincing those swords can be. They want to help with the Prime Elector, but we gave them the slip and snuck to The Underground. They don't know where we are."

I sit up straighter and brush my hair from my face. I'm on a futon stuffed in the corner of the room. "Good. They've done enough. What about the mess at the Boathouse?"

"The police don't know what to make of it," says Troy.

Blake smirks. "The news is calling it the 'Bloodbath at the Boathouse.' They don't have any suspects."

"Gagarin would have killed me if it wasn't for you guys." I smile at them and feel my heart burst. I'm not alone. We've become a team, closer even — a family. "Thanks."

"We didn't do anything you wouldn't have done for us." Blake looks taller, standing straighter with his head held high.

"That was some wind funnel you created."

"Well, of course. Child's play." Blake grins and forms a miniature tornado by his side.

We all laugh and it feels good. "What about the drug in the water supply? We have to stop them." A jolt of adrenaline shoots into my body. "If they activate that cellular signal, millions of people will die."

"Landon knows all about it, Jules," Troy says. "His friend at the hospital is working on it. Apparently she's made progress. She thinks magnesium will dissolve it in the water. They just have to figure out how much to add to the aquifers. Landon thinks she's close."

Blake adds, "I wired him enough money so funds won't be a problem. The hospital's lab is working around the clock." He lifts a water bottle. "Until then we drink only from these."

Connor lifts the broken crystal tablet from the Boathouse. It's blackened and shattered. "What about the Prime Elector? Did you learn anything from this to help? We all tried to start the bloody thing, but it's cracked. I couldn't get anything from it."

"None of us could," adds Akari.

All their eyes turn to me.

Their desperation and my responsibility twist together until it becomes a heavy woolen blanket that threatens to suffocate me. We have no other leads. I could tell them nothing. Maybe I should send them on their way, find the Prime Elector on my own, and leave them out of it.

I stroll toward the bar and let them follow in my wake, to allow me a moment to think. When I reach the bar, I've made my decision. They *are* Chosen like me. I can't hide this from them. It's not that I can't go on without them, but it would be wrong to rob them of their voice.

"I know who the Prime Elector is. He's young and lives part of the time in Guernsey and London. He's strong. He's much stronger than Gagarin. I... I don't know how we'll defeat him, but I've made my decision. *I* have to go after him, but each of you should make your own choice. I'll understand if you want to sit it out." I smile at Connor. "Go to Fiji if you like."

"What rubbish! I don't know about anyone else, but I'm with you. There's no way I fancy letting you save the world while I sit on my arse. Besides, I burn like toast in the sun." He grins. "I'm in."

"Well, now that I'm badass, I figure this Prime Elector guy should be a breeze. Get it, a *breeze*." Blake makes a short burst of

318

wind and laughs that genuine real laugh that took so long to come out of him. "I'm in."

Akari playfully elbows him in the side and he squeals. "Yeah, you are a killer all right. We're a team."

Troy shrugs. "I'm in if you guys will have me. I know I'm not a Chosen or special."

Connor shoves him in the back. "Of course you're in. I don't know why Juliet was so hard on you. We tried to tell her that you'd come in handy in a pinch. She can be a bit stubborn."

"Right." I chuckle. "I'm not the only one who's stubborn around here."

A squeak emanates from the corner and Blake jumps. "What's that?"

"Just a mouse, *Mr. Badass*," Akari teases.

"What about Sydney?" I ask.

"Sydney owns the Inn," says Blake. "Stuart deeded it over to her before we went to the Boathouse."

"He was full of surprises," I say. "He was braver than he seemed. He must have known that if we failed, Gagarin would have killed him."

"I guess I had him pegged wrong," says Troy. "I think he loved Sydney. He knew what it was like to live as a slave. Maybe he didn't want Sydney to live that way under the Deltites."

"Maybe. That might explain those romance novels he always carried with him. Where's the bathroom in this place?"

Connor points to a small door in the corner.

I go in and wash two days worth of grime from my face, then stare in the mirror. I'm the Alpha. I'm different from the others, but that's not so bad.

A vibration in my front pocket startles me. It takes a few moments for me to realize what it is.

The vial from my room, the one with the Fusion I'm supposed to take when I'm ready, has come alive. It has turned crimson and the top has vanished.

I guess I'm ready to learn the next crucial bit of information, the secret the Alphians wanted only me to know. I tip back the glass.

My mouth freezes and a million tiny pinpricks stab at my insides. Then, as the coldness melts away, a whoosh of thoughts and ideas whip through me.

Oh no! What have they done?

THE END

ACKNOWLEDGEMENTS

Many thanks to our awesome beta reads who helped us take random ideas and make them special. We'd list them all here, but we might forget one and feel crummy for weeks. You know who you are.

Much thanks also to Evolved Publishing and in particular to Lane Diamond, our fabulous senior editor and publisher, and Whitney Smyth, our junior editor.

Mallory Rock worked her usual magic on the cover and internal elements. Pavarti Tyler does a super job helping the *Chosen* series get noticed, and a special thanks to Ruby Standing Deer for her technical knowledge of all things Native American and her invaluable wisdom and support.

And lastly, we need to thank the readers of *Wind Catcher* for their enthusiastic support and encouragement.

ABOUT THE AUTHORS

Jeff Altabef lives in New York with his wife, two daughters, and Charlie the dog. He spends time volunteering at the Writing Center in the local community college as a certified writing instructor. After years of being accused of "telling stories," he thought he would make it official. He writes in both the thriller and young adult genres. As an avid Knicks fan, he is prone to long periods of melancholy during hoops season.

Jeff has a column on The Examiner focused on writing, designed to encourage writing for those that like telling stories.

You can find Jeff online at:

www.JeffreyAltabef.com Also visit him on Goodreads, Facebook, Twitter, or email Jeff at JeffreyAltabef@gmail.com.

Erynn Altabef is an avid reader, dancer, and community activist. When she's not in High School, she loves Starbucks, performing in school musicals, baking, and watching movies with her friends.

Some of her favorite authors are Veronica Roth, Joelle Charbonneau, and her dad! (That would be Jeff Altabef.)

You can find Erynn online at:

Facebook.com/ErynnAltabefAuthor.

WHAT'S NEXT FROM JEFF ALTABEF & ERYNN ALTABEF?

SCORCHED SOULS
(A Chosen Novel – 3)

Watch for the third book in this young adult fantasy series,
coming in the fall of 2016.

~~~~~

Fate and destiny clash in the explosive, heart-pounding
conclusion to the award-winning Chosen series.

~~~~~

Survival is not enough.
Alliances will be formed.
Loyalties tested.
A choice made.

Juliet Wildfire Stone is not just a Chosen, she's the Alpha. The fate of Earth may well rest in her hands, but when she meets the Prime Elector at last, the mortal enemy at the center of her new destiny, he proves not to be what she expected.

Plunged into a conflict between two ancient foes, one that threatens to rip Earth apart, Juliet must navigate her new path, form unlikely alliances, and solve ancient mysteries. She needs to set aside her fears, make the tough choices set before her, and become the Alpha Chosen once and for all.

The cost to Juliet does not matter; too much depends on her. She cannot allow Earth to be cast into a darkness from which it might never escape.

Yet she cannot do it alone. Will the other Chosen follow her? Or will the people of Earth be enslaved for all time?

MORE FROM JEFF ALTABEF

WIND CATCHER
(A Chosen Novel – 1)

This multiple award-winning first book in the *Chosen* series of young adult fantasies is now available.

~~~~~

Juliet Wildfire Stone stands between two worlds. Her eccentric grandfather tells her stories about the Great Wind Spirit and Coyote, but he might as well be speaking another language. She's started to hear voices and see visions, but even they don't make any sense. All she wants to be is an average sixteen-year-old girl, but she has never been average—could never be average.

She is the Chosen and the Seeker Slayer, and our only hope.

Recently transferred to an exclusive school, Juliet is forced to choose between her new wealthy life and her Native American heritage. Unsure where she fits in, she stumbles upon a series of murders. Worried that her grandfather is involved, she discovers an ancient secret society, the Order of the Twisted Arrows—a society formed over two hundred years ago to keep her safe.

When the mysterious Seeker learns of Juliet's existence, he threatens everyone she loves in the world, willing to kill to have her.

Betrayed by the young man she loves, she must decide whether to run or to fulfill her destiny as the Chosen.

SHATTER POINT

This multiple award-winning suspense thriller is now available.

~~~~~

When her 19-year-old son Jack miraculously recovers from a serious head trauma, Maggie is sure her luck has changed. But when she's abducted by a shadow from her past - a phantom with dangerous sapphire eyes - it's up to Jack and his younger brother Tom to unravel the mystery and save their mom from a deadly psychological battle.

The brothers seek help from their colorful great aunt, who exposes them to a world of nefarious family secrets, explosive government conspiracies, and a series of horrific murders. Together they must navigate a dark underworld full of political subterfuge and class warfare.

Yet as they search for their mother, Jack changes—he's raked by skull splitting headaches and weird visions. How exactly did he recover from his coma, and how does this tie into the psychopath who's abducted their mother?

Will Jack and Tom save Maggie before Cooper reaches his shatter point? Does Jack have enough time left?

MORE FROM EVOLVED PUBLISHING

CHILDREN'S PICTURE BOOKS

THE BIRD BRAIN BOOKS by Emlyn Chand:

Courtney Saves Christmas
Davey the Detective
Honey the Hero
Izzy the Inventor
Larry the Lonely
Polly Wants to be a Pirate
Poppy the Proud
Ricky the Runt
Ruby to the Rescue
Sammy Steals the Show
Tommy Goes Trick-or-Treating
Vicky Finds a Valentine

Silent Words by Chantal Fournier

Bella and the Blue Genie by Jonathan Gould

Maddie's Monsters by Jonathan Gould

Thomas and the Tiger-Turtle by Jonathan Gould

EMLYN AND THE GREMLIN by Steff F. Kneff:

Emlyn and the Gremlin
Emlyn and the Gremlin and the Barbeque Disaster
Emlyn and the Gremlin and the Mean Old Cat
Emlyn and the Gremlin and the Seaside Mishap

I'd Rather Be Riding My Bike by Eric Pinder

SULLY P. SNOOFERPOOT'S AMAZING INVENTIONS by Aaron Shaw Ph.D.:

Sully P. Snooferpoot's Amazing New Forcefield
Sully P. Snooferpoot's Amazing New Shadow

THE ADVENTURES OF NINJA AND BUNNY by Kara S. Tyler:

Ninja and Bunny's Great Adventure
Ninja and Bunny to the Rescue

CHILDREN'S PICTURE BOOKS (continued)

VALENTINA'S SPOOKY ADVENTURES by Majanka Verstraete:

Valentina and the Haunted Mansion
Valentina and the Masked Mummy
Valentina and the Whackadoodle Witch

HISTORICAL FICTION

Galerie by Steven Greenberg
SHINING LIGHT'S SAGA by Ruby Standing Deer:

Circles (Book 1)
Spirals (Book 2)
Stones (Book 3)

LITERARY FICTION

Carry Me Away by Robb Grindstaff
Hannah's Voice by Robb Grindstaff
Turning Trixie by Robb Grindstaff
Cassia by Lanette Kauten
The Daughter of the Sea and the Sky by David Litwack
A Handful of Wishes by E.D. Martin
The Lone Wolf by E.D. Martin
Jellicle Girl by Stevie Mikayne
Weight of Earth by Stevie Mikayne
White Chalk by Pavarti K. Tyler

LOWER GRADE (Chapter Books)

THE PET SHOP SOCIETY by Emlyn Chand:

Maddie and the Purrfect Crime
Mike and the Dog-Gone Labradoodle
Tyler and the Blabber-Mouth Birds

LOWER GRADE (continued)

TALES FROM UPON A. TIME by Falcon Storm:

Natalie the Not-So-Nasty
The Perils of Petunia
The Persnickety Princess

WEIRDVILLE by Majanka Verstraete:

Drowning in Fear
Fright Train
Grave Error
House of Horrors
The Clumsy Magician
The Doll Maker

THE BALDERDASH SAGA by J.W.Zulauf:

The Underground Princess (Book 1)
The Prince's Plight (Book 2)
The Shaman's Salvation (Book 3)

THE BALDERDASH SAGA SHORT STORIES by J.W.Zulauf:

Hurlock the Warrior King
Roland the Pirate Knight
Scarlet the Kindhearted Princess

MEMOIR

And Then It Rained: Lessons for Life by Megan Morrison

MIDDLE GRADE

FRENDYL KRUNE by Kira A. McFadden:

Frendyl Krune and the Blood of the Sun (Book 1)
Frendyl Krune and the Snake Across the Sea (Book 2)
Frendyl Krune and the Stone Princess (Book 3)

NOAH ZARC by D. Robert Pease:

Mammoth Trouble (Book 1)
Cataclysm (Book 2)
Declaration (Book 3)
Omnibus (Special 3-in-1 Edition)

MYSTERY / CRIME / DETECTIVE

DUNCAN COCHRANE by David Hagerty:

They Tell Me You Are Wicked (Book 1)

Hot Sinatra by Axel Howerton

NEW ADULT

THE DESERT by Angela Scott:

Desert Rice (Book 1)
Desert Flower (Book 2)

NOTHING FAIR ABOUT IT by Linda Kay Silva:

Nothing Fair About It (Book 1)
Nothing Fair About It: Something Always Changes (Book 2)

SCI-FI / FANTASY

Eulogy by D.T. Conklin
THE PANHELION CHRONICLES by Marlin Desault:

Shroud of Eden (Book 1)
The Vanquished of Eden (Book 2)

THE SEEKERS by David Litwack:

The Children of Darkness (Book 1)
The Stuff of Stars (Book 2)
The Light of Reason (Book 3)

THE AMULI CHRONICLES: SOULBOUND by Kira A. McFadden:

The Soulbound Curse (Book 1)
The Soulless King (Book 2)
The Throne of Souls (Book 3)

Shadow Swarm by D. Robert Pease
Two Moons of Sera by Pavarti K. Tyler

YOUNG ADULT (continued)

THE DARLA DECKER DIARIES by Jessica McHugh:

Darla Decker Hates to Wait (Book 1)
Darla Decker Takes the Cake (Book 2)
Darla Decker Shakes the State (Book 3)
Darla Decker Plays it Straight (Book 4)

JOEY COLA by D. Robert Pease:

Dream Warriors (Book 1)
Cleopatra Rising (Book 2)
Third Reality (Book 3)

Anyone? by Angela Scott

THE ZOMBIE WEST TRILOGY by Angela Scott:

Wanted: Dead or Undead (Book 1)
Survivor Roundup (Book 2)
Dead Plains (Book 3)
The Zombie West Trilogy – Special Omnibus Edition

CPSIA information can be obtained
at www.ICGtesting.com
Printed in the USA
FFOW05n1824031115

9 781622 533169